"Five Minutes, Goodlove. You and Your Crew, Out of Town in Five Minutes."

"And if I don't feel like it?" Goodlove said.

"You're a damned fool," Travis said evenly. "And too old for what will happen. Five minutes, Goodlove. You know me, I don't repeat an order more than once. Move out!"

Goodlove placed his hands on his hips and said, "All right, Travis. I'll see you again, late this summer. I'll come back down the trail with the biggest crew this god-forsaken town ever saw. We'll ride into your town on our way home, and then we'll wipe this town off the map. You understand me, Travis? Next time you won't be big enough. I'm warning you now."

It Started with a Threat . . . And It Ended with a Pledge of *Violence at Sundown.*

Books by Frank O'Rourke

Blackwater
Latigo
The Professionals
Violence at Sundown

Published by POCKET BOOKS

FRANK O'ROURKE

VIOLENCE AT SUNDOWN

PUBLISHED BY POCKET BOOKS NEW YORK

POCKET BOOKS, a division of Simon & Schuster, Inc.
1230 Avenue of the Americas, New York, N.Y. 10020

Copyright 1953 by Frank O'Rourke
Copyright renewed 1981 by Frank O'Rourke
Cover artwork copyright © 1987 Mort Kunstler

Published by arrangement with the author

ISBN: 0-671-63685-5

First Pocket Books printing October 1987

10 9 8 7 6 5 4 3 2 1

POCKET and colophon are registered trademarks of Simon & Schuster, Inc.

Printed in the U.S.A.

VIOLENCE AT SUNDOWN

One

THE TOWN DOZED IN DUSTY SILENCE UNTIL LATE AFTER-
noon, scattered gadabouts leaving shallow imprints of their
passage before Lockland's store and the Bighorn Saloon.
At five o'clock, with the sun heat abating and shadows
crawling from the west-side false fronts on Pioneer Street,
the town stirred lethargically into life. People appeared
in the upper town where the substantial houses stood in
white-painted, respectable aloofness. On lower Pioneer the
saloons prepared for business, and Big Annie filled her
doorway facing the tin-can-littered cul-de-sac just off Pioneer, yawning prodigiously and studying the street with
fat-pouched, infinitely wise eyes. In the pleasant stillness
Marshall Travis emerged from the hotel and walked leisurely toward the jail office.

Jim Murphy, the day marshal, had swept the office and
cleaned the purplish-stained pen nibs on the battered golden
oak desk. The windows facing the street were glowing with
late sunlight and the office was comfortably warm when
Travis took the swivel chair for his daily inspection of the
books. The office was a bare room with unpainted pine
floorboards and patched gray plaster walls, but Travis de-
rived a sense of old-shoe comfort from it. The desk was

7

adequate and clean, like a housewife's back porch table used for secondary purposes, and the big gun rack against the east wall beside the door leading to the cell block was dusted, the guns oiled until they reflected a dull bluish sheen. Behind the hard-coal burner, Travis had nailed up a long bookshelf which contained a collection of mixed reading—*Harper's* magazines, novels with dark mottled board covers and imitation leather backs, a doctor book of home remedies, and a well-thumbed Bible. The books went untouched during the summer; not until the hard-coal burner was going did Travis sit at the desk, boots up, pursuing his reading.

Travis opened the day book and read the names of prisoners currently occupying the cells beyond the inner door. Just three today, he counted with relief, two vagrants and Mexican Joe. Joe had beaten his wife last night and turned himself in before she recovered and attempted vengeance with the nearest solid object. Joe was a fine man until he drank beyond his limited capacity. After that he followed the course of such volatile souls who turned with animal instinct upon the dearest object of their combined love and hate. Travis checked off the prisoners and made a quick study of the cash ledger, meals served against meals purchased at the Acme Café, a box of .45's, fifty cents worth of sweeping compound for this month of June. Travis closed the books and lit a cigar, leaning far back in his swivel chair with meditative eyes.

He was thirty-eight this summer, an old man for a town marshal. He was tall and angular and prematurely gray, a deliberate man with large hands and feet, with blue eyes washed pale and shiny, with the heavy belt and holster lying against his right thigh, so much an integral part of the man that it had become, through the long years, a natural appendage, a piece of his body, to be scratched and cleaned and carried like a third arm, a third eye, looking down, but always ready to come up and out, unseeing but seldom missing. He wore a suit of blue, lightweight serge cut by a good tailor in Omaha, baggy and unpressed, but spotlessly clean, the coat riding upward in a telltale bulge above the holster. He was always neatly dressed, and his body was as clean as his clothing.

The cell block door opened and Jim Murphy led the vagrants and Mexican Joe into the office. Murphy said, "Here's the marshal," and grinned at Travis as he slumped into the barrel chair beneath the gun rack. Murphy was soft and loosely built, with a thick brown beard and reddish hair hiding most of his pleasant, apple-cheeked face. He had been day marshal for six years and had a pretentious air about his most casual movements, but nobody was fooled by his gun belt. Murphy was a fearless man in routine work, but he couldn't hit the side of a barn with his revolver. His favorite weapon was a double-barreled shotgun and he hesitated to use that since the night a bull ran wild through Ferguson's back yard and carried away Mrs. Ferguson's unmentionables. Murphy made a good shot that night as the bull roared down Pioneer, one horn flaunting lace bloomers, the other waving a silkier object. Mrs. Ferguson had never forgiven Murphy for the badly timed placing of that shot.

"Hot," Murphy said wearily. "Ain't it?"

"Some," Travis said. "Well, boys?"

They faced his desk, blinking owlishly against the fading sunlight, two dirty young men with the tiredness that lived continually in the mind once the body gave up the fight to find a real life. They were the drifters who rode a freight and slept free in a jail, and wandered on into nowhere. They made Travis angry, just trying to locate a spark of pride in their sour, whiskered faces.

"Thanks for bunking us, Marshal," the tall one said.

"Want a job?" Travis asked curtly.

They shuffled nervously, shying from the cruel words. The tall one said, "Well, Marshal, I don't know . . ."

"Get a meal at the Acme Café," Travis said. "Take the night freight toward Omaha. You work in this town or keep traveling. And wash before you eat. Jim, see they get away tonight.''

"Come along, boys," Murphy said. "The pump's out back."

The tall one looked at Travis and shook his head in secret wonder. They were going to wash and get a free meal, leave town decently, not booted out on their backsides. Everything they'd heard about the marshal of Olalla was true. He was fair, but tough, and you didn't argue. The tall one said sheepishly, "Many thanks, Marshal," and herded his partner down the cell block hall behind Murphy. When the door closed, Travis relit his cigar and smiled at the remaining prisoner.

"Joe, where did you hit her this time?"

Mexican Joe was fidgeting around, plainly afraid that his wife might erupt through the front door with a skillet or a hunk of cottonwood. Joe was a slender, stoop-shouldered little man with smooth brown skin, white teeth and wavy black hair. He was a happy little man who played his guitar with magic fingers and dodged all work with even greater magic. Now he spread both his hands in resignation and shrugged expressively.

"All over, Señor Bob, but so very softly. I was pretty drunk."

"Think it's safe to go home?" Travis asked.

"I will chance it," Joe said cautiously, "and I will stay sober . . ."

"Until next time," Travis said. "You scoundrel."

"Time is heavy," Joe grinned. "What else can a man do, Señor Bob? All the time Lupe is driving me to work. Have we not a roof and food and clothes? Pretty soon she drives me to a little drink, and then she pays for her worry."

"Give my regards to Lupe," Travis said. "And lay off the drink, eh?"

"You want me to work like Johnny Cork?" Joe asked.

10

"Not that," Travis smiled. "Like Joe Gonzales, my good friend. Adios, amigo."

Mexican Joe said solemnly, "You have my promise, Señor Bob," and left the office with dignity, much as a steady customer might take a familiar route from his regular trading store. Travis had known Joe for three years, and during that time Joe beat his wife once a month, so that Travis and the little man were close friends through association in the jail and down in the Mexican quarter where Travis was always welcome at the *bailes*. Everybody liked Joe, and nobody could make him work steady. He sang and played, day after day, allowing Lupe the honor of worry over food and clothing. Only when dire necessity appeared did Joe go forth to labor honestly for a week or two with the section gang.

Joe spoke gaily to someone outside the door, and John Lockland came from the street with a backward, "I've got those new guitar strings, Joe," and smiled gravely at Travis. "Regular customer again, Bob."

"Couldn't do without him," Travis said. "How did Tommy fish today?"

"A one-pounder," Lockland said. "Margaret's frying it for his supper."

"Good boy," Travis smiled, "but you didn't stop by so near suppertime to tell me fish stories."

The storekeeper nodded soberly and advanced to the desk. John Lockland was the quietest and most orderly man in town, a gray-eyed merchant who never raised his voice in accusations or threats. But he was a man with the courage of his own beliefs and a great love for his wife and son, all of which made him respected and listened to during town board meetings and along the street. Lockland had come out from Omaha five years ago and bought the general store, built up the stock, and made it the center of trade for the entire area.

"Goodlove brought his herd in yesterday," Lockland said. "You know that, of course."

"Biggest ever to come this far north," Travis said. "I hear Stacey will ship one trainload to Omaha for expense money, but the herd is going north into Dakota territory. They are stocking those ranges, John, more every year. We're watching the start of a new era."

"I appreciate the economics," Lockland said. "I'm worried about tonight and tomorrow. Goodlove's outfit is wild and his trail boss won't control them in town. I'd hate to see any trouble."

"Speaking for yourself," Travis said, "or the others?"

"Both. Can you handle them, Bob? We could deputize a few men to help out."

"That's Ferguson speaking," Travis said. "I always recognize his confidence in me. No. I'll get along. You forget I've known Stacey a long time. He's never promoted trouble. His crew deserves a good time. What difference— some windows, a few fights and rebel yells, a few raped women. Annie's girls ravish fairly easy, and glass is cheaper this summer. Plug up your ears, sleep sound, and let them roar."

Lockland flushed at the easy words and Travis saw the streak of New England stubbornness light up the gray eyes. Lockland said, "I understand all that, Bob, but I'm sick of having my store turned upside down every time a herd pulls into town."

"Nobody begged you to come here," Travis said quietly. "You knew this was a trail town, a railroad town, a tough town. But it's changing now, getting better all the time, John. Change doesn't happen overnight. Remember that, be patient. And listen to me, John. You're my friend and I know your temper. If a young fool barges in, drunk and happy, and wants to break a lamp or dance a jig on your counter, let him dance. Charge him double and wish him good luck."

Lockland smiled despite his worry. "I'll try, Bob. There's something else now . . ."

"I can read your thoughts," Travis smiled.

"Good. Makes it easier to say. Is it true that your're resigning?"

"As of July 1st," Travis said. "I told Ferguson yesterday."

"That makes me feel very happy," Lockland said. "But what then, Bob? Will you stay in town, or try the land?"

"I don't know," Travis said. "I've got the money for either. I'm going to loaf all summer, fish with Tommy, eat supper at your house and work Margaret's fingers to the bone baking me coffee cake. I recommended Jim Murphy for my job. He deserves the raise, he can handle. it. The town won't need my kind much longer, John. Now I can see you didn't think I meant it before."

"No," Lockland said. "Not when you told us, Bob."

"I'm the luckiest man in the world," Travis said soberly. "Fourteen years in this work, John, and still alive. Do you understand what that means?—no, don't try to. I won't press my luck another year. I'm quitting while I can walk away on my own two feet."

"I'll tell Margaret," Lockland said. "She'll be happy. Now I'm late for supper—good night."

Travis waited until the door closed, then rose and gave his belt a tug, settling the holster against his thigh. He had expected Lockland since noon, and it was a good feeling to have his resignation known to the town. He had given it serious thought through the winter, watching the changing tempo of the town, and had realized he could finally step down with no loss of pride or self-respect, no stigma of ducking an unfinished job.

Olalla had never been a wild town like Dodge and Ellsworth and Abilene. The Union Pacific had driven across Nebraska territory and made the town, and during the seventies only a few herds were pushed on north beyond the Kansas railroad and shipped east to Omaha. Now the great new range country—the Dakotas, Montana and Wyoming—was opening, and the herds were driving north to stock that land. They stopped at Olalla, but there was less wildness coming with the crews.

Olalla was not a lady by any means, but the town's meanness was the natural spirit and growing pain of any small town changing slowly into a respectable community. It no longer needed his gun. His three hundred dollar salary was a burden on the community. He could step down and buy a business, or homestead a piece of the high land north of the river. In five years nobody would remember his past. Travis pictured himself behind a breaking plow, gee-hawing to a pair of mules, and smiled at the vision. In the aftermath of this early thought he stepped from the jail office and turned down Pioneer Street. Lea Ferguson was hurrying along the west boardwalk to visit the milliner about a new hat, carrying the white feathers for whatever creation Maggie could dream up for the banker's daughter. Lea waved her greeting, smiled hopefully and Travis gravely tipped his hat.

TWO

ON THE WEST SIDE BEHIND THE BUSINESS DISTRICT, Johnny Cork hung his battered saddle in the stable alley of Herbelsheimer's livery barn where he had been breaking horses all day and turned into the side shed, walking as if he was treading on soft-boiled eggs and feeling the top of his sandy-haired skull bounce loosely somewhere high above the sky. He stripped away the blue shirt and dirt-caked pants, tugged worn boots from his tired, burning feet, and crawled wearily into the water trough. He ducked under and then lay back and sloshed himself liberally, washed the dirt and sweat from his skinny body and closed his eyes for a restful ten minutes in the sun-heated water. The loafers hadn't fouled the trough today and that was thanks enough for any man.

He remembered the last horse he had broken to saddle and decided there was a quicker way to make his fortune. As he dried himself with a stained gunny sack he ruminated that tonight he would lie in his bunk and ask himself for the thousandth time, "How can I get ahead, improve myself?" and the silent walls would offer no solution.

Johnny Cork dressed and walked slowly through the alley to Pioneer Street, his movement accidentally coinciding with the marshal's and Lea Ferguson's. Travis paused on the opposite corner, smelling the evening breeze, and saw Johnny Cork come from the alley in time to catch a fleeting look at Lea's skirt as she turned into the milliner's shop.

Johnny Cork felt the old surge of anger, not at Lea, but against the parents who had filled her with false ideas about her position in life. Her easy living came from the bank, that differed in no way from a hundred others, but Lea could not understand. Johnny Cork saw the bright flash of her skirt and crossed the street to stand beside Travis, slight and youthful against the marshal's bulk. He looked upward with his quick, old man's stare of acute knowledge. Travis saw the fresh scratch on Johnny's left forearm.

"Will you ever learn?" Travis asked.

"I caught the devil the last trip," Johnny said. "He rubbed the fence on me."

"The job pays good," Travis said. "The lumps go with it."

"True," Johnny said. "But I'm sick of it, Bob."

"Time goes," Travis said quietly. "You'll be an old man soon. Is that the trouble?"

Travis smiled at Johnny Cork, nineteen this summer, handling a man's rough, thankless job for Herbelsheimer, breaking wild stock for army sale at three dollars per head. Travis remembered the day Johnny had come to town last winter, broke and cold, asking for a bed in the jail. Within two days Johnny was sweeping out Lockland's store, candling eggs, unpacking merchandise, then in the spring hauling hay for Calderson from the river bottoms, and thence to breaking the wild stock for Herbelsheimer. Johnny hadn't taken a backward step since arrival, but he was impatient now, and Travis read this urgent desire plainly in the thin, sun-blackened face, knowing the reasons well, approving one and distrustful of the other.

"That's it," Johnny said. "I'm getting old fast, Bob. How does a man make his stake, his start?"

"Two ways."

"The straight way," Johnny said, "but just as easy as possible."

"I can't tell you," Travis said. "Any idea is good. It might fail, but one leads to another. One day you'll get it, right in your hand."

"Where I stand," Johnny said, "that day looks ten years off. I've got to improve myself."

"Any other reason?" Travis asked dryly.

Johnny flushed and looked instinctively toward the millinery shop. "Maybe."

"I can offer sound advice in that department," Travis said. "If it's only the money she expects you to make, she's not worth the time. If it's you first and money second, she'll be easy to convince."

"I'm hoping it's my handsome face," Johnny Cork said sharply. "And then the money."

"Is it?"

"Bob," Johnny Cork said miserably. "I don't know."

"If it was me," Travis said soberly, "I'd take Mary Summerhays to ten of Lea."

Johnny shook his head and moved off toward his room at Calderson's house, walking fast in the yellow sunlight. Travis watched him and thought, if they were all like Johnny, he could move through town with peace of mind. He wondered if Johnny really cared for Lea Ferguson or was struck by her so-called position in the town and Johnny's lack of position. Lea was a pretty girl but a rattleheaded little fool, vain and given to childish outbursts of foolish talk, badly spoiled by her mother. But Johnny couldn't see that. Lea wasn't half the woman Johnny thought he saw, not fit to carry water for Mary Summerhays, but Johnny was blind to the look in Mary's face whenever they met. Travis sighed and crossed over to the Bighorn Saloon, forgetting problems of the heart as food smell drifted from the hotel dining room.

He looked into the Bighorn and waved to Dick Burnett, and went on down the boardwalk to the hotel. From lower

17

Pioneer came the familiar sounds of approaching night, lifting and hanging on the wind—a tinkling piano, someone singing behind Big Annie's curtains, a waterbucket dropped on a dirty porch. Olalla was making ready for the first big night of the summer. Travis entered the hotel and took his customary table in the dining room. He ate slowly and looked around for Stacey Goodlove. He realized that he was actually waiting, as all the rest of the town was, for the beat of hoofs and the rebel yell announcing the arrival of Goodlove's crew. Then the night would start with a roar.

He sat back with coffee and a cigar, thinking of the past years in Dodge, when the herds were coming up the trail and the Texas men poured into the town, the wildest bunch of hell-raisers on the face of the earth. And he should know, Travis thought dryly, for he had come up that trail ten years ago and nobody was meaner, wilder, nor more ready for trouble than young Bob Travis. It took a lot of years and a lot of living to change a man and make him see those days with the proper insight. Wyatt Earp had told him one day that the only way a man could understand the marshal job was to put himself in the boots of the wild ones, the young punchers and the old hellers and try to understand that every man must blow off steam in some way. The catch to that understanding was, a man had to come from their life or never see the logic of getting drunk and shooting out windows, riding horses through open doors and scaring peaceful merchants half to death. Now it was all behind him and better forgotten, and he had no desire to become a dead legend like so many of the others who, like himself, had taken the star and walked the streets of the towns. Goodlove's crew tonight and tomorrow night, one or two more during June, and he was through.

He looked up as Stacey Goodlove entered the dining room, saw him and crossed immediately to his table. Goodlove was a barrel-chested, blocky man with massive shoulders and a heavy, forward-thrust head crowned with coarse black hair. There was an individual look to the manner in which Goodlove combed that shaggy hair, brushing it straight back and over his large ears, as if accepting no insubordinate cowlicks or silly curlicues. Fresh off the trail, washed and barbered, Goodlove wore a stiff gray woolen suit that looked awkward on his body, for the truth was that no suit could ever civilize this man. Goodlove was driving the largest herd in the history of the trail, going north to stock a virgin range and help open up a new empire. There was a feeling of fate and destiny hanging over men like Goodlove. They understood nothing but their own passionate ambitions and desires. They walked roughly, but with innocent bullishness, throughout their lives. Stacey Goodlove was an honest and forthright man, faithful to his friends and outspoken to his enemies. Tonight, as though they had spoken only yesterday and not three years ago, he shook hands warmly and sat beside Travis.

"Boys are coming in tonight, Bob."

"Good," Travis said. "You don't change, Stacey. Was it an easy drive?"

"Fast and easy," Goodlove said. "The bad part comes when we head north."

"You'll make out," Travis said. "I wish you all good luck. About tonight. Your boys know the rules?"

"They've got a big thirst," Goodlove said, "and a yen to quench it, Bob. Go easy on them. Two nights here and they see nothing but beans and dust until Dakota."

"The town is theirs," Travis said. "They know about checking guns in the saloons, no raising hell or riding horses on upper Pioneer. If they want to sleep over, there's plenty of room in the jail. I'll stay open just in case."

"Same old Travis," Goodlove chuckled. "I'll buy the drinks tonight."

"Same trail boss?" Travis asked quietly.

"Sam Thompson," Goodlove said. "Best in the world."

"I know that," Travis said. "But remind Sam that I'll stand for no foolishness. By and large, your crews are fine.

When trouble starts, you always find Sam at the bottom of the pile. He's getting too old for that foolishness. I know damned well I am."

"Why don't you quit?" Goodlove asked bluntly.

"Maybe I have," Travis smiled. "Stacey, I'll take that drink a little later."

He shook hands again, bridging the three years' gap with this simple gesture, and walked from the hotel with at least another hour of quiet before Goodlove's crew reached town. It was nice to see Stacey once more, to find the big man healthy and still pounding toward whatever goal he desired, but it would have been much better if Sam wasn't along. Too many memories, Travis thought, too many years behind them to forget.

Turning up Pioneer, he saw the little maple trees far up the street, planted before Ferguson's house and a few others, and wondered as he had for two years why people tried to bring in eastern trees that wouldn't grow in this sandy Platte country. Why didn't they stick to the cottonwoods and the gray-green tamarisks that grew naturally out here?

But that was the way it went in the new towns. The Fergusons tried to perpetuate an alien form of society, and carried this forced change from trees to dresses, from pie crust to the Ladies Aid meetings on Thursday afternoons. But only in their small part of town, thank God. Across the tracks in Mexican town, along the other streets in the little houses, people understood their country. Cottonwoods shaded the houses and humped along under the earth, breaking into the wells with their searching roots, giving the water a funny taste, but nobody cared. People planted gardens and hammered up window boxes and grew the bright, simple flowers. It was always a fight between different people when a new town started, and that was all to the good because out of argument and change and experiment came the real town, the town that would outlive them all.

Travis smelled the night wind off the river and thought

suddenly, "It's summer and I haven't gone fishing yet."
He yearned for a cane pole and time to take Tommy Lockland out to the river, at the big hole in the bend where the
catfish lay along the sandy bottom. That was the best part
of the summer, time to fish and dream and he'd be doing
it every day in one more month. The town was changing,
all right, but not fast enough to suit him.

Three

THE HAZY SUMMER DUSK APPEARED TO COME FROM THE river as sunset faded, and descend in a soft, blue darkness over the town. Beside the river, in the willow thickets and above the backwater pools where the black bugs darted and the dragonflies swooped in graceful streaks of green, the mosquitoes hummed in great clouds. Fireflies glowed intermittently along the white-wedged sandbars that thrust outward against the lazy, gurgling water. In the hour before full darkness, sitting in his customary place outside the jail office, Travis seemed to understand most clearly the strange paradox of life in his town.

He sat there in the early summer evening, smoking his cigar in peaceful solitude. Yet, a few miles to the west, the wild riders—really strangers from a foreign land— were saddling up. Around him was the town that welcomed those men with a last dying throwback to the old days of Dodge and Abilene. But really not the town, Travis thought, just a small part extended the physical welcome. The town was at its supper tables, home from work, railroaders from the depot and roundhouse, switchmen and yard engine crews, the watertank man who checked his level a last time on the wobbly platform beside the tar-calked redwood tank that overshadowed the track east of the depot. The Fergusons and Locklands were saying polite grace on upper Pioneer, the saloon-keepers were eating a hasty sandwich at their back bars, and Big Annie's girls were fortifying their stomachs against the coming night's excessive labors. The clerks and workers and common folks were all at home. These people in their houses, were the real town. Sitting in the cane-backed chair, tilted against the office wall, Travis could see the entire town in his mind.

On the streets east and west of Pioneer lived the railroad men, the clerks, workers and the old-timers, in small houses with little lawns and flowers under the cotton-wood trees. He could smell cabbage and frying onions and fresh bread with the butter drying on the hot brown crust. Children were playing a last game before answering the stern call to wash ears, face, and hands, and come to supper.

On upper Pioneer, Travis could see the bigger houses with the half-glass doors and the big doorbells that cranked like eight-day clocks, where the dark parlors were filled with ugly horsehair furniture and stiff pictures of ancestors. Down below the depot, beyond the tracks, Pioneer dribbled away into a sandy cowpath lined with weeds and sunflowers, cut deep by buffalo before man came, and now worn deeper by the people who lived in that part of town.

Mexican Joe and the section men lived there, with their wives and mistresses and many children. They couldn't make good dobe this far north, but they had managed to build with a poorer grade of home-made bricks, plus odd pieces of lumber and hunks of tin hammered flat from discarded oil barrels and abandoned signs. Their yards were neatly defined by stick fences, or rocks, and the chimneys were rusty stovepipes thrust upward from the kitchen roofs at cockeyed angles. Almost any night Travis could hear Joe and his friends playing a guitar and singing "La Go-

londrina" or another of their songs. They had a bottle—
with luck—and a song; and they sat late into the summer
night, smiling lazily at the warm darkness.

And all of this was his town, Travis thought, with roots
in the past but all of its future foreign to those roots. The
future was growing solidly in the little houses, on the quiet,
dusty streets, in the churches and schoolhouse, in the town
hall. The trail crews might come a while longer, but eventually the town would give a final heave of labor pain and
cast out the past. The saloons would become quieter, Big
Annie would move on, and lower Pioneer would settle into
stodgy respectability. In one way that wasn't the best thing
in the world for Olalla. Every town needed a pinch of
wildness. Travis couldn't stand any town made up entirely
of Fergusons and their kind, with nobody like himself and
Mexican Joe to jar them loose once in a while. But he was
worrying needlessly about such a condition in Olalla. The
change was coming, and tonight was one of the last acts
in the drama he knew so well.

Travis dropped his cigar beside the tilted chair and
placed one boot-heel over the coal. He heard no sound
from the west, over the rolling plain, but his ears seemed
to stretch their sense of hearing into the smoky dusk and
discover that familiar noise long before the earth echoes
telegraphed the rataplan of hoofs. He stood beside the
doorway and saw Lea Ferguson step from the milliner's
shop, call good night, and walk swiftly toward home.
She had stayed downtown too late and Travis wanted to
give her a piece of his mind. If a puncher happened in
from the west and gave her a salute, or jumped from his
horse and kissed her out of sheer animal spirits, Lea was
the type to enjoy the sensation secretly and then scream
bloody murder. Travis watched and heard, at last, the
rising drum of hoofs.

Lea had stayed too long, watching Maggie fuss with
the white feathers and the hat form covered with purple
velvet. When they finally settled on the number—Maggie

swore three was the latest eastern style—it was almost suppertime. Lea hurried up Pioneer, sniffing disdainfully as the shrill voice of a Big Annie girl floated from below. She reached the intersection of Cottonwood Avenue when the Goodlove crew galloped furiously out of the dusk and made her leap back with a little scream of fright.

They swept past her, cutting the corner, leaving a suction of dust and clods and fierce yells. A straggler waved his shapeless hat and shouted, "Wait for me, girlie!" and made a lewd gesture as he rounded the corner. Lea half ran across the street and kept running until she touched her front gate. She didn't know why, and the feeling never lingered, but she had an emptiness whenever she saw the trail crews and watched them roar into a world of fun she would never experience, much less understand. Travis might have explained if she had asked, that she had a lot of bitch in her, only it was buried so deep beneath starched manners and underwear that she'd never realize her true role in life.

Her mother rose from the porch swing and tapped her blunt fingers impatiently against the corner post as Lea mounted the steps. Mrs. Ferguson was a stout woman with lovely gray hair that came out nearly silver after a careful rinse. She had been a handsome girl, but age deposited another inch on her jaw and gave her long nose a peculiar sharpness that somehow reminded observant people of a dripping waterspout in cold weather. Mrs. Ferguson was completely selfish about having her own way, and this ingrown feeling did not soften the harsh lines of her jaw and nose. In fact, there were times when Lea wondered how her mother and father had ever managed to sire her. But this feeling came only when Lea was studying her face in the bureau mirror. For on the whole, Lea was well on the way to becoming a carbon copy of her mother in every respect.

Mrs. Ferguson's house was spotlessly clean, her washing on the line Monday mornings by eight o'clock. Her kitchen was a model of neatness. She was an excellent cook in a heavy-handed way but lately it seemed that no matter what she served, her husband ate his food in a silent, absentminded way. Mrs. Ferguson didn't understand that good food wasn't everything, that the table must be naturally cheerful and the faces around it bright with something more than gossip and dry words repeated a hundred times. There was more to eating than food, but she didn't understand. And it really didn't matter, because Lea was too young to notice, and Ferguson was even blinder than his wife to the beauty of such things.

Mrs. Ferguson had no time for the homesteaders and the railroad men and the Mexicans. They existed in Olalla, in her mind, simply through the generosity of such men as her husband who owned the bank and the storekeepers who gave credit to such irresponsible fools as Mexican Joe. But not too much credit; just so far, then draw the line. When she thought of that young tough, Johnny Cork, she fairly winced with hurt pride. Even his name was immoral. And he had the gall to make eyes at Lea. Mrs. Ferguson was a strong-minded woman, and this quality never appeared in better style than while sitting on her front porch, peering down Pioneer Street through the morning glory vines.

"Ah," she said. "Those roughnecks came in."

"Mr. Goodlove's crew," Lea said.

"Did they bother you?" Mrs. Ferguson asked suspiciously.

"No, Ma," Lea said. "They . . ."

"You stayed too long," Mrs. Ferguson said. "You know better than to linger down there this late. It's dangerous and those men are—well, please remember in the future."

"I will," Lea said. "But they wouldn't bother me, Ma. You know that."

"Probably not," Mrs. Ferguson said, "but be sensible.

That Travis wouldn't do much to help if some man did insult you. Now, how was the hat?''

Lea Ferguson sat beside her mother on the porch swing and described the new hat, and far downtown a red-faced puncher was telling how he scared some skinny little fool near out of her pants when he rounded the corner. Goodlove's crew, thirty strong, was already scattered among the saloons, making up for lost weeks on the trail.

Travis showed himself plainly against the lighted doorway of the jail office when the Goodlove crew rode past. He saw the lone puncher frighten Lea and wondered if she would complain and make an international incident out of youthful horseplay. Then he forgot Lea, watching the riders. He wanted them to see him, which they did as was proved by their shouts as they swept past the jail office. He reminded them that he was the law in town and it was time to check their guns and remain on the lower end of Pioneer Street.

He waited until they dismounted and scattered among the saloons and dance halls before starting his first tour of the night. He entered the Bighorn as Dick Burnett locked the wall-box door on a full depository of guns. Burnett said cheerfully, ''All clear, Bob,'' and hurried away to help his bartenders set up the drinks. Johnny Cork came off the street, looking for an odd job and an extra dollar, and grinned knowingly at Travis.

''Cut off their horns?'' Johnny asked wisely.

''Maybe,'' Travis said. ''Don't go running your nose along the stumps. They can still bite.''

Johnny Cork grinned and passed by, intent on getting Dick Burnett's attention in case Burnett needed extra help behind the bar tonight. Johnny was never too tired for more work, for the chance to get ahead. Travis watched him for a moment and then crossed to the Big Nugget where he received another favorable report from Clem Wilson, also more good news later on from Big Annie. Finishing his walk down Pioneer to the tracks, and back along the alley behind the saloons, Travis was fairly satisfied with to-night's beginning.

Goodlove had kept his crew in hand so far and that was half the battle. Once the guns were locked away, they could fight all they wished, drink until they rolled in the dust. Nobody got badly hurt in a drunken brawl. Now he could have that drink with Goodlove and relax until midnight. But entering the Bighorn, Travis had the old worry over that one puncher, whoever he might be, who might have shoved a hideout gun under a shirt. His second worry was that tomorrow night would be wilder than tonight.

----------------------- Four -----------------------

STACEY GOODLOVE HAD TAKEN OVER THE FAR END OF
the bar, and stood with his elbows spread wide, occupying
a generous expanse of walnut and brass. His face was red
and his black string tie was hanging in two bedraggled,
twisted shoelaces, and his blue serge suit was already
stained with spilled whiskey and the odd dust pigment a
careless man seemed to gather no matter how carefully he
stepped.

Sam Thompson stood at Goodlove's elbow, back to the
corner facing the door, the way Sam always remained in
any room from backhouse to bedroom. Goodlove was arguing happily with Dick Burnett and pushing at his glass
with his thick fingers, relaxed now and completely at home
in the only atmosphere he understood. He was worth half
a million dollars and would never see the day he balanced
a coffee cup in somebody's formal parlor or wore a coat
and tie with ease. He saw Travis and lifted one big arm in
greeting, shaking his bottle and pointing at the extra glass.

"You're late," Goodlove roared. "Join the party, Bob."

Travis pushed through the bar crowd that resisted his
passage momentarily, then eased away as the punchers gave
him their quick, sidelong stares, faint smiles or scowls,

depending on the memories and stories each man had collected about the marshal. Travis worked along the bar, speaking to men he knew, nodding to the bartender, and finally reached the rear, where Goodlove thrust the glass under his nose and shouted, "Say when, Bob!"

"Three fingers," Travis said. "How are you, Sam?"

"Fair," Sam Thompson said. "You're looking good, Bob."

Travis lifted his glass and saluted them. "Your good health, gentlemen."

They drank together and Goodlove refilled the glasses as he pawed through his rumpled pockets for cigars. Travis accepted a wrinkled perfecto and held the match, watching Sam Thompson above the bright flame while Goodlove blew smoke across the bar. Sam had watched Travis's progress through the Goodlove crew and silently enjoyed the small pressure his men placed in the marshal's path, knowing exactly why it was offered and how Travis reacted. Sam would never change, Travis thought, would live out his days in the same way. And he could be worse now, after three years. What lay between them was better forgotten.

Sam was a scrawny little man who had sloughed off his excess flesh years ago, leaving a leather-tough shell of sandy-colored, thinning hair, long nose, thin lips and sloping shoulders. Also there was the once-broken right leg that gimped slightly when Sam was forced to walk more than fifty steps. Sam was the best trail boss in the business, and his long years with Stacey Goodlove spoke eloquently of that ability. Sam drove his men, but never spared himself. His one god was cattle, and whatever stray drop of love and devotion that possibly lay hidden in his dark brown face with its overhanging brows, long nose, thin, wide mouth covered by the drooping moustache, was so deeply buried in layers of sour distrust for all mankind that Sam himself was undoubtedly ignorant of its existence. In his own field Sam was nearly perfect, but he had one failing—

he could not tolerate resistance and he dearly loved a fight, with guns or fists or clubs, not so much the chance to join in but to start and then stand back and watch. He never forgot a grudge, and had been known to ride five hundred miles to even an old score. He feared nothing and he paid fealty to one man—Goodlove. Theirs was a union of spirit and temper, bound by common love for the only life they knew.

"And your health," Goodlove said. "Well, the boys raising hell yet?"

"Too early," Travis said. "Give them time, Stacey."

"True," Goodlove said cheerfully. "They're sure a bunch of wild ones. Does 'em good to see how other folks live, then they know how lucky they are. How's that tightwad, Ferguson, the old sonofabitch?"

"The same," Travis said.

"Would be. There's your example of how never to ripen. Dry as dust, runs his bank like he wouldn't give credit unless a man left his wife in the vault."

"Not that bad," Travis said. "Just a cautious, hardheaded businessman."

"Say, where'd he get that daughter?" Goodlove asked wonderingly. "And where'd he get that wife? Jesus, what a woman! I'd head for Pecos if I ever found her in bed the next mornin'."

"Every man to his own taste," Dick Burnett said dryly. "Ferguson was young once, so was his wife. I know it's hard to believe, but maybe they were different then."

"That I doubt," Sam Thompson said. "Some people are born that way."

"It depends on who was the worst in the beginning," Travis said. "Blame that one, Sam."

Sam Thompson's face lifted in a quick flash of understanding, and slipped as quickly back to somber blackness.

"That's true, Bob. In that case, I'll pick the wife."

They talked on, drinking from the two bottles, while the noise around them increased with a steadily deepening note of intensity. Travis saw Johnny Cork washing glasses over the water tub and smiled when Johnny raised two fingers, meaning he had caught Dick Burnett shorthanded and had driven a two-dollar bargain for the night's work. Burnett tried to strike a happy medium between his important customers and the mob, talking with Goodlove for a few minutes, then moving down the bar to serve drinks or change money at the cigar counter. Travis finished his first drink and nursed the second along, answering questions and nodding quiet agreement as Goodlove talked approvingly of cattle and land and the great future of the new northern ranges.

". . . and more railroads," Goodlove's voice came through Travis's thoughts. "Ain't that right, Bob?"

"Yes," Travis said. "But how many?"

"Got to be," Goodlove said doggedly. "Up there she's open country, no roads, no nothin'. Got to be a railroad built to the Missouri from Omaha or out from St. Paul. We can't be driving down here to ship east, can we?"

"No sense," Travis said. "There'll be a road, Stacey. Give them time."

"I ain't got time," Goodlove said, staring into his glass. "God, man. We got just so long to do a lot of things. I can't wait on those eastern bankers forever. Sometimes I get so goddamned mad I feel like going out and building everything we need myself."

Goodlove was just as drunk as he ever became, which meant that he was red-faced and sweating straight through his shirt and coat, but steady on his feet and sharp with his tongue. Goodlove had never been put under the table, and liked to brag about the times he closed deals over the second bottle and laughed at his opponent's discomfort in the morning. Tonight he was feeling good inside, the long half of his drive finished, and something brand new just ahead. The unknown was a challenge to such men, Travis knew, and it was a good thing for the country that men like Goodlove kept growing up.

Travis had stayed long enough. He took advantage of a minor argument down the bar to say good-by and move quickly through the mob, settle the difference between two men, and continue through the doors into the street. He made a slow and thorough round of all the saloons, and entered the jail office at midnight for the usual talk with Murphy who was on duty tonight and would be tomorrow, giving Travis a much-needed second hand if trouble came.

Murphy had lodged a friend of Mexican Joe's in the back cell for getting drunk far too early in the evening and stumbling over a case of eggs just taken from a homesteader's wagon. Pablo Manero had a dollar and forty cents, not enough to pay for the eggs, but the homesteader recovered his sense of humor in time to laugh it off and help Murphy lead Pablo to jail. Travis could hear him now, singing a happy song and calling for Mexican Joe between verses.

Travis took his shotgun from the rack, checked it carefully, placed two buckshot shells in the chambers, and set it against the wall behind the desk. It was the only extra protection he ever made on a big night, for as he often told Jim Murphy, "What else can you do? Just keep the shotgun ready, more as a persuader than a weapon. As for the rest, well, that's up to you."

Travis left Murphy patrolling the street outside the jail office and walked north to Cottonwood Avenue, west on the silent street, and south along the alley that ran behind the saloons. It was time to keep a sharp watch for trouble, and moving along unseen behind a street of drunks was not so easy as many people believed. Travis went on with his tiresome round and the night passed slowly with very little trouble until two o'clock.

They had a stem-winder of a fight then, in Big Annie's. Sam Thompson slipped away from the Bighorn and went up the cul-de-sac to Big Annie's parlor where a dozen of his crew were singing and drinking and chasing the girls. Sam had a drink with Annie and sat on the bottom stairstep to watch the fun, and probably reminisced over a dozen years of such nights in a score of trail towns. Maybe he wondered with his dry, cynical mind whether there was really any sense in all of this.

But that didn't stop Sam from starting the fight when a stray railroad man wandered inside and tried to take his favorite girl away from the red-haired puncher. Nothing much was coming of the argument until Sam slipped up behind his puncher, gave him a push at the railroader, and yelled, "Take him, Red!" When it was over, the parlor resembled a junkyard after a tornado. Big Annie stood beside her front door with a sandsock, ordering the last bruised, bleeding warrior out of the house, not in anger but with a kind of resigned good humor. Sam Thompson was again seated on the stairstep, and Big Annie shook her sandbag at him meaningly.

"Wonder who started this?" she asked.

"Who?" Thompson said innocently.

"You trickster," Anne snorted. "But what the hell, Sam. I enjoyed it, I'm still ahead for the night. Chairs and windows are cheap. I'll keep 'em out for an hour, then we'll open up again. How about some coffee? Where the hell is Stacey? I ain't seen him in three years."

Travis entered the kitchen as they came from the front hall, and Annie said, "Just in time, Bob. I'm serving tea and crumpets. Draw up a chair."

"Too late," Travis said. "Have a little trouble?"

"Nobody hurt," Annie said. "Forget it, Bob."

Travis had watched the fight from the back window, and knew exactly what part Sam Thompson had played. He wondered how Sam, older than himself, could go on in this way with age and reason and good judgment solidly implanted in his sharp mind. It was a gutter rat's trick, this egging men into a whorehouse brawl, like a ferret-faced little kid pushing another into the mud puddle and turning the blame on somebody else. It didn't make sense, but it always happened when Sam was around. And one night,

Travis thought, something would backfire and Sam would pay the final price. But not before innocent people were hurt.

"Stacey gone to bed?" Travis asked.

"Most likely," Thompson said. "Get your sleep, Bob. The boys are running down."

"I'll do that," Travis said. "Annie, you look tired yourself."

"Don't mention it," Big Annie said wearily. "My feet are killing me."

"Tomorrow's Saturday, Sam," Travis said. "Homesteaders coming in to trade. Don't be too hard on them."

He saw the flicker of meanness in Thompson's face. Sam had been thinking of homesteaders long before Travis made the point. Sam liked nothing better than a good brawl between those easy-going, muscle-bound men and his punchers. A farmer stood no chance against the Texas men in a street fight, and worse things came from such beginnings. Travis waited for the reluctant answer that was not quite a promise, "Won't be, Bob," before nodding good night and leaving the kitchen.

Pioneer was quieting down when he reached the jail office. A bunch of riders swung from the Bighorn rail and rode slowly from town, and other men wandered unsteadily into the hotel. The night freight from Omaha, stopping for coal and water, whistled hoarsely and began the long run up the plateau toward the mountains. The night was spent and big trouble was averted for another day. Jim Murphy came from the cell block, wiping his face with a red bandanna, and sighed heavily.

"All clear, Bob. Let's knock off."

"For tonight," Travis said. "Start worrying about tomorrow, Jim. See you at noon."

He left Murphy to lock up and walked north, wanting only to get away from the jail at this time of night, past three in the morning, when all the smells and sounds and memories of the past crowded in between the jail walls and gave him little peace of mind. He paused on the corner of Cottonwood Avenue for a last look down Pioneer, and then took the side street to his house, the little one at the very end on the north side, shaded by cottonwoods and made pleasant by the flowers Mexican Joe had planted last year.

He had rented the house a year ago from a railroad man who was transferred to Cheyenne. Travis had never felt better than the day he moved from the hotel into this house. He had a kitchen, bedroom, and living room, and felt as if there was room for an army. After a year of sleeping in the morning quiet, with no more boots on hotel hall stairs and hacking coughs from awakening drummers and breakfast smells from hotel kitchens drifting up the hall, Travis knew he could never go back to that life. Not only that, just living in this house had done something to his way of life, his way of looking at the supposedly simple business of living. Maybe it had quickened his decision to resign. He wasn't certain, but he knew the house had changed him inwardly.

He could take off the belt and gun, build a fire in the cookstove, drink his coffee and sit back in his socks. He could sleep soundly and wake the next noon, and walk sleepy-eyed to the kitchen and douse himself in the blue-veined marble washbowl, brush his teeth and gurgle water like a kid playing in the washtub, with nobody around to hear the marshal betraying his dignity. He could take his own sweet time about dressing and going outside to face another day. The house had given him a taste of life as the Locklands and Summerhays, and even the Fergusons, knew it. Whatever the real feeling was, he would soon understand that unknown side of living. Just a few more nights, he thought, and it was all over.

Five

HENRY FERGUSON ATE HIS BREAKFAST IN SILENCE, chewing methodically through ham, eggs, hot biscuits, honey, and three cups of coffee with plenty of sugar and cream. Ferguson never spoke until he rose from the table, and his wife confined her remarks to conversation with Lea, their woman talk sailing far above Ferguson's ears as his mind stirred and woke slowly, considering the new day ahead.

Ferguson was getting fat but his health, at forty-seven, was excellent. Besides, weight gave dignity to a man and in his business dignity was an important asset. From his first year in the Omaha bank, Ferguson had used its president as his model, copying that stern man's conservative brown and gray suits, spotless white collars and cuffs, silver collar buttons, and gold watch chain that hung primly across a plain colored vest beneath the coat. Ferguson had been detested by everyone, but the milksop hatred of junior clerks meant nothing to him. He knew exactly what he wanted and worked relentlessly toward that goal. Today he could sit back and belch over his coffee and say, honestly, that he had made good.

Six years ago he had been cashier of the Omaha bank,

a position higher than the presidency of many smaller banks. When the president offered him the new branch at Olalla, explained the growing possibilities in that small western town, Ferguson did not hesitate a minute. The deal included twenty percent of the stock with a chance to buy fifty percent in the near future. It was really a great honor, for the position was coveted by a dozen other men in the organization, many of them senior to Ferguson in years and experience. Most people believed Ferguson made the move for the money, but Ferguson had never admitted, even to his wife, that his true reason lay much deeper.

It was the chance to become the big man in a new town. Here in Olalla Henry Ferguson was the BANKER. Here, in six years, he had become the number one citizen, at least in his own eyes. If anyone cared to express the doubt openly, that man's chance of a loan was the same as a snowball in hell. Ferguson knew how to crack the whip and his wife was not long in realizing the advantages of her new position. Ferguson had watched her shed the frightening shadow of the Omaha president's wife, and blossom forth as the social leader in Olalla. Ferguson was in complete accord with his wife, and Lea was proving to be a fine daughter, growing into a beautiful girl, worthy of a fine match in the near future. But not here . . . back east where she would attend school this fall.

Ferguson rose from the table and patted Lea's head, kissed his wife dutifully, and spoke for the first time, "Looks like a hot day."

"Yes," Mrs. Ferguson said. "Be careful today, Henry."

"Lea," Ferguson said. "I don't want you downtown after dark, hear?"

"Yes, Father," Lea said, and added, "do you think we'll have trouble tonight?"

"Who knows?" Ferguson said grumpily. "Well, time and tide wait for no man."

Having delivered this ancient proverb, Ferguson lifted his black fedora from the hall tree and stepped outside. Each step beneath the cottonwoods brought him closer to the immalleable egotist he became the moment he entered the bank and took his seat. He walked with dignity, a plump man of medium height with graying hair cut neatly and trimmed in rather thick sideburns along his small white ears. Johnny Cork had once called Ferguson's face the spitting image of a potato left too long in the seedbin. While this description never got back to Ferguson, a lot of people admitted the sagacity of Johnny's words.

Ferguson's face was almost round, actually in the oval shape of a gourd, with a short, thick nose and fleshy red lips and, a bony jaw, and eyes that were never dull. Everybody knew why Ferguson wore the heavy sideburns. He had a wart on the right side of his face beside the ear, and all the needles and salves he could find had no effect on it. So Ferguson grew sideburns just thick enough to mask the wart, and sat at his desk facing the door with his right ear next to the wall. He didn't hide it when he talked business, but it was there and deep in his mind he was angrily conscious that, like certain unlucky people, he was marked for life.

He saw John Lockland on his store steps across the street and glanced at his watch. Ten minutes of eight, time for a little chat. Ferguson crossed and stood beside Lockland in the shade of the candy-striped awning. Lockland's clerk was unpacking a shipment of dry goods, and the faint, sweet odor of peppermint candy tickled Ferguson's nose as he rocked back on his well-polished black Congress shoes and regarded the dusty emptiness of the street below them. Ferguson said cautiously, "How was business yesterday, John?"

"Fair," Lockland said. "It will be good tonight, Henry."

"Watch those bad risks," Ferguson said. "Don't let the

punchers take advantage of you. Goodlove promised to hold them down, but I trust none of them."

"Bob will handle them," Lockland said. "Don't worry about it, Henry."

"I'm almost glad Travis is resigning," Ferguson said. "We can get along nicely with a cheaper man."

"I hope so," Lockland said. "Well, time to get at it. Have coffee with me at ten, eh?"

"If I can get away," Ferguson said.

Passing down the short hall to his office, Ferguson sat at the big walnut desk. His papers were arranged neatly, waiting for his decisions, mortgages and loans, and a talk with Goodlove. He slipped a pair of black silk armguards over his cuffs, adjusted the rubber bands below his fat elbows, and got to work. It would be a pleasure this month, mailing the report to Omaha. Not a bank in the organization could boast his cash on hand, his growing assets. It was enough to dissipate the rising day heat.

While Ferguson added his totals, Johnny Cork approached his first horse of the day, a wall-eyed claybank with a broom tail. Mexican Joe escorted Pablo Manero from the jail to the depot where Pablo had to face a day's work and collect his weekly pay and lend Joe the money to buy a new set of guitar strings at Lockland's. Stacey Goodlove rolled over and grunted thickly in his hotel room, drained the water pitcher, and told himself that last night was the last time. Then Goodlove grinned at the dirty ceiling.

He always felt this way after a big night, but his headache would vanish at breakfast. And today he was paying a call on old Ferguson who wanted him to start an account in the bank. Goodlove knew it was a wise idea but he hated to give Ferguson the business. Then Goodlove thought of tonight and how his men would rip the roof off before renewing the drive to the Dakotas.

He was proud of them and he hoped they'd leave a mark on the town, not in blood but with plenty of fights and good spirits. Travis was a tough man and Sam Thompson had never really cottoned to the marshal; that was the one weak spot in letting the crew run wild. Goodlove wished half-heartedly that he could control Sam's impulse a little, but that was impossible. Sam was unchangeable.

Goodlove shaved and dressed, went downstairs to eat a big breakfast of steak and potatoes. Lighting a cigar as he stepped onto the veranda, he squinted up the street against the hot, rising sun that cooked the mist above the river. The commission man from Omaha joined him and said, "I'm ready any time you are, Stacey."

"My price," Goodlove said shortly.

They were not far apart on the price for a trainload of cattle, and Goodlove had agreed last night to ride out and give the commission man one last look before they reached the figure.

"Within reason, Stacey."

"My price," Goodlove said stubbornly. "Figure on that, or you're wasting your time. I'll drive 'em all north before I lose good money."

The commission man smiled faintly and lit his cigar. He knew Goodlove from long experience in Dodge City. They would growl and haggle and eventually Goodlove would accept a fair offer. He said easily, "You won't lose money, you old mossyhorn. Call me when you're ready."

"Give me an hour," Goodlove said.

Walking toward the bank, Goodlove saw the first wagon rumble down the street from the river crossing, a bearded homesteader with a slab-shanked wife and four kids piled atop their produce, come to town for groceries and candy and what they figured was a helluva time. Goodlove snorted and turned into the bank, glowered at the cashier who came forward hastily, and entered Ferguson's office without knocking. Ferguson glanced up with angry words on his tongue, then nodded stiffly and motioned to the empty chair. "Didn't expect you yet, Stacey."

"Couldn't sleep," Goodlove said. "Helluva night, woke up dry as a buffalo chip."

He saw Ferguson wince and bend over a paper, and smiled happily, always pleased when he hurt the banker's tender feelings. He said, "Got the same argument this morning?"

"No argument," Ferguson said. "Just common sense. You're going north where there are no banks. You need access to a good bank. I'll give you the best service in the west. What more can a man wish?"

"All right," Goodlove said. "Make out a draft for fifty thousand on my New Orleans bank. Now listen, you honor no checks except with my signature, the way I showed you. If I send a man down with a check, it'll be Red Dohney or Sam Thompson. Anybody else shows up, kick 'em out or shoot 'em."

"I will," Ferguson said. "If you'll come out to the window, Stacey, we'll fix things up right now. Will you have dinner with us tonight? Mrs. Ferguson mentioned it this morning. She's a wonderful cook."

"Thanks just the same," Goodlove said hastily, "but I ain't got the time. Let's get this business done."

"I hope your men enjoy themselves tonight," Ferguson said. "They certainly were decent last night."

"And if they buck over tonight?" Goodlove said. "What happens then?"

"They won't," Ferguson said. "We have your promise. Your word is good."

"Well, now," Goodlove chuckled. "I didn't make any hidebound promises. And I sure as hell can't control those rannies when they get on the prod."

Ferguson heard the words and realized that a smile was called for, and did his very best. With a small, dry contortion of his fat lips while walking to the front window, he felt the shadow of real fear. Then Goodlove's big hand clapped him on the shoulder, and Goodlove said, "Jesus Christ, man! You talk like a deacon. You think this place is all settled yet? We ain't done with this town. When the last herd comes through, then you can have those Ladies Aid parties and lawn dances. Until then you've got lower Pioneer Street and Big Annie, and you got Travis, and if that don't spell something, you tell me. Where's that draft? I got business at the herd."

---------------- Six ----------------

Waking at noon, Travis heard the town noises from what seemed a great distance. He went leisurely into the kitchen, started his fire, and began breakfast. Then he washed and dressed slowly, laving his face and getting a fine tingle from the cold water, and shaved with the straight edge he had used for nearly twenty years, honing it carefully on the worn leather strap hanging from a corner of the mirror. His nose distorted a little in the mirror's wavy surface, and his graying hair fuzzed against the tops of his ears when he trimmed there with short, careful strokes. Time for a haircut, maybe a shampoo, if the afternoon was slack.

He took the nearest chair and crossed one leg, knees sticking out of his baggy nightshirt like a pair of knobby red apples. He trimmed his toenails square across their tops, separating the bent toes that were cramped from natural shape by too many years in boots, and chuckled as he thought of the town catching him in this undignified position. To the town he was just a gun with bones attached. They didn't really see him as a man, doing the everyday tasks of their life, burning a finger on the frying pan, mixing a batch of biscuits, sewing on a button, but that was just as well, he knew, for he had built an illusion and it must be kept a few more weeks.

Travis washed his hands, broke two eggs into the spitting bacon grease, and dressed while breakfast simmered. He sat down hungry as a bear, wondering how the day would go, what the night might bring. He thought of others starting their day five hours earlier. Ferguson, for instance, who rose at seven and tackled breakfast like a man adding up ledger totals, when breakfast ought to be the happiest meal of the day. Thank God, Travis thought, he might be worried about the coming night but that would never spoil his appetite or chase a smile from his face. Eat a good breakfast, smile at the world and think about tonight.

Saturday was the big night in Olalla. The railroad men and workmen were paid off, and the homesteaders drove in for the weekly trading. It was no accident that new shipments of goods from the east arrived on Friday, to be unpacked and displayed by Saturday night. There was usually a church supper or a dance, and sometimes an ice cream social if enough cream, rock salt and ice could be rounded up. Travis enjoyed the ordinary Saturday nights because railroad men and homesteaders caused no serious trouble, understanding that he was protecting them rather than waiting for a chance to toss them in jail and fine them a week's pay from sheer official meanness. The railroaders respected him and the homesteaders, long ago, had judged him their kind of man.

He had ridden through the country many times in past years, visiting farms, eating in their kitchens, helping with the chores. He could plow a straight furrow, milk a cow, even darn a sock, and he wasn't a bad cook. He had become fast friends with the Summerhays two years ago, and found time to visit them once a month for Sunday dinners. After Johnny Cork met Mary Summerhays, Travis tried to bring him along, but Johnny couldn't see any girl but Lea Ferguson. He wished the Summerhays would stay home today, with Goodlove's crew in town, but nobody could request that of Fred and his neighbors. They might be clod-hoppers, rednosed gougers in the eyes of Goodlove's crew, but they could teach anyone plenty about real guts and strength. And most of all, their strength was the kind that endured and, eventually, would make the real future of this country.

Travis washed his dishes and put on his coat, smoothed it over the belt and holster, and began his walk downtown. He met Ferguson at the corner of Pioneer, heading back to work after a heavy noonday meal. Ferguson for once couldn't ignore their meeting. They matched steps on the boardwalk, and Ferguson nodded soberly, "We were lucky last night, eh?"

"Could be," Travis said. "Tonight's another story."

"I doubt we'll have serious troubles," Ferguson said curtly. "Goodlove opened an account this morning."

"That's nice," Travis said, "but it has nothing to do with his crew."

Ferguson cursed himself inwardly. Travis was the only man who could upset him, make him feel like an incompetent fool; and worst of all, apparently pierce his brain and read his innocent thoughts. In this case, Ferguson was really saying that Goodlove, now a customer, would certainly keep his crew in line. Beyond that, Ferguson was playing his usual mealy-mouthed double role, detesting violence but willing to accept a certain amount if the dollars flowed in and the violence passed over his bank and family. Travis knew all this, said nothing, and smiled faintly. Ferguson felt obliged to add, "I did not mean Goodlove's account has exempted him from obeying our laws."

"Neither did I," Travis said easily. "Well, good banking."

"Wait," Ferguson said. "Are you serious about resigning?"

"Do I have to repeat myself once a day?" Travis said.

"Not at all. I just want to be certain. We will hate to see you go."

"I'm staying around," Travis said. "You haven't got rid of me yet, Henry. I may be in for a loan."

Travis crossed to Lockland's store and Ferguson marched into the bank with red cheeks. Staying around, come in for a loan! It would be a fine day when he lent Travis money. Ferguson turned abruptly and riffled through the account ledger. He was surprised then, for Travis had a current balance of three thousand, two hundred dollars, much more than he had realized. Then Ferguson's face turned redder as he understood belatedly that Travis would never approach him for a loan, had been baiting him as usual and was probably laughing now, well aware that Ferguson was checking his account.

"The bastard!" Ferguson whispered. "I wish . . ."

Across the street in the pleasant, cool interior of his general store, John Lockland turned from his high-topped desk and called, "It's time you got up, you night owl. Going fishing with Tommy?"

"If I have time," Travis said, boosting himself on the main counter and dipping one hand into the candy jar beside the scales. "Appears that you anticipate large profits today."

"Now what makes you think that?"

"Oh," Travis smiled, "the rundown appearance of your shelves, the lack of stock."

Lockland gave a proud look at his bulging shelves and counters. They both saw the fresh bolts of dry goods, bright prints and calicoes and percales, the shoes and boots, bandannas, shirts and pants and underwear, the gun rack, all the goods that spoke of thriving business. In a dozen other stores Travis visualized this identical scene: the restocking of shelves, the marking of price tags, getting ready for the big night. The jeweler and the blacksmith, the furniture store, the billiard parlor, the saloons, the hotel, the cafés. Everybody was waiting for the rush. Travis thought of the furniture store advertising parlor and chamber suites, and where would a homesteader put a parlor suite in a soddy?

47

But that was the whole point. The furniture dealer wasn't crazy. The time would come, and the people would remember who had early faith in their future buying power. Travis chewed his peppermint and watched Lockland wrestle three new saddles onto the rack facing the counter.

They talked about prices and the best method of selling. Lockland had never really understood why Travis showed so much interest, unless Travis was actually thinking seriously about making an offer to buy into the store. They had discussed that a few times, never in seriousness, but Lockland's mind was set on one point: if Travis wanted to become a merchant, a blacksmith, a farmer, a banker, whatever he tried when he resigned would turn out a success. Lockland smiled and thrust his cigar toward the street.

"The day you resign I'll learn how serious you are about saddles and dry goods, not to mention eating up my profit in peppermint. Now go fishing. You need it."

"Yes, sir," Travis said. "About tonight. Remember what I told you. Don't argue with Goodlove's men if they come up to buy. Let them have their way."

"Just so far," Lockland said stubbornly. "I won't be insulted, Bob."

The humor melted from Travis's eyes and his face turned stiff with sober thought. "You listen to me," he said flatly. "I've warned you once. I expect cooperation."

He left the store and went down Pioneer Street to the livery barn, and heard from out back the uproar and the shouts around the corral where Johnny Cork was breaking a horse. Dust rose in thin clouds and the loafers on the top rail shouted encouragement as Johnny sweated for his three dollars a head. When Travis saddled his mare and rode up toward Lockland's house, half a dozen wagons were grouped in the vacant lot behind the courthouse and people were moving into the store. The night was starting about five hours earlier than expected, and fishing was a luxury he had to forego today. The mare stopped without command at Lockland's front gate and Travis went up the red brick walk, cupping his hands and calling, "Where's the fisherman?"

From the depths of the big square house, the boy's shout came strongly.

"Your mother home?" Travis asked.

"In the kitchen. Come on."

Travis followed Tommy Lockland down the hall and smiled when Margaret turned from her worktable, hands white with flour, fine brown hair tucked beneath a white headcloth that showed only the curly ends and the tanned nape of her neck. She was a tall woman with a perpetual air of serenity and a smile that never left her mouth. Five years ago she had entered town with absolute loathing; now, in her own words, they couldn't drag her away with a mule team. She had grown up in St. Louis, oldest daughter of a well-to-do merchant family, and until she married John and came west she hadn't known such a world existed.

"Well," she said, wiping her hands. "Fishing?"

"Too busy," Travis said. "I'll make it up to him during the week."

"I understand," Margaret said. "Tonight could be bad."

"Possibly," Travis said. "But right now I happen to have time for coffee cake and a glass of milk. Don't lie to me. I can smell it."

She smiled and turned to the pantry. "You're a regular bloodhound, the way you smell baking. Sit down, Bob. I'll join you."

When Tommy came back from the back porch, loaded with fishing tackle, Travis looked up from his plate and shook his head. "Hate to back out," he said. "I've got to stay in town, Tommy. Understand?"

He saw the disappointment, then acceptance of the day's work, that was known even to a boy of nine. "Sure," Tommy said. "Those punchers are gonna get drunk and—"

"Never mind the details," Margaret said. "Why don't

you find Joey Collins and take him fishing. Maybe Bob can go tomorrow afternoon.''

"Can you?'' Tommy asked eagerly.

"We'll see,'' Travis said. "Sorry, Tommy. I wanted to go bad myself.''

Tommy left the house and they heard him in the alley, shouting across the neighbor's fence for Joey Collins.

Margaret asked quietly, "Do you think there'll be trouble tonight, Bob?''

"You never know,'' Travis said. "The boys ride in for their fight, have their fights and make their drunken threats and forget everything one day up the trail. That kind is the good kind. The others—'' he frowned, thinking of Sam Thompson, "you never know.''

"You know, of course,'' she said, "what I am trying to say.''

She was worried about John, knowing her husband's temper and pride, remembering past incidents when John had been close to trouble with drunken punchers in the store. She had been hearing the gossip about Goodlove's crew, and last night's fight at Big Annie's, and her woman's keen intuition sensed that tonight might be wilder than usual.

"Don't worry,'' Travis said. "Part of my job. I'll be around tonight.''

"Thank you, Bob,'' she said. "I wish—no, I guess what I'm doing is wondering why they have to settle everything with their guns?''

"You ask me that,'' Travis smiled. "Me, of all people.''

"I never think,'' she said quickly. "When you come to our house to eat with us, play with Tommy, I forget about the guns and the other things. Mostly, I suppose, because you are different with us. I wish I could understand men like Goodlove.''

"When a land is being made,'' Travis said slowly, "out of dirt and blood and the good part of our lives, the making never comes cheap, Margaret. Someday the guns will not be important. You never know when that day will come, but it will be here sooner than you think. Maybe a month or two in Olalla. Today the herds are still coming north and the town is wide open, but the end isn't far off. Then the town will settle back and start to grow the way you and John and your friends want to see it grow. The way I want to see it. Then the guns won't be needed. I've watched the towns grow and have their day and die while I stood on the street and felt the dying. But you never know when. Does that sound foolish?"

"No," she said. "I can understand all that. I've been here long enough to know. Maybe I should have stayed in St. Louis."

Travis smiled. "St. Louis was wilder than this a few years back. Now you use it for your example of piousness. See how fast time passes?"

"Yes, it passes," she said. "I wish tonight was gone and John was home. I don't know why, Bob, but I'm afraid about tonight."

"I'll walk home with John tonight," Travis said. "If I get more coffee cake."

She smiled warmly. "You do. And thank you, Bob. You always make me feel better."

"Nothing to worry about," Travis said. "It will be like a hundred other nights, and not many more like it left to come. Now I've got my work."

The mare wheeled reluctantly away from the smell of open country and the distant river, and trotted back to the livery barn where Travis fed her a lump of sugar and spoke a few gentle words in her ear. The street was filling up at mid-afternoon, wagons were rumbling into town, riders were tying up at the rails, and a good volume of sound rose above lower Pioneer. Travis walked to the jail office and stood in the doorway, hat pulled low over his eyes as he took up his watch of the street. It meant a long day for him and Jim Murphy, from mid-afternoon until almost morning, but there was no choice. After tonight he should have a month of quiet nights, and then he was finished. It was worth one last stretch of uncertainty.

Through that long, hot afternoon Travis remained in the office, watching the street and wondering where the people came from, suddenly aware that he no longer knew them all. It was a fact, then, and not just advertising that homesteaders were fairly swarming out of the East. He counted a hundred wagons by dusk, and an equal number of horses, in the vacant lots and along the hitch rails. The railroad men came from work and stopped along the street for their glass of beer before supper, and the homesteaders grouped outside the stores, talking quietly and smoking cigars. The Bighorn Saloon was swelling with noise and the alley path to Big Annie's was busy long before darkness fell. Goodlove appeared on the hotel veranda at five-thirty wearing his old riding clothes, and Sam Thompson stood beside him a moment, then wandered down the street with the red-haired puncher named Dohney. Travis marked Dohney in his mind. If that puncher was sticking close to Thompson, he was starting the wrong kind of thinking.

Jim Murphy brought his supper from the café and took up the door station while Travis ate at his desk. Sunset was a blaze of orange and red and intermediate colors, then hazed over into a gentle pink and finally the first soft gray of nightfall. All the stores would stay open until the last customer was served tonight; the lamps were bright and shiny, advertising the goods just inside those big open doors. Children played around the wagons and in the vacant lots, and the church bell tolled merrily, calling hungry people to a chicken dinner at fifty cents per head. Travis stepped to the doorway and saw Mexican Joe coming from the south, fairly sober, smiling broadly and weaving just a little on his feet.

"Well?" Travis asked.

"New guitar strings," Joe said happily. "Pablo got paid."

"How long will they last?" Travis said.

"Who cares," Joe laughed. "I will play a dozen songs just for you."

Travis smiled and watched Mexican Joe wobble through the crowd and duck into Lockland's store. There'd be a big time in Mexican town tonight, with Joe playing his guitar and everybody getting drunk and singing sadder by the hour. Lea Ferguson showed up before the bank and picked her way daintily across the street to Lockland's, sniffing at the homesteader girls' dresses, showing her superiority as she avoided contact with them. Travis caught her glance and tipped his hat, forcing her to acknowledge the greeting, knowing exactly how he made her feel. Behind her, coming from their wagon, he saw Mary Summerhays and the comparison was so vivid in his mind that he wished for Johnny Cork right then, with clear eyes for once in that young fool's life. Mary crossed over and shook hands, smiling up at Travis from the boardwalk, tall and strong and happy, a fine, honest girl who made Travis wish he was twenty years younger.

"Where's that lazy father?" Travis asked.

"Spending our money," Mary said. "Are you coming out to supper tomorrow?"

"See me before you start home," Travis said. "I'll let you know then, Mary."

"You're past due," Mary said. "Three weeks, Bob."

"Is this worry strictly for me?" Travis said.

There wasn't an ounce of coquetry in Mary Summerhays. She said honestly, "No, not just you. Bring Johnny along. What's the matter with him, Bob? Is he scared of me?"

Travis lowered his head and said softly, "Johnny's a little slow on the draw. Give him time. He'll wake up."

She moved up on the step beside him and turned looking down Pioneer toward the bright smoky lamps of the saloons. Johnny Cork was there now, behind the bar in the Bighorn, washing glasses for Burnett, picking up another two dollars tonight. She knew that, and she was wishing that Johnny would be like the other young men, willing to come uptown where she had to stay, buy her a soda and talk a lot of pleasant words. She said, "I wonder why I like him, Bob? Do you know? Can you tell me?"

"For the same reason I like him," Travis said. "I can't put it in words, Mary. Don't worry about Johnny and you know who. When September comes, Johnny is due for a change of feeling about a lot of things. If you still think he's ace-high then, things might happen pretty fast. Now you run along, and don't be coming down this far again tonight. It's pretty early, but we might get some rough stuff in an hour or so."

"Don't forget about tomorrow," Mary Summerhays said. "We'll have fried chicken."

Travis did not move for a full second when the gunshots came from up the street. Perhaps that was why he did not react, for gunshots had no business coming from upper Pioneer among the stores. Then he was running, pushing Mary out of his path, pounding up the boardwalk through the crowd, reaching Lockland's store where people were crowding inward. He called harshly, "Give way here, give way! What's the matter?" and someone near the door answered. "Lockland's shot a man!"

Seven

TRAVIS MADE A CROSSED WEDGE OF HIS FOREARMS AND battered through the crowd, shoving men aside with brutal haste, climbing the steps and pushing toward the door. An elbow raked his ribs and he gave that unfortunate man a smashing blow in the chest, opening up the last six feet and gaining the doorway in one jump. Half the crowd was made up of homesteaders, the others railroaders and townspeople, all filled with curiosity and very little violence. Travis spread his arms across the door and called, "Back up, off the porch!" and when they stared blankly at him and kept surging inward he spotted Fred Summerhays and shouted, "Fred—Fred, get your friends off the porch, and don't block the street!"

Fred Summerhays nodded and began pushing men away, calling at his friends, lifting one big tow-headed youth by the arm and tossing him a full ten feet into the street. Travis called to other men and watched them nod agreement and move slowly off the porch. Jim Murphy came from lower Pioneer, pounding through the dust with a riot gun, taking up a position beside Travis in the doorway and holding the short barrels downward at a suggestive angle. Travis said, "Keep them back and quiet. I'm going inside."

"Dead?" Murphy asked softly.

"Don't know. Let me know how it goes to the south."

Stepping inside, he saw Mexican Joe pressed against the south wall beneath the harness rack. Beside the dry goods counter Lea Ferguson stood in stiff-backed terror, staring wildly at the body on the floor. John Lockland was behind the counter, left hand holding his right arm, the small bulldog .38 still dangling loosely in his right hand. Lockland's face was white with anger and a mild surprise, as though he could not believe that he had shot a man. When Travis came down the aisle, Lockland looked up and the relief brought color to his drawn face.

"Well, John," Travis said quietly. "What happened?"

He really didn't need an explanation; the story was plain before him, needing only a few words to tell of the beginning and the subsequent action. John Lockland wiped his face with his left hand and told it haltingly. One of Goodlove's young punchers had wandered uptown, across the invisible line between upper and lower Pioneer, and drifted into the store. The puncher hadn't caused any disturbance in the street. He seemed like any man looking for a shirt, pants, boots—any one of a hundred items needed for the long ride north into the Dakotas. It was from this everyday occurrence that the trouble began.

The puncher had been drinking and complained about the price of a saddle. Lockland had explained patiently about high freight charges forcing the price so high. The puncher suddenly boiled over and cursed Lockland, until Lockland could stand no more and ordered him to leave. There was good and decent reason for this order, because Lea Ferguson was shopping at the dry goods counter and the puncher knew she was within earshot. Mexican Joe was on the other side, examining guitar strings, and both were in the path of any possible argument. Lockland ordered the puncher to get out, but it was too late and Lockland had never learned how to soften his voice when he knew he was in the right.

The puncher had carried a revolver inside his shirt—this directly against Travis's regulations—and the puncher leaped back, upsetting the cracker barrel, and went for his hideout gun. Lockland had no choice; it was kill or be killed. And there was Lea to consider. Lockland reached under the counter for his own revolver and shot the puncher a moment before the puncher's bullet, deflected by Lockland's shot, cut Lockland's sleeve and thudded into the wall. The puncher fell face down on the floor, his head coming to rest in the spilled white crackers. That was all there was to it—one shot by each man, and one man dead.

"That's all, John?" Travis asked.

"No more," Lockland said. "I had to, Bob. He was drunk and crazy. It was one of us for sure."

"Self-defense," Travis said soberly. "Carrying a concealed gun north across the line, and coming north of the line after dark. Below the line he was also breaking the law. The young fool. Who was he?"

"I don't know his name," Lockland said. He's red-haired."

Travis knelt beside the dead man and lifted the battered brown hat and saw the sun-burned, roughly handsome face of Red Dohney. Now it would come, he thought dismally—the trouble he had hoped to escape. A man's death in Olalla was not a rare occurrence. It happened about once a month the year around, but mostly by accident in drunken quarrels along lower Pioneer, or in the railroad yards or along the river. The last shootout was almost a year old, he remembered, and nobody was hurt that time but an innocent bystander who took a ricochet in the fleshy part of his right calf and ran all the way to Doc Steven's office holding the wrong leg. But this was different, and everything was wrong. Red Dohney had gotten drunk and somebody had egged him into crossing the line. Now he was dead, and Sam Thompson was down the street with too much guilty knowledge in that shriveled heart. Anyway, Travis thought, he was lucky in one respect. The trouble had come before Goodlove's crew had the time to get completely drunk. That was one factor in his favor now. Travis covered the face with the hat and rose slowly.

"John," he said. "Lock your back door and windows. Go to your office and stay there until I call you."

"No . . ."

"Go on," Travis said. "This is no time for moralizing."

"Very well," Lockland said. "But I've no reason to hide, Bob."

"Not for this," Travis said. "For what comes next, I wish you were in Omaha."

Lockland walked reluctantly through the archway into the back room, and Travis crooked one finger at Mexican Joe and said easily, "Did you see it, Joe?"

"Si," Mexican Joe said, in a thin and whispery voice.

"Was it like John told me?"

Joe nodded. "Señor John, he had no choice, amigo."

"All right," Travis said. "You go in back with John."

"I better go home," Joe said quickly. "Pretty fast. I think I go home."

"You go in back," Travis said, "and you stay there!"

"But that Goodlove . . ." Joe began.

"Stay there," Travis said. "Understand?"

Joe vanished into the back room and Travis turned to Lea Ferguson for the first time. He had no sympathy for her tonight. She had been warned a dozen times about coming downtown after dark when a trail crew was in, and she always managed to break that rule in one way or another, enjoying the thrill of showing off a pretty dress and snatching those veiled glances at men like the one on the floor. The only good part about her presence was the fact that she could testify for Lockland. Travis nodded at the body and said bluntly, "Did you see it happen, Lea?"

"Yes," Lea Ferguson said thinly. "I saw it."

"Was it the way John told me?" Travis asked. "Self-defense?"

"Oh, yes. Mr. Lockland had to shoot. Oh, yes."

"Good girl," Travis said. "Kept your wits about you. That takes guts."

Lea looked up and then swayed weakly against the counter. She was basking in the limelight, all at once, and waiting for Travis to put his arm around her and speak some more nice words. But mostly, he thought, to feel an arm around her shoulders. She was running pretty true to the way he had judged her long ago, and he did not move while she swayed and finally recovered her balance with an angry look.

"I want to go home," she said coldly. "I want my father."

"Don't you want to help John?" Travis asked.

"Why, yes."

"Then you step around behind the counter," Travis said. "You're a witness and I'll need you for a little while. Your father will be here any minute."

"I want to go home," Lea said stubbornly. "I don't know anything about all this."

"Get over there," Travis said coldly. "I thought you had some backbone."

He saw angry pride brighten her face. She might be scared, mostly of what her father would say when he found her here, but she'd stay now out of pure spite. She hadn't gotten her craw full of secondhand thrills yet, and she knew what was coming. Travis faced the door and at that moment Jim Murphy called from the porch, "They're coming, Bob!"

"All right," Travis said. "Send for Judge Clark and Doc Stevens. Then come inside."

Murphy gave a sharp command to someone and stepped into the store and took a position on the south side, in the shadows against the wall. Travis remained in the center aisle, the overhead lamps halfway between him and the door, and heard the sound of boots walking as one, coming from lower Pioneer, walking steadily and without haste.

Travis unbuttoned his coat and cleared the holster. He waited there with his right hand held loosely just above the gun butt.

"Want a shotgun?" Murphy asked. "I can grab one off the rack."

"No," Travis said. "No need, Jim."

"You know who he is?" Murphy asked suddenly, looking down at the puncher.

"Red Dohney," Travis said.

"Sure," Murphy said, "just another puncher, I thought. I just heard outside who he was. Goodlove's nephew by marriage, his first trip up the trail and the apple of Goodlove's eye. What about that, Bob?"

"I knew it," Travis said quietly.

"You knew it!" Murphy said. "God, Bob. Why didn't you tell me before? Listen, you want that shotgun now?"

"We won't need it," Travis said. "Not tonight."

He heard the movement of the crowd as it edged back across the street, and then he saw the silhouettes of the hats against the opposite side lights, forming a solid circle before the porch steps. One man came up the steps and barked something at the others, and then Goodlove entered and came forward three steps before halting. Goodlove was armed and outside, twenty strong, his crew was armed and waiting. Goodlove looked through and beyond Travis, saw the body, and clenched his big fists until the skin over the knuckles turned snow white.

"Easy, Stacey," Travis said. "Let's have no more trouble."

This was the harsh and decisive moment. Goodlove was filled with whiskey and a great, unreasonable anger, as any man was bound to feel in such a time. Goodlove wanted Lockland, and while he was dangling on the edge of furious action, he saw Travis and controlled himself with the vanishing ends of his common sense.

"Red!" Goodlove said thickly. "Dead?"

"Dead," Travis said. "Couldn't be helped, Stacey. He

was drunk, he started it, John had no choice. It was cut and draw. John was lucky, that's all. Self-defense pure and simple.''

"Red?" Goodlove said. "Nothin' but a boy!"

Travis said, "I'm sorry, Stacey."

"Sorry?" Goodlove said. "That's small help. Where's Lockland?''

"No arguments tonight," Travis said. "Stacey, the street is closed as of now. Take your crew out of town. We'll hold an inquest tomorrow morning at nine o'clock."

Goodlove glanced around the store and saw Murphy, and then saw Lea Ferguson for the first time. He was fighting himself hard by that time, trying to hold back his rage, and he had no time for manners. He said, "She see it?"

"Yes," Travis said. "She'll testify. I want to get her home now.''

"Anybody else?" Goodlove said.

"One other man," Travis said. "He'll testify, Stacey. I'm hiding nothing from you."

Goodlove looked at the body again, and Travis knew the big man was reading the signs and seeing the action as it had taken place, but refusing to admit the truth. Feet clattered on the porch and Ferguson burst wildly through the door and ran to his daughter and took her in his arms, and began shouting at Travis in a hoarse, frightened voice. Goodlove turned slowly and glared at Ferguson and said, "Shut up, little man! Get your pup out of here!"

"Now," Ferguson said squeakily. "Now . . ."

"Take Lea home," Travis said quietly. "She's all right, Henry. Just take her home . . . now!"

Ferguson said, "Gladly," and led Lea from the store, strangely obedient for the first time Travis could remember. Doctor Stevens and Judge Clark came then, stepping around Goodlove and approaching the body. Clark studied the scene while Doctor Stevens knelt beside the body, and in this moment Goodlove spoke with a thin, odd voice,

"Any objection to taking Red out of here?"

"Doctor?" Travis said.

"Nothing to be done," Doctor Stevens said. "If you have the facts, Bob."

"Everything," Travis said. "All right, Stacey."

Goodlove turned and called, "Joe, Ed! Come in here." Two punchers came up the steps and into the store, and Goodlove pointed to the body and said, "We'll take Red along, boys. Carry him gently."

They advanced on Travis, shoulders touching, and at the last step split and went around him, the wild anger riding high in their faces, but his presence and his right hand still holding them down. They lifted Red Dohney and only then Travis stepped aside as they carried the body from the store and down the steps out of sight.

"Inquest at nine tomorrow, Doctor?" Travis asked.

"Yes," Doctor Stevens said. "Agreeable, Judge?"

"Nine," Judge Clark said. "Courthouse. You have the witnesses, Bob?"

"They'll be present," Travis said. "All right, Stacey. There's nothing more we can do tonight. The street is closed."

He felt the words coming, the outburst that was certain to fall upon them all. Goodlove backed deliberately toward the door and stopped there, big and bent and gray, face shadowed by his wide hat brim. "God damn you!" Goodlove exploded. "Witnesses and all, everything nice and legal. Come to the inquest, pour Red in a hole, keep riding. Travis, I know this mealy-mouthed Lockland. I know how he thinks and I can guess what happened. Self-defense, sure it was, any fool can see that. Red had a few drinks, felt his oats, and this stiff-backed sonofabitch couldn't let it ride, give the boy a chance to cool off. Sure, self-defense, fifty other times down the trail we saw it happen, you and me, Travis, but not this time. Pat me on the back, tell me to keep my men in line, then why don't you keep your damned storekeepers in line? It won't settle with me, Travis, not this time."

There was no use arguing now. Travis said coldly, "Five minutes, Stacey. You and your crew, out of town in five minutes!"

"And if I don't feel like it?" Goodlove said.

"You're a damned fool," Travis said evenly. "And too old for what will happen. Five minutes, Stacey. You know me. I don't repeat an order more than once. Move out!"

Goodlove placed his hands on his hips and said, "All right, Travis. I'll see you again, late this summer. I'll come back down the trail with the biggest crew this god-forsaken town ever saw. We'll ride into your town on our way home, and then we'll wipe this town off the map. We'll have Lockland. You understand me, Travis? I've no time now, I've got to move north and I need every man. Well, next time you won't be big enough. I'm warning you now."

"I'll be here," Travis said, "and you won't ride down the trail, Goodlove."

"You're wrong," Stacey Goodlove said, suddenly quiet and soft spoken. "And if you're wise, you'll resign before I come again. Nobody gets in my way the next time."

He was gone then, outside and down the steps among his men. Their voices rose in angry protest before they moved down the street in a close-packed wedge toward their horses. Goodlove led them past the store and around the corner to the west on the run. They were gone in a flurry of dust and clods and one harsh yell that echoed behind the hoofbeats. Judge Clark mopped his sweating face in the following silence and said painfully, "Great God, Bob! We're lucky tonight."

"I want this legal tomorrow," Travis said. "I'll have the witnesses there. Lea Ferguson and Mexican Joe."

"Will Goodlove show up?" Doctor Stevens asked.

"What do you think?" Travis said.

"I say no."

"He'll send a man," Travis said. "He's too proud to come himself. But he'll be represented."

"Who?" Clark asked.

63

"I could not say for sure," Travis said. "But I can guess. Well, gentlemen . . ."

Doctor Stevens grunted and said, "Yes, time to go home," and turned Judge Clark toward the door. When they left the store, Travis called, "John," and watched Lockland come from the back room and join him beside the counter. Lockland had heard it all, and his face was filled with uncertainty. Travis said moodily, "Stacey means business, John."

"You mean he'll come back?"

"I'm afraid so," Travis said.

"How long do I have then?" Lockland said steadily. "I heard him, Bob."

Travis smiled and put one hand on Lockland's arm. "The rest of your life, John. They'll be back in September, you'll be here when they come. You'll be here when they leave. I think you'd better close up for tonight. Wait here, I'll walk home with you."

Murphy came from the shadows and leaned his shotgun against the counter and puffed out a huge burst of breath. Travis said, "Stick around," and went through the door and down the steps to the street. He walked south and felt like the only man in town, the loneliest man at any rate, walking the center of an empty, dusty street. He stopped at each saloon and gave the signal to close up; and as he traveled to the far end and back, the lamps went off and the doors slammed shut. Pioneer withdrew into uneasy, black silence. Nearing the store again, Travis began selecting the words to use with Margaret Lockland, and then thought with weary belated anger, "How can I resign now?"

Eight

JUDGE CLARK HAD COME TO OLALLA BEFORE TRAVIS
took the marshal's job. Clark was from Coon Rapids, Iowa,
a lawyer who farmed on the side and gradually became
bored with what seemed to him an increasingly humdrum
life. He practiced law for three years in Olalla before the
voters elected him county judge. During those years he
proved his fairness a hundred times over to all people, no
matter their creed or color. He collected a thousand dollars
for the widow of Carlos Pavez, who was killed on the
section, invested her money in good bonds, and started her
in a dressmaking business. Then he charged her fifty dollars for a case that ran six months. No man could have a
better endorsement among the people of Olalla.

When Clark was elected by an 85 percent majority, he
growled about folks buying a pig in a poke, and proceeded
to run the courthouse gang with stern honesty. He was a
rotund little man in his mid-forties, brown-eyed and nearly
bald, with a monkish tonsure of bristly yellow fuzz clinging to the tanned skin above his ears. He had big feet and
hands, and a long, thin nose that thrust out from his fat
cheeks and double chins like an inquisitive raccoon's. He
was a widower of fifteen years, and that was his only fault

in the eyes of the ladies. They wanted every man married and Clark resisted all applicants with courtly defiance. With Travis and Doctor Stevens, Clark formed a bachelor trio that boasted impregnable bastions.

Judge Clark got down early that Sunday morning and settled himself at his desk while the clerks and bailiff opened the big courtroom for the inquest. Clark hadn't slept well for pondering the shooting and the people involved. He wasn't concerned with the verdict—clearly self-defense—but he was deeply worried about possible complications. Stacey Goodlove had lived outside the law all his wild life, and it was unreasonable and unfair to the man's nature to assume that he would change; and in that volcanic anger lay the very real danger to John Lockland's future. Clark could finish the inquest business in a few minutes, but any man who believed the case closed was simply a damned fool.

He watched the courtroom fill with spectators, dressed for church but stopping by to see if Goodlove would appear. Ferguson and his wife, stiff in their black Sunday clothes, brought Lea down the aisle to front seats behind the railing. Jim Murphy and Travis entered a minute later with Mexican Joe, led Joe through the gate to the prosecutor's table, talking quietly, trying to calm Joe down. Judge Clark nodded at them and waved to Doctor Stevens who came from the inner office and dropped into a chair beside Travis.

"Any sign of Goodlove?" Clark asked.

"None," Travis said. "He won't be here."

"Then let's finish this," Clark said. "George, get the Locklands."

The bailiff hurried in the side hall and returned with the Locklands who took seats across the table from Travis. It was plain that Lockland hadn't slept a wink, and Margaret was not her usual self. Travis said, "Cheer up. This isn't a wake."

"I couldn't sleep," Lockland said. "Thinking about that boy."

"Man," Travis said. "Don't lose sleep over it. Margaret, I don't like to see you with that hangdog look. What are you ashamed of?"

"Nothing," Margaret Lockland said. "I'm frightened, Bob."

"Of what?" Travis said. "Do you see the bogyman? Of course not."

"Nine o'clock," Judge Clark said. "George, shut the doors and earn your pay."

The bailiff signaled one of Sheriff Conroy's deputies to swing the big double doors. Johnny Cork slipped inside at the last moment, glanced down the sloping row of seats, and took a back bench on the right side. Just before the doors thudded together Travis saw the man he had expected for the past ten minutes. Sam Thompson entered the courtroom and took a rear seat beneath the balcony overhang in the deep left corner. Sam was dressed in his dusty riding clothes but he wore a new pearl-gray Stetson, and Travis saw the belt and gun worn in deliberate violation of the rule. Travis could not see his face plainly, only the tilted-down brim of the Stetson and the sharp, angular jawline as Thompson hunched down and folded his short, thick arms across his chest. John Lockland stiffened and touched Travis on the arm.

"Thompson's here," he said.

"What of it?" Travis said. "His privilege."

"But . . ."

"He will not start trouble here," Travis said. "Forget him, John."

Judge Clark rapped his gavel and gave his orders. His clerks immediately swore in an inquest jury from the first three rows. The judge carried them through the technical opening and into the recorded testimony of the previous night concerning the shooting, the man's death, and brought them speedily to the entire crux of this business, the testimony of the witnesses who would verify and place John Lockland's self-defense on the record. Judge Clark said pleasantly, "Lea Ferguson, will you come forward."

Lea rose hesitantly from her seat, bent down as her mother spoke in her ear, and came through the gate to the stand. She repeated the oath and sat gingerly in the big walnut chair, no doubt thinking about soiling her pretty new Sunday dress on the same wood that, in past years, had cushioned the hips of killers and horse thieves and rapists. Judge Clark leaned down and said, "Lea, tell us what you saw last night in John Lockland's store. Take your time, tell us everything you saw."

Lea glanced toward her parents and fidgeted with her handkerchief. "Judge Clark, I can't remember anything."

"What?" Clark said. "Well now, Lea. You were in the store."

"Yes, sir."

"At the dry goods counter?"

"Yes, sir."

"And Red Dohney came into the store?"

"I guess so," Lea said. "I didn't know him."

"So you had to hear the argument that started between Dohney and John Lockland, didn't you?"

"They were talking," Lea said. "I didn't pay much attention. I was looking at material."

"But you heard them?"

"Well . . . the cowboy was talking awfully loud."

"And then the fight started?" Clark asked.

"I guess so."

"Now, Lea," Clark said. "Dohney jumped back and upset the cracker barrel, didn't he?"

"I think so," Lea said.

"The cracker barrel is ten feet from the front end of the dry goods counter," Clark said. "You heard it tip over, didn't you?"

"Yes, sir," Lea said. "I guess I did."

"And then Dohney drew his gun and John drew his, and both shot at nearly the same time. Isn't that right?"

"There were two shots," Lea said.

"Very well," Clark said. "Now tell us, did John Lockland shoot in self-defense, to save his own life?"

Lea crushed her handkerchief between her hands, looked quickly at her parents, and bit her lower lip. She said breathlessly, "Judge Clark, I wasn't looking at all. I heard the shots and I guess I screamed, and everything was terrible. I was so frightened I don't remember what happened. When I looked around that—that man was on the floor and Mr. Lockland was standing there with his gun. That's all I remember."

Judge Clark leaned heavily on his desk and squeezed his short fingers cruelly around his gavel. He had listened to countless witnesses lie and fumble and worm around the truth, but Lea was doing one of the best jobs he had ever heard. She was playing the poor, helpless girl who had been so confused and frightened she couldn't remember a thing, and she was putting it over in fine style. Clark wondered how Stacey Goodlove had worked this deal so fast, and for what reason, and how many hours last night and this morning Ferguson had labored to make Lea perjure herself, literally give an openhanded slap to Lockland's word of honor. For Lea was lying, with the stupid and unknowing cruelness of the young, and everybody with an ounce of common sense knew it. There was nothing to do. Lea had effected a stalemate and rendered her testimony valueless.

"You're sure that's all?" Clark said.

"Yes, sir," Lea said faintly.

"Step down," Clark said. "Next witness . . . all right, Joe."

Mexican Joe was given a helping boost by Murphy. He came forward and took the oath, and looked up at Clark with wide, trusting eyes. Joe was freshly shaved and wore clean pants and a blue shirt. He was doing his level best to stay calm in the presence of so much law and order, but his eyes jumped around the courtroom and his long brown fingers began folding accordion pleats in the front of his shirt when he took the chair. Clark thought, "He's all right, this will be better," and gave Joe a warm smile of encouragement.

He heard Travis's chair squeak as Travis pushed back from the prosecutor's table and half-turned toward the rear of the courtroom. Then Mexican Joe was suddenly frozen in place, staring toward the left rear corner. In that back row, under the balcony shadow, Sam Thompson had sat up and pushed his pearl-gray Stetson far back on his forehead, showing the white skin just beneath his hairline. Thompson placed both hands on the bench before him and looked directly at Mexican Joe, and stayed in that position with his Stetson showing up as a pale blob against the gloom.

"All right, Joe," Clark said quickly. "Tell us what you saw last night in John Lockland's store?"

Joe looked up and Clark saw fear growing in his brown face. Joe had closed his mouth tightly and there was no more white-toothed smile or little grin of hopeful admiration for the judge's kindness. Joe wanted to tell them, and then his head dropped and Clark knew that Joe was really not sitting in this courtroom, but seeing the world outside and Sam Thompson waiting behind every tree and up every draw of that world, from now on until Joe looked into the barrel of a gun.

"Well," Clark said. "Tell us, Joe."

"I don't know much," Joe said, so softly that Clark had to lean down to catch the words.

"You were there," Clark said patiently. "You heard everything, Joe. You saw the fight. What were you doing in the store?"

"Guitar strings," Joe said.

"Did you get them?"

Joe nodded. "Yes, sir. I got 'em."

"So you remember that," Clark said. "All right, Joe. There's nothing to be afraid of. We want you to tell us what you saw, and that's all there is to it. Go ahead."

"I guess," Joe began, "I guess I wasn't looking, Judge."

"Bob," Judge Clark said, "when you entered the store, do you remember where Joe was?"

"On the south side," Travis said, "against the wall, facing the aisle."

"Remember that, Joe?" Clark asked.

"Yes, sir," Joe said, looking at Travis with a sad, forlorn movement of his shoulders.

"If you were like that," Clark said, "you had to see what happened. Now go on and tell us, Joe. Did you see John Lockland and Red Dohney draw their guns?"

"I guess so," Joe said faintly.

"And you heard the shots?"

"Yes, sir."

"And John Lockland had to draw and shoot, to save his own life?"

Joe shrank back in the big chair until the top of his black head was below the chair back. He looked small and confused and very frightened, and he couldn't seem to turn his eyes from that rear corner of the room. And then Travis spoke softly from the prosecutor's table, his words meant only for Joe and barely reaching the stand.

"You do not remember your true friends, amigo?"

Mexican Joe would not look at Travis. He said desperately, "I don't remember nothing, Judge."

"But you heard the shots?" Clark said.

"Yes, sir."

"And Red Dohney knocked the cracker barrel over?"

"Somethin' fell," Joe admitted.

"Did John Lockland have to shoot?" Clark asked. "Did he, Joe, to save his own life?"

Mexican Joe retreated visibly into a private shell of his own kind, like a turtle withdrawing head and flippers. Clark knew that once Joe dropped into this hard-cased cover of the mind and soul, nothing could draw him out and make him speak. Joe was fighting the evil that had been ground into his people for centuries, remembering his own childhood far to the south, and with that instinctive memory came the past hurts suffered by his parents, and their parents, and all their forgotten ancestors who had feared men like Sam Thompson.

There was nothing much to do. Mexican Joe possessed nothing tangible in his body and heart but a great, childish love of living; and if he lost that love, the living itself would mean nothing to him. It was impossible to force Joe into telling the truth when he could see Sam Thompson, and know that for some reason beyond his understanding, his life was hanging literally by a thread. Judge Clark moved his head in a tiny, negative gesture, and Travis nodded in return.

"All right, Joe," Clark said. "That's all."

Joe tried to smile, show Clark he was grateful and that he hated to be this way, but it was something that he dared not do today . . . maybe tomorrow when Thompson was riding far north on the trail, but not today . . . and maybe not tomorrow either, or next week or next month or next year. Joe slipped from the big chair and almost ran to the table. Clark sighed and decided to go ahead with the business and get it over with. The jury knew what had happened. There was no need hashing everything over again. The testimony actually wasn't essential.

Clark pushed it through in a hurry, and the jury didn't bother to leave the courtroom, just glanced around and nodded together. The foreman stood and gave their verdict, self-defense, and that was an end to the farce. The inquest was on record now, John was cleared, and everybody could go to church or have a drink. Clark rapped his gavel and the deputy opened the big double doors and people rose and began filing outside. Clark saw Sam Thompson move leisurely through the doors and disappear down the steps into the sunlight. Ferguson and his wife hustled Lea up the aisle, out of the building, heading for church. They were going to do a little righteous praying, Clark thought, and whatever confessing Ferguson might deem necessary on such a Sunday morning. When Clark came down from the bench to join Travis and the others, Doctor Stevens touched his arm and nodded to Travis.

"Join me," Stevens said. "I need some refreshment . . . and a lot of talk."

"In a few minutes," Travis said. "At your place, Larry?"

"Yes, come around the back way."

Travis said, "I'll need that drink," and left them at the table, walking for the doors and the meeting with the man they all knew was waiting outside on the street. Clark took one look at Lockland and frowned.

"Margaret," he said. "You and John go home and forget all this. You hear me?"

"Yes," Lockland said. "But I don't understand why . . ."

"You will," Clark said. "In due time. Now run along."

Nine

JOHNNY CORK EDGED NEAR THE FRONT DOORS AS THE Fergusons hurried past. Lea saw him but all she did was turn her head away and clutch tighter at her mother's arm. Then she was gone down the steps and up Pioneer toward the church. Johnny Cork drifted with the crowd and watched until Lea's skirt flickered a last time in the sunlight outside the church. Turning away with a sick, wondering hollow in his stomach, he saw Sam Thompson going along lower Pioneer. Johnny Cork's mind jumped like a cricket, trying to unravel the testimony and make sense of the inquest—or the lack of sense in everything that happened.

People were talking all around him, on the grass and under the cottonwood trees, delaying their midday meal and church to discuss the inquest. Johnny Cork flushed with anger at one speech, "What did that fool girl testify that way for? Hell, she saw Lockland shoot. She knew he had to save his own hide. What's her idea, you tell me?" Johnny Cork was asking himself the same question, but that didn't stop him from hating the speaker, wanting to punch all of them in the face. It wasn't Lea's fault, he told himself stubbornly. It was easy to get flustered and forget everything you saw, especially when it happened so unexpectedly. And what was the difference? Judge Clark had acquitted Lockland, nobody was hurt. And then Johnny Cork thought, belatedly, "What about Mexican Joe?" and didn't feel honest inside.

He guessed accurately at Joe's sudden choke-up. Thompson was a Mex-hater, and scaring Joe out of his wits was probably Sam's idea of a fine joke. Johnny Cork wandered down the street, kicking at the dust with his fresh-polished boots, trying to think up some way to spend the day. He wanted to see Lea but that was getting tougher all the time. His best chance was a walk along the river, on the south bank above the bend. Lea sometimes went up there with the other girls right after supper in the summertime. Johnny Cork stopped outside the jail office windows and glanced at his reflection in the glass. Wasting time again, he told that skinny figure. For God's sake, get to thinking and try to get ahead before there's no time and no more chance.

Travis caught up with him there and slapped him gently on the shoulder. Johnny Cork grinned and faked a punch at Travis's stomach, and stepped back out of range. "Nice morning, Bob."

"Is it?" Travis said. "How's your appetite?"

"The same," Johnny said. "Always hungry."

"Saddle up," Travis said. "We're invited out to evening supper."

"Summerhays?"

"Nobody else," Travis smiled. "Fried chicken and cherry pie and grape wine."

Johnny Cork rubbed his sunburned nose. "Next week, Bob. I can't make it today."

"Well," Travis said absently. "Another time then, Johnny."

Johnny Cork realized that Travis wasn't going to eat with the Summerhays either, was just talking to pass time while he watched the hotel veranda. Travis patted his shoulder once more, and headed across the street where Sam Thompson was sitting in one of the wicker-bottomed rocking chairs. Watching Travis climb the steps and take the adjoining rocker, Johnny Cork felt young and useless. He was standing here, mooning over a girl, worrying about his future, and Travis was facing something that even the town hadn't begun to understand.

In the veranda shade, Travis sat beside Sam Thompson and lit a cigar. Sam was staring into nowhere, hands dangling loosely over the chair arms, dusty boots thrust far out toward the railing. Travis got his cigar going satisfactorily and said, "Herd on the trail, Sam?"

"Got away early," Thompson said. "No trouble at all."

"You staying around?" Travis asked.

"I'm pulling out in a minute or two," Thompson said. "Just come in to see how you folks run an inquest. Stacey figured it was only polite for one of us to be present."

"Glad you came," Travis said. "Everything go like you expected?"

"Pretty near," Thompson said. "That Clark sure knows his law talk, don't he?"

"A good man," Travis said. "Sometimes he has trouble with witnesses, but he gets what he wants in the end."

"Like just now?" Thompson asked.

"Like now," Travis said. "Maybe you're thinking he didn't get what he wanted, Sam. He did."

"All cut and dried," Thompson said. "You got it on your record. Lockland's cleared."

"He was clear last night," Travis said. "You all knew that, Sam."

"Yes," Thompson said thoughtfully, "pretty good judge. Well, time I cut the dust. See you in the fall, Bob."

Thompson brushed ashes from his shirt and rose slowly, gave his belt and holster a deliberate tug, and started for the hitch rail. When he reached the first step, Travis said, "Sam—"

"I got a minute," Thompson said. "No more."

"Sam," Travis said, "turn around."

Thompson turned on his heels and placed his left hand on the smooth, hand-worn porch rail. "What's the trouble, Bob?"

"With you, Sam," Travis said quietly. "That's the trouble. You're wrong inside. You like to play it nice and easy, act like a gentleman, and underneath you're boiling over like a hot spring. I know what you'd like to do right now, but I can tell you something about that idea, Sam."

"Tell away," Thompson said. "Not being familiar with my own mind, I'd appreciate you reading it, Bob."

"You never could read your own mind," Travis said. "About this little idea of yours, I don't know if you planned it, or Stacey did the brainwork, but it won't go. It won't work. I want to straighten out a couple of facts before you head north, Sam. First off, I never hid behind a woman's skirt and I never expected Stacey to pull that carpetbagger trick. Tell him for me it makes him out a good deal cheaper than I ever judged him. As for Mexican Joe, leave him alone. Don't bother him, Sam."

"Want me to pass this along to Stacey?" Thompson asked.

"Word for word," Travis said. "I don't want any misunderstandings."

"There won't be," Thompson said, "Not between us, Bob. Never again. I'll tell Stacey. We'll be seeing you in the fall—if you don't resign and pull stakes."

"I'll be here," Travis said. "Whether I resign or not, it won't matter."

Thompson smiled then. "Good! You're making a long ride a lot happier, Bob, just knowing you'll be here. If that's all you got to say, so long."

"One more thing," Travis said.

"Well?"

"Take off that belt and gun," Travis said. "Drop it on the porch. You know my rule, Sam. You can pick it up in the fall."

Watching Thompson, he stood suddenly and kicked his rocker out of the way, against the wall, and waited patiently, knowing exactly what Thompson would do. Goodlove had sent him in to listen, and do a certain job, and return with all the news. Not to make trouble, or be tricked into trouble. Besides that, Sam Thompson would never go crazy enough to stand against Travis. He wasn't that good a man, he knew it from long experience, and the inferiority rankled in him like salt on a raw wound. Travis was grinding him down in public and he couldn't do a thing about it. But he wouldn't give up without some word.

"No," Thompson said. "Nothing doing, Bob."

"Drop it," Travis said evenly. "Drop it, or I'll take it off you, Sam. Standing up or on your back. All right . . ."

Thompson fumbled at his belt, disengaged the hook, and let it drop to the veranda floor. He stepped backward, down the first step, and said, "Now I'll sure be looking forward to this fall, Bob."

"I want you to," Travis said easily. "Me keeping your gun ought to make you come back, Sam. I always felt you were a man who liked to keep track of his personal property. Give my regards to Stacey and tell him I'll be waiting if he's fool enough to make the try."

Thompson turned and walked to his horse, climbed up, and rode straight through town and out of sight without a side glance. Travis lifted the gunbelt, unloaded the Colt, and went into the lobby. He pushed the belt and gun across the desk and said, "Store this in your safe. I'll call for it."

"Under what name, Bob?"

"Sam Thompson," Travis said. "Print it plainly so there'll be no mistake."

Johnny Cork was waiting on the veranda when he came out. Johnny said, "About that fried chicken. Reckon we can make it this afternoon?"

"Changed your mind?" Travis said. "Why, Johnny?"

"Don't know," Johnny Cork said. "Guess I just want to get the hell out of town for a while."

"I feel the same way," Travis said gravely. "Tell you what, Johnny. I've got some business until noon. We'll ride out about two o'clock."

"I'll saddle your mare," Johnny said. "See you at the barn. Say, Bob—"

"Yes?"

"Was he trying to get mean?"

"Mean," Travis said. "No, Johnny. That was me trying to get mean. There's a lot of difference in that. Or didn't you know how mean I am?"

Ten

DOCTOR STEVENS WAS LEAN AND RAWBONED, WITH A long, hollow-cheeked face that grew belligerent reddish orange whiskers whenever he missed his daily shave. That happened often when he was in the country setting broken legs and delivering babies and fighting fever. Stevens had come to Olalla four years ago, one of the few young doctors who passed up a safe, lucrative eastern practice and took a gamble on the west. He was thirty-one on arrival and his age, at the start, was naturally a drawback. People instinctively distrusted young doctors, and it took them a year to realize that age had nothing to do with competence.

In that time Stevens proved his skill and demonstrated a refreshing lack of the professional bedside manner to those vaporous women who wasted a busy doctor's time. Stevens stopped that foolishness in a hurry, among those ladies so inclined, and only grinned when Mrs. Ferguson went to Omaha twice a year for treatments from a "specialist." Stevens didn't give a tinker's damn about her kind. The homesteaders had adopted him and while his cash balance was never high, his credit in hams, eggs, butter, bacon, comforters, jellies, jams and love was never on the debit side.

Ordinarily Stevens liked nothing better than a good argument with Judge Clark and Travis, the three of them in his living room locked off from the town. Stevens bought the Purtle house six months after he started practice, it being the last house on the west side of Pioneer Street before the business district began, a small four-roomed place badly run down. He remodeled the front rooms into an office and operating room, kicked out the rear partition to form the big living room, and had a kitchen and bedroom built on the side. He cooked his own breakfast and Hertha Svoboda came in to clean house and prepare his evening meal. The rest of the day he lived alone and loved it. His living room was a clutter of books and medical trivia, guns and boots, fishing rods and never less than half a dozen well-cured hams hung along the back wall, with the names of the donors etched into the dark brown skin in red ink, showing the credit allowed and for what purpose. Mexican Joe and Pablo Manero built three heavy chairs with rawhide backs and seats, and each chair was the private property of a certain man: namely Clark, Travis, and the doctor.

Stevens and Judge Clark waited for Travis that morning, sitting deep in their chairs, coats off and suspenders down, drinking coffee and holding back their thoughts until Travis arrived. Finally they heard a horse pass and turn west on Cottonwood, and Clark sighed with relief. "He'll be along in a minute. Pour me a drink, Larry."

"So early?" Stevens asked.

"Man," Clark said. "I need it. Don't split hairs with me today."

"You're turning into a sot," Stevens said cheerfully. "Well, don't mind if I join you."

They were sipping cherry brandy when Travis came from the kitchen and saluted them with a handwave and wry smile. Travis took the third glass, drank it neat, and dropped into his chair. Judge Clark said, "Did he leave town?"

"Few minutes ago," Travis said. "God, I needed that drink. You got coffee hot, Larry?"

"Help yourself," Stevens said. "We've been holding off for you, Bob. I think Ed is close to busting a gut, worrying about this inquest."

"Why?" Travis asked. "We settled it."

"In a pig's patoot," Clark said bitterly. "Legally speaking, we rammed it through without evidence of self-defense and you damn well know it, Bob. I'm not saying we're wrong. We know John is innocent of any crime in the broadest sense. But I can't understand why Lea Ferguson sat there and lied so badly."

"I can't say it in the legal words," Travis said. "All I can tell you is what Stacey Goodlove is thinking, and what he did about it. We've got the record on file. John's innocent, proved so, and Goodlove knew it would be that way. But Goodlove can't reason that way. Nothing can change him. Something happened last night or this morning between Goodlove and Ferguson. You saw how Lea backed water, Then Thompson showed up and scared Joe. That was open and aboveboard. Maybe I'd have done the same in Stacey's boots. Anyway, he knows we've cleared John, but the written evidence won't show any direct statements by the witnesses to that effect. And Goodlove wanted us to do it just that way."

"But why?" Stevens asked. "What difference can it make, Bob?"

"It's in Goodlove's mind," Travis said. "I guess in his soul. There's a feeling in that man that if there's nothing on paper that says he isn't wrong, then he can go ahead in his own way and right a wrong and not have to suffer for it."

"Go over that again," Clark said.

"What I mean," Travis said, "is now he can come back in the fall and make his play, and if he gets John, he'll just keep riding for Texas, knowing damned well we can't bring him back. That way he squares the book for Dohney and himself, and the way he feels, he's done it fair and square because we can't show on the record that John shot Dohney in self-defense. And if he gets John, we can't bring Goodlove back, I'll tell you that. Who could go down there and bring him out? And he won't come through here again, heading north. He'll come up through Denver and Cheyenne, and even if we knew about that, who knows when he's coming."

"You know the man well," Clark said.

"I should," Travis said. "I was like him once. Maybe I still am, I don't know."

"I see what you mean now," Clark said. "But what about this: perhaps Lea will change her mind in a few weeks. Maybe Ferguson will see how wrong he is. And what about Mexican Joe? Bob, can't you work on him, take plenty of time, make Joe understand that he's got to testify and help John out, and we'll protect him. If we can get just one of the two to reverse their testimony, put the truth on record, then make certain Goodlove hears about it, we might avert a lot of future trouble. We might even change Goodlove's mind about this coming back and causing trouble."

"No," Travis said. "We can't change his mind. But about the record, we can try that."

"All right, by God!" Clark said. "We'll start today."

"I agree with you," Stevens said, "but we're sitting here, cool and happy, talking all around the one thing that really counts. What about John?"

"He's alive," Travis said shortly.

"Man," Stevens said, "You've just told us that Goodlove isn't fooling, that he'll actually come back. We can't yell for a troop of cavalry, keep them here indefinitely because of something that might or might not happen. And we can't watch John day and night without help. What about that, Bob? If Goodlove comes back this fall, what can John do?''

"Nothing," Travis said.

"But Goodlove may have fifty men," Stevens said. "Doesn't that scare the very hell out of you?"

"It does," Travis said.

"Then why think about facing them?"

"You mean John?" Travis said. "He won't."

"All right," Stevens said testily. "I mean you."

"I've got to," Travis said. "What else can I do?"

"Oh, hell's fire," Stevens said. "I ought to know better than argue your business with you. I always end up on the short end of the stick. Let's get back to John Lockland. Does he stay here?"

"Would you?" Travis asked mildly.

"I'm not married," Stevens said. "I don't have a wife and son. John does. And I say the devil with foolhardiness. We're not living in the days of chivalry. John ought to get out of town this fall, take a trip east."

"I don't know," Clark said cautiously.

"It's up to John," Travis said.

"What if he asks you?" Stevens said. "You know he will. What will you tell him, Bob?"

"Stay," Travis said.

"But why?"

"A man can't do otherwise," Travis said. "I can't. You and Ed can't. What else does a man have in him that's worth the salt, worth holding onto? If we back up on one thing, we never stop backing the rest of our lives. It's up to John. Maybe he'll stay, maybe he won't. If he asks me, I'll tell him to stay."

"And if he asks you what you're going to do?" Stevens said swiftly. "There's the catch, Bob. What about that?"

"Good Christ!" Travis said patiently. "He's not going to be standing in the middle of Pioneer with a bull's-eye painted on his belly when Goodlove rides in. I don't ask that. But he'll stay, I know that, and I'll be here. Just remember, this is my deal. If they want John, they come to me first.''

"It comes down to one thing," Clark said heavily. "We'll leave it to John and Margaret, just as you say, Bob. And while you're manning the bridge with Horatius, a few of us won't exactly dig a hole and pull the cover on about that time."

"I know you won't, Ed," Travis said. "But that's where you're all wrong. This isn't your kind of business. It is my kind. I'll handle it. Let it rest there."

"You're a damned fool," Stevens said, "but I admit a tiny kernel of admiration for your bullheadedness."

"Something like a boil?" Travis smiled.

"Exactly, and right where I sit," Stevens said. "Which brings us to another point. What about your resigning next month?"

"What difference does it make?" Travis said. "None to Goodlove. None to me."

"Well, are you?" Clark asked.

"Ed," Travis said, "I'll tell you next month."

"So let's get back to Lea and Joe," Clark said, "and forget the rest. Right?"

"I'll talk with Joe," Travis said. "Don't expect any miracle. He's scared. It'll take time."

"As for Lea," Clark said moodily. "Sometimes I wonder what that girl needs."

"I can tell you," Stevens said, "but her mother wouldn't like it."

"Her mother," Clark said emphatically, "hasn't liked it for about eighteen years."

Travis joined Steven in laughter and Clark's round face broke into a pleased smile. They were doing their best to help Travis over a tough moment, knowing too well that all the talk about staying and changing evidence and wishing, within themselves, that Goodlove would forget to come back was so much eyewash. There was so much more to it than the things a man could say, and it wouldn't start working on them until a few days passed by and they slipped into the summer. They were thinking of Travis's future, his plans for a farm or a business, and the years ahead in which he could lay aside his gun and be like other men. They were considering the trick of fate that had put a different ending on that dream. For now Travis could not go away, dodge the future, with all his life behind him an open book as to the way he had met such crises in the past. But there was the beginning of the argument, not in words, but in his mind and his heart. They would worry every day from now on until July and August slipped away, and September came, watching for stray bits of news which might trickle down from Fort Robinson, Deadwood City or Cheyenne, stories telling where Goodlove was and what he might be doing. It was all pointing toward one day—nobody could even hazard that date—in late September or October. And that day would affect the lives of everyone in this town. It was not a problem to be talked out in an hour, in a cool room, over a glass. It would grow and hurt them all through the summer days, and they could not guess the ending.

"Well," Travis said, "that about brings this session to a close. I've got some work, then I'm going to dinner."

"Summerhays?" Stevens asked.

"Chicken and cherry pie," Travis smiled. "Name me a better way to spend a Sunday evening."

"I'll have to invent some excuse," Stevens said, "and happen by there more often. That woman can really cook."

"So can Mary," Clark said. "Johnny Cork wouldn't be riding with you, Bob?"

"He is," Travis said. "But I'm afraid he'd rather be hanging around Ferguson's front gate."

"The damned fool," Stevens said. "No, that's not fair. Johnny's a good boy, he'll be all right, given the time."

Travis finished his coffee and went to the back door. He looked at them soberly for a moment, feeling the very solid and apparent weight of their friendship, valuing his luck at finding and having such friends. "See you tomorrow," he said. "And don't worry about it, eh? There's a lot of time till fall."

·····················Eleven·····················

F RED SUMMERHAYS MET THEM AT THE YARD GATE AND helped put their horses in the barn, talking a blue streak all the while about the inquest and the way Sam Thompson had tried to gum things up. Travis let him go on, knowing how Fred enjoyed talking with visitors, living as he did eight miles from town and having only women to argue with seven days a week. Johnny Cork was glad to be a silent listener for the time being, and after the first bad moments of meeting Mary and the family, and sitting down to supper a few minutes later, he got over his feeling of embarrassment with Mary and pitched into the fried chicken. Talking with Mary and kidding her young brothers, Johnny watched them all and couldn't help but feel their closeness as a family. But that wasn't strange, knowing where they came from and how they loved each other.

Fred was a big man who always smelled of hay and wind and Bull Durham tobacco. He wore overalls and blue workshirts, and his overall suspenders left their dark sweat cross-stitch on every shirt. He was forty years old and weighed two hundred pounds, and was rather flat across the cheeks below his high forehead and straw-colored hair, but wide-jawed and firm-mouthed, with just a trace of stubbornness at the corners. Fred smiled a lot and his teeth seemed to laugh when his full lips pulled back, the front upper pair far apart and slightly yellow. He was the strongest man in the district, and the easiest going until somebody crossed him. Then he could be holy terror with his big arms and fists.

Fred's parents had come from Wisconsin after the war and homesteaded in the northeast Nebraska hills above North Fork, east of the North Fork River. They came to farm new land, Fred's parents and many of their Wisconsin neighbors, and each man had a profession to help him make a little money during those early years. Fred's father was a stonemason and from him Fred picked up a working knowledge of that trade. He helped build one of the first niggerhead barns in the area, hauling the stone from Wisner and thatching the roof from the long hay grass. Fred grew up there and married Annie Brinkoph, and just when they were getting ready to buy a farm and stay, took a trip west with a cattle feeder to help bring home a load of yearlings. He stayed in Olalla five days, saw the country, and changed his mind about the place to live.

Fred liked the rolling hills, the high sky, the color of the grass and the river that was a mile wide and one foot deep. The ground was thin and sandy, but along the river a man could grow good crops and feed cattle. Fred bought his farm from a Bohemian who had the itch to see big mountains, and that fall they made the move. To the folks back home it seemed they were going to another continent, but letters traveled fast and it wasn't two years before several of Fred's neighbors were coming out themselves.

It wasn't an easy life. A man had to be blessed with good health and a good wife—and there Fred was lucky. Annie was skinny when they were married, but the combination of Mary and the two boys, plus her own cooking, changed the pig-tailed girl into a strong, generously-padded woman who worked beside Fred in the fields if necessary and kept up her house work.

Johnny Cork volunteered to dry the dishes after supper, but Annie shooed them out of the house. Johnny sat on the hog yard fence and looked across the fields toward the trees that lined the river's course a half mile to the south. Travis and Fred came down a minute later, smoking their cigars, talking with the lazy, easy slowness brought on by a good meal. Olalla and all the day's worry seemed far away. Johnny Cork half dozed, his stomach full of good food, listening absently to their talk.

Mary came from the house and leaned against the fence beside Johnny. She smelled of soap and hot water, and she pushed her thick brown hair back, fumbling with the hairpins in the darkness. Johnny slid down and stood beside her, and Fred began talking cows and moving toward the barn with Travis. Johnny was ill at ease then. He didn't like to be alone with Mary these days. Maybe she was remembering that dance last winter when he acted the fool.

He'd only been in town two months when he met her in Lockland's, and danced with her that night at the town hall. During intermission they took a breather outside and Johnny felt so good, having a job and money and good prospects, that he kissed her before he realized what he was doing. She wasn't a girl who took those gestures lightly, he realized instinctively when she stepped back and looked at him gravely, but neither did she squeal or slap his face. Instead, she invited him out to dinner; and that started it. He went with Travis several times, until people were beginning to talk, and then he met Lea Ferguson and everything changed. Now he felt guilty with Mary, and she couldn't help knowing what was going on.

"Cat got your tongue?" Mary said.

"So full I can't talk," Johnny Cork said. "That was a fine supper."

"You should come oftener, Johnny."

"You know how it goes," Johnny said. "I'm trying to save money, get that break."

"What about the place east of here?" Mary asked. "The one I told you about."

"What do I use for money?" Johnny Cork asked.

"Six hundred down," Mary said. "You can get a loan."

"No loans," Johnny said firmly. "When I start, I want to own everything."

"You're a darned fool," Mary said flatly. "Owing money is no crime if you work hard and pay off. Don't you want to farm?"

"I don't know," Johnny Cork said. "Got to wait and see."

"How long?" Mary asked bluntly.

"Damn it!" Johnny Cork said impatiently. "How do I know? Besides, I've got other worries now."

"You mean Bob," Mary said gravely. "And John Lockland."

Johnny was glad to change the subject. He said, "That's it," and then wished he hadn't when Mary said, "We heard about the inquest and I can't understand what got into Lea. She's not that flighty."

"She's not?" Johnny said.

"Her?" Mary laughed. "I went to school with her four years. She's no more flighty than me."

"Maybe," Johnny said, "but you never looked down a gun barrel that way."

"I won't argue with you," Mary said. "I just don't like the way it went, that's all."

"Well," Johnny said, "all we can do is wait and be ready to help Bob. I guess it's about time to start home."

He turned from the fence and brushed her arm, and for a moment he wanted to stop and talk some more. It was funny how he didn't want to kiss her while he dreamed about kissing Lea, and yet he still liked talking with Mary. He couldn't understand it but he'd better not get any closer now, feeling as he did about Lea. That wasn't fair to Mary. Johnny Cork said awkwardly, "Well, I better get the horses."

He hurried into the barn and found Travis throwing the bridle over his mare while Fred tightened up the cinches and turned Johnny's gelding toward the door. Travis looked around and said, "All set, Johnny. We'll thank Annie again and cut the dust."

"Remember what I told you," Fred Summerhays said.

"And I told you," Travis answered. "Don't be stubborn, you big ape."

Fred walked between their horses to the kitchen door and Annie came out, wiping her hands on her dish towel. She accepted their thanks and invited them back as soon as possible. Johnny Cork said, "Good night, Mary," and didn't feel relaxed until they topped the ridge and lined out for town.

"Fine girl," Travis said.

"Sure," Johnny Cork agreed. "What were you warning Fred about?"

"Nothing," Travis said shortly. "Let's ride."

They didn't talk much until they crossed the river and cantered slowly into town. Then Travis seemed to loosen up, make some decision that was bothering him, and act his old easygoing self. "Back there," Travis said while they unsaddled in the livery barn, "there's what you want, Johnny. Your own boss, a good farm. Those folks like you."

"Sure," Johnny grinned. "I'm the breath of spring."

"Breath," Travis said. "You're a March wind, you hellion."

"In like a lion, eh, out like a lamb?"

"Don't we all come and go that way?" Travis said gently.

"You're right," Johnny said soberly. "I don't mean to talk down about those folks. I just can't make up my mind.

I'd better sit tight and worry about things that count right now.''

"Enough of that," Travis said. "Worry only makes a man fuzzy."

"Now you're steering me off," Johnny Cork said. "You can't sidetrack me, Bob. I'll be around to help when the time comes."

"I know that," Travis said. "I counted you long ago."

"You did?"

"You never asked before," Travis said. "Now you can't back up. How do you like that, fire-eater?"

"I like it fine," Johnny Cork smiled.

"And now forget it," Travis said. "Time you hit that bed."

"What about you?"

"Later," Travis said quietly. "I'll take a walk right now, Johnny."

Travis walked from the barn and faced south on Pioneer, waiting patiently for Johnny Cork to cross over and go home. Johnny hesitated a moment, scuffling the dust, and said, "Bob, when does a man know he's picked the right woman?"

"I can't answer that," Travis said. "Nobody can."

"Then what can a man do?"

"That's the question a man answers himself," Travis said. "But I'll tell you something else, Johnny. The girl a man always wants the most is the one he can never have. And you don't know yet how lucky a lot of men are, never getting that one. Good night."

Travis walked away before Johnny Cork could answer, moving down Pioneer between the silent, dark saloons, feeling better inside for the meal at Summerhays. But only for the moment, he knew that too well. Riding out and eating with them, and talking, was just one way of easing the mind, taking his thoughts off the business at hand. Standing at the fence and talking in the barn, he had found his mind turning to Mexican Joe, and he was anxious to saddle up and ride back to town and have a talk with Joe.

He passed the Bighorn and heard two men talking on the porch outside the Drovers Bar. Then he left the saloons and crossed the tracks beside the depot, onto the sandy, grasslined path that led down into Mexican town. He caught the faint, halfhearted sound of a lazy guitar, but it wasn't Mexican Joe picking out the tune. Travis walked faster, wondering at his sudden worry, and for the first time today thought about Sam Thompson and just where Sam really was tonight.

------------------------------ Twelve ------------------------------

Ferguson suffered a mild attack of stomach gas that night, brought on by too much potato salad and cold rhubarb pie. He took a pinch of baking soda at nine o'clock and stood on his front porch for a breath of air. He saw Travis and Johnny Cork ride by, kicking up little dust shadows that caught on the wind and tickled his nose with astringent dryness. Ferguson smiled frostily as they trotted down Pioneer into the Sunday night gloom of the closed, shuttered street. He had finally gotten the best of Travis, proved that the marshal was far from infallible. Ferguson turned inside, his stomach rumbling, and joined his wife in her sewing room.

"Rose pattern?" he asked cheerfully.

Mrs. Ferguson was quilting, her finger moving ponderously over the bright-colored scraps of silk patching. "What?" She looked up, her eyes squinting above her glasses, disturbed as always at an interruption. "Oh—yes. Are you hungry?"

"Just thinking," Ferguson said. "I should walk over and see Lockland."

"Tonight?"

"John is bound to be worried," Ferguson said. "He needs a few kind words."

"John is a grown man," Mrs. Ferguson said calmly. "You can't shoulder the town's troubles, Henry."

"Now," Ferguson said modestly. "John's young, inclined to be flighty. Want to come along?"

"No, thank you," Mrs. Ferguson said. "I know Margaret too well. You go, but don't promise him the moon."

"No danger," Ferguson said. "He'll be around for help soon enough, once he finds that Travis can't help him this time. I'll just put the bug in his ear."

"Yes," Mrs. Ferguson said proudly. "It takes a man like you to stop Goodlove. Say good night to Lea before you go. The poor child is nervous as a cat."

"Yes," Ferguson said. "I'll be back soon."

He lifted his hat from the hall rack and paused at the stairs to call, "Lea—Lea," and heard his daughter's voice faintly, muffled in her pillow. Ferguson said, "Coming downstairs again, Lea?"

"Not tonight, father," Lea said. "Did you want me?"

"Just to say good night," Ferguson said. "I'm going out for a minute."

"All right," Lea said. "Good night, father."

"Sleep well," Ferguson said warmly. "You're my very best girl, you know."

He smiled fondly and went down the steps and turned north toward Lockland's house in the next block, sniffing the wind and estimating the chances for rain. Rain meant grass and crops, and interest money, and Ferguson was never too preoccupied for a weather guess. He mounted Lockland's porch and rapped firmly with his knuckles, remembering that John's doorbell was always out of order. Steps sounded on the hall carpet and John Lockland spoke through the locked door, "Who is it?"

"Me," Ferguson said. "Gone to bed, John?"

Lockland opened the door and stepped back, motioning

Ferguson into the hall. "No. What are you doing up this late, Henry?"

"It's been a bad day for us all," Ferguson said. "I thought you might want to talk things over."

Lockland said, "Very well," and led Ferguson down the hall to the kitchen. Margaret closed a book and rose from the table when Ferguson smiled and gave her a little nod of greeting.

"Henry can't sleep either," Lockland said. "We'd better have some coffee."

"Good evening," Margaret said stiffly. "Are you hungry?"

"No thank you, Margaret," Ferguson said. "But coffee would be fine. Well . . . I hope you two haven't been worrying about that foolish threat that Goodlove made."

Lockland had shown his worry before, and did nothing to conceal it now. He brought cups from the sideboard and went to the pantry for cream and sugar before he answered. "I can't agree with you, Henry. Goodlove doesn't make foolish threats."

"Come now," Ferguson said, "we're not living in the dark ages. Goodlove can't come here and destroy our town. It can't be done. After you've thought it over a few days, you'll see how utterly foolish it is."

"Does Goodlove know that?" Margaret asked.

"He certainly does," Ferguson said. "Once he gets over his anger, he'll be sensible."

"But you didn't come over tonight to tell us that," Lockland said quietly. "Did you?"

"Well, no," Ferguson said. "I wanted to talk about Lea."

"I'd rather not," Margaret said curtly.

"Margaret," Ferguson said, "don't condemn Lea for her action this morning. She's young, she was frightened to death last night. Surely you understand that. Then add that foreman, Thompson, standing in back like the devil's disciple, and ask yourself how a young girl would feel."

"Feel or not," Margaret said. "She saw everything. Why did she lie?"

"She didn't mean to," Ferguson said. "We've had a bad day with her. Getting her down there, then all day she was sick in bed. She seemed to get hold of herself at supper, but she's still half-sick. John, you don't think—?"

"Think what?" Lockland said. "You tell me what I don't think."

"Good for you," Ferguson said. "I'd feel the same way, and that's why I came over. I don't want you to believe that Lea was frightened before the inquest. I should say, threatened by Goodlove through me, or directly. I can imagine what people are saying, that Goodlove came to my house last night and threatened us with something or other if Lea testified for you, John. Nobody enters my house, threatens my family. Lea simply lost her head and became utterly frightened to death this morning. She saw you defend yourself, John, and she knows it was self-defense."

"And all it took was one word," Margaret said coldly. "No one is so frightened he can't answer a single question with one simple word. Yes is the word, in case you've forgotten how Judge Clark worded the question."

"Please," Ferguson said. "You're a grown woman, a brave woman. Could you say the same about yourself at Lea's age? Please be kindly in your thoughts. Remember too, it doesn't matter. Clark followed everything through in the right way. John is acquitted, the record is on file. What have we lost? Not a blessed thing. Lea will come over just as soon as she can and apologize. You wouldn't close the door in her face, would you?"

"I'm liable to break it over her head," Margaret said. "I'm sorry, Henry. I can't afford pity when my family's future is at stake."

Ferguson gave Lockland an appealing look and sipped his coffee slowly. Ferguson had expected an outburst from Margaret; but this reply was not so much instantaneous anger as a new feeling of distrust and fear apt to continue for a long time. Still, she was a woman and she'd be herself in a few days. Then she'd do some apologizing herself. Ferguson said, "Forgive me, Margaret. I'll say no more. I'd better run along. We'll all feel better for a good night's sleep."

She remained at the stove, her back to Ferguson, until they left the kitchen and entered the hall. Stepping outside with Lockland, Ferguson said, "I don't blame her a bit. Amanda's been the same way all day."

"What about it?" Lockland said suddenly. "What about this fall?"

"Don't give it a thought," Ferguson said. "I give you my word that Goodlove will carry out no wild threats."

"How do you know?" Lockland asked. "What can you do to stop him?"

"A good deal," Ferguson said. "Remember, I have a few connections. I'll see that he comes here peacefully or not at all."

"Bob thinks he'll come back," Lockland said.

"Travis again," Ferguson said shortly. "John, that reformed gunman has blinded you. Do you think the man is perfect, can do everything? Travis deliberately angered Goodlove that night."

"How do you know?"

"I heard."

"From Lea?" Lockland said. "I thought she was hysterical."

"Not from Lea," Ferguson said. "I hear things, John. Travis isn't the only man who has an ear to this town. Now, as I was saying, Travis angered him. Then after the inquest this morning he tried to pick a fight with Thompson. Does that make sense? Is that soothing them, trying to patch things up?"

"Travis had a good reason," Lockland said. "Thompson was wearing his gun."

"A good excuse, you mean," Ferguson said sharply.

"John, it's time you looked around and realized who your friends are in this town, the people you'll be living with for many years. Not a vagabond like our marshal. He's resigning soon. God knows where he'll be this fall. John, face the facts. Travis will only cause you additional trouble if you continue to let him influence you and Margaret and your son."

"I can't agree with you," Lockland said stubbornly. "Bob isn't leaving after he resigns. He's not running from anything."

"I won't argue the point now," Ferguson said. "But promise me one thing—look around, see conditions as they actually exist. Don't let people use you to promote their own future. And above all, stop worrying about that stupid threat." Ferguson laughed jovially and slapped Lockland's shoulder. "Man, we'll look back twenty years from now and wonder at our own foolishness. You'll be mayor and I'll be in my wheelchair, and our grandchildren will be begging for tales of our wild days, and we'll certainly have a bushel of them at our fingertips—if we stretched the truth a little. Right?"

"Possibly," Lockland said dryly. "Well, I'm tired, Henry."

Ferguson took the abrupt dismissal in good spirits. He started down the steps and then turned with a final thought on his tongue. "John, I think we should take up a collection for that puncher's family, send it to Goodlove."

"What?" Lockland said. "Are you serious?"

"Why not? It's the human thing to do."

"My God!" Lockland said. "You can't do that. Don't you understand Goodlove? To offer money is the worst kind of insult. If you don't believe me, ask Clark or Stevens. Ask Travis. They'll tell you."

"I think you're exaggerating," Ferguson said. "A little decency and kindness never made anyone mad. But we'll discuss it tomorrow. Now stop worrying. You have friends. Trust them."

John Lockland watched him down the steps and turned into the house. He locked the door and went through the silent hall to the kitchen, and met his wife's angry stare with a rising anger of his own. Margaret said, "That pompous little man is either a complete fool or we don't know the first thing about him, John. Coming over here, defending that empty-headed daughter, trying to tell us about a man like Goodlove. John, I wish you'd kicked him into the street."

"I can't understand him," Lockland said wonderingly. "He was too quick with that story about Lea simply being too frightened. What happened last night, Margaret? What happened to Ferguson, and who frightened Lea? Damn it to hell, I wish Bob was here."

"Bob is busy," Margaret Lockland said. "He'll come as soon as he can. Remember, he has a few things to worry about, too."

"I know," Lockland said. "But I can't get this business straight. Ferguson was right about one thing."

"What?"

"We've got to stop worrying." Lockland said firmly.

"Right this minute," Margaret smiled. "Between breaths?"

Lockland crossed the kitchen and gave her a quick tight hug. "Right this minute. Now, for some reason, I'm hungry as the devil."

"About time. You didn't eat a thing at supper. Sit down, I'll fry some eggs and bacon."

Sitting in the safety of his own kitchen, smelling the bacon and the eggs, Lockland stirred his coffee and watched his wife move before the stove, and thought of their son sleeping upstairs.

"I wonder where Bob is tonight," he said. "Sometimes I think that man never stops moving or thinking."

Travis came to the sandy depression that marked the old buffalo wallow, where the cottonwoods began and grew taller as they marched southward toward the shacks of Mexican Town. Here the path grew narrow branches, single foot tracks snaking down the slope behind the houses. Travis stopped halfway along the first path and rolled a cigarette with no real desire for smoking. That was habit from the past, on the nights when a man had nothing to do but smoke and watch the herd, and wonder what lay up the trail. He had put in ten years of that, from sixteen to twenty-six, before he broke away. He didn't like to think about those years. He threw the loose-wrapped cigarette away and went down the path to Mexican Joe's house.

The lone guitar had stopped playing on the street, and only one window reflected yellow lamplight. Tomorrow was a workday and the sun bound to burn bright along the tracks. Mexican Joe and his friends might carouse on Saturday night, but a wise man got his sleep on Sunday and kept his job on Monday. Travis stepped around the white-washed rocks marking the small yard and knocked gently on the door. Bare feet shuffled inside, calloused soles on sand, and Lupe whispered, "Go away, go away."

"Lupe," Travis said. "Too late for me?"

"Señor Bob!" Lupe said. 'One moment, please."

She hadn't been sleeping, and Joe wasn't home. She opened the door and looked upward into his face, holding the lamp aside to keep smoke from their eyes. Her long black hair was combed smoothly and she wore one of her shapeless cotton gowns, tied at the waist with a piece of linen cord. Travis had never seen her face move in excitement, no matter what happened. Even tonight it was brown and unlined and ageless. He removed his hat and stepped just inside the door and said, "Where is that worthless man, Lupe?"

Lupe shrugged her thin shoulders and padded to the table. She set the lamp in the exact center of the lace coverlet.

"I do not know," Lupe said. "Somewhere about. Who can follow him in the night, Señor Bob?"

"Not I," Travis smiled. "He's a ghost at night. Don't be frightened, Lupe. I came to talk with him."

"Of what?"

"You heard what happened today?" Travis said.

"Yes."

"Then you know what talk I want," Travis said. "Do you think Joe was wrong?"

"Let José say that, Señor Bob."

"Joe was frightened this morning," Travis said. "Of Sam Thompson."

"Yes," Lupe said. "A cruel and bad man. We know his kind."

"I don't blame Joe for that," Travis said. "But we are friends of John Lockland, and we must help him. Isn't that true, Lupe? We must always help our friends."

"But how much?" Lupe said quietly. "Must we die?"

"That's coward talk," Travis said. "No harm will come to Joe, or you. If I can't find Joe tonight, I want him at my office tomorrow noon. Understand?"

"I will tell him—if I see him."

"Another woman?" Travis said casually.

He saw the flash of anger in her face, a brief coloring of her thoughts, and as quickly Lupe swallowed secret laughter. "I am all the woman he needs, Señor Bob."

Travis said, "And more, Lupe," and left her at the table with her hands placed flat on the scrubbed wood, her face again expressionless in the smoky lamplight, all the patience and immovable spirit of her race showing tonight. She knew where Joe had gone, but death wouldn't open her mouth. Travis walked south from the house, counting off other houses in the darkness until he reached the sixth. The house was dark and wind fluttered a curtain in the glassless window beside the closed door.

"Pablo," he called. "Pablo, open up."

He heard again the sound of bare feet on clean-swept sand. Pablo's wife said, "Señor Bob?"

"Pablo there?" Travis asked.

"No, Señor."

"Where is he?"

"I do not know. He went at dusk."

"Go back to sleep," Travis said. "I am sorry to disturb you."

He went on south between the houses and came to the edge of town where a few piles of tincans and rubbish soiled the earth, and the cottonwood trees finally gave up fighting the thick prairie sod that began here and ran endlessly over the hills. He could search every house and find no sign of Joe tonight. Joe was gone, with Pablo helping him, hours out of town along the river riding north.

Joe had a better reason for running away than the fear of talking with him; it was a big fear that made Joe warn his wife sternly about keeping her mouth shut. Travis knew only one fear big enough for that. Joe was running from Sam Thompson and it could mean just one thing. Thompson hadn't ridden north to rejoin his herd. How Joe knew this was one of those mysteries they kept to themselves down here in Mexican town.

He couldn't do a damned thing about it tonight. Tomorrow he'd check all the stores and see if Joe or Pablo had purchased supplies. He could search their houses for missing blankets and clothing, make a count of their guns. He could check their horses; after that he could wait for Pablo to come back and go to work. That wasn't hard to do, making sure Joe was gone, but then it wasn't easy in any way. He could search for Joe, all right, but Sam Thompson might be camped outside Olalla, thinking in the same way and making that same search. There wasn't good sense in Thompson's gunning for Joe, but nothing seemed to add up and make sense.

Travis rolled another cigarette and held it between his fingers, thinking of the hideouts around town. He dropped the match when a man whispered from the high grass, "Señor Bob!"

"Yes," he said. "Who is it?"

"A friend. Don't move from the path. I have a message from José."

"Good," Travis said. "What does he say?"

"He says that it is bad for him to stay in town. So he has gone away for a little time. He says please don't chase him because sometimes the wolf tracking the rabbit leads the coyote to his hole."

"I see," Travis said. "Many thanks."

"You will stay in town, Señor Bob?"

"Tell Joe I've got to see him," Travis said. "I'll stay in town until tomorrow noon, waiting for him. Then I'll have to look. Tell him that."

"His blood will be on your hands, Señor Bob."

"What has happened to the brave men I knew in this place?" Travis said. "So many yesterday, now I talk with ghosts. *Buenos noches*, Nino. Put a quarter in your mouth next time. Then I won't know your voice."

He walked swiftly through the street and up the slope to the path. Crossing the tracks and approaching the jail office, he felt like going inside and sitting in the darkness for an hour or two. Sometimes that helped, but it was doubtful if any thinking would help him tonight. Goodlove was a forthright man who promised one thing and didn't change his mind. Sam Thompson was something else, as Joe knew all too well. This was the way it started so many times. Lockland was the only man directly involved, and now innocent people were pulled into the affair. He'd better go home and get some sleep because there wouldn't be much time for quiet nights from now on. Instead of peaceful weeks through the summer, he faced the prospect of finding not one man but two, and the second would be looking for the first, with a twisted, crazy purpose and a ready gun.

"God damn you, Sam!" Travis said savagely. "If you're around tonight, God damn you!"

-------------------- Thirteen --------------------

DOCTOR STEVENS WOKE TRAVIS AT EIGHT O'CLOCK, knocking loudly until Travis came sleepily through the house and let him into the kitchen. Stevens gave him a professional look and started breakfast without delay, clattering the pans and digging vigorously into the cookstove firepot with the poker.

"You look a little peaked," Stevens said. "How many eggs?"

"Three," Travis said, "and what are you doing up so early?"

"Checking my clients," Stevens said blandly. "How's the state of your health?"

"Po'rly," Travis smiled. "Hold that breakfast, Larry. I'll wash up."

While Stevens set the table and told a rambling story about Mrs. Ferguson's strange and recurring case of vapors which required an Omaha specialist, Travis filled the wooden tub with lukewarm water from his roof tank and lowered himself onto the upturned stone crock that served as the seat. He soaked for ten minutes before soaping and washing off, thinking wryly that at least he'd slept in his own bed while Mexican Joe was on a blanket among the rocks. That was small consolation, but he wished Joe no material comforts this morning.

"Ready," Stevens said. "Hurry up, man."

They sat at the table and Travis found his appetite surprisingly good. Buttering bread and beginning on the eggs, he pointed his knife at Stevens. "Judge sent you for something, didn't he? Or is this your idea?"

"Ed's," Stevens said. "He had a lot of work this morning, but we had questions that couldn't wait. We didn't know what you had planned today, so I came over early."

"Fire away," Travis said. "I'm not going anywhere."

"Until when?"

"Just what have you two heard?" Travis asked.

"That Joe ran away," Stevens said. "Lupe visited Ed late last night, after you saw her. She thought Joe had done something she didn't know about. She wanted legal advice, but mostly some kind words you had no time to offer."

"I wasn't feeling kind last night," Travis said. "Joe's spoiled this business for me."

"That's the point Ed and I discussed," Stevens said. "In fact, we disagreed. Ed was wondering just half an hour ago if perhaps we hadn't exaggerated the danger."

"And you disagreed?"

"Why, I don't know," Stevens said, "but the way I see this, time doesn't lessen danger. It just dulls the senses and lulls the mind, until the danger returns and stabs you in the back. Ed maintains that Joe will sneak back into town soon. Then we can corner him. I've got a hunch he won't. How do you feel about him?"

"He'll come back," Travis said, "to see Lupe, his friends. But not in daylight, and only when he knows it's safe. He won't show up until late fall, if you want my opinion."

"And mine," Stevens said. "There's our argument. We want to know if you're going after Joe, and how we can help."

"I gave him until noon to see me," Travis said. "He

won't come in. I'll go after him, Larry, but there's nothing much you and Ed can do to help. Lupe didn't tell Ed something else, I see that. Sam Thompson didn't go north and rejoin his crew. He's looking for Joe right now, and for one reason. See what I've got to buck?''

"Why do you say that?" Stevens asked curtly. "It doesn't make sense. Thompson has an important job with Goodlove. They can't spare him."

"For this," Travis said, "Goodlove could spare half his crew. Sam's around town somewhere. Put that in your pipe and remember it."

Stevens went to the stove for the coffeepot and lifted it gingerly with a rag, frowning soberly as he thought of Sam Thompson. "It won't add up, Bob. If you say so, I'll believe you, but why should Thompson want to—you mean kill Joe?"

"Not pat him on the back," Travis said.

"But why? Joe means nothing either way. An innocent bystander, a man who hasn't hurt Goodlove or Thompson in any way. Damn it, this was cut and dried yesterday. We're worried about John, but not too worried because we feel we can protect him. This business of threatening innocent people is an outrage."

"I told you yesterday," Travis said. "Stacey Goodlove follows no pattern that people around here can ever understand. Sam is worse than Stacey. He's a *lobo*, a wild one. Goodlove puts an idea into his head and Sam goes on from there in his own way. You've got to know the inside of their minds, Larry. Even then it's hard to understand. It goes back so far, and there's so much you people don't know."

"But you know them," Stevens said. "Tell it to me, Bob. Sometimes I think medicine is the easiest of all the sciences when I try to fathom the workings of a man's mind."

Travis pushed back from the table and lit his morning cigar. He had never tried to explain men like Goodlove to anyone because he had lived their life, in their home country, and their thinking and living had grown in his own mind until it was second nature. A man seemed to understand his neighbors with a strange insight that came from riding and roundup and going up the trail together. But they were so busy doing their jobs, alone so much of the time, with speech a luxury, that Travis couldn't remember a single instance in which he had talked of other men at any length. You just didn't think about sizing up a man in so many words. You simply knew, inside, what a man was and how far you could trust him, and what he could be expected to do at any given time, how he would react to love or hate or kindness. The words were in his mind, and ten years had given him the gift of explanation. Not like a lawyer, he thought, or an educated man with a fluid tongue, but clear enough to serve the purpose—if he should tell it all now.

"I've got to have your promise," Travis said. "This stops with you and Ed. The way things are going now, I've got to tell you. Otherwise, I wouldn't open my mouth."

"It'll go no further," Stevens said. "You know that, Bob."

"All right," Travis said suddenly. "I can't tell it in a few words. If you've got any calls, better make them. We can meet tonight."

"Now," Stevens said. "Tonight you might be along the river."

"Prod me if I'm hazy," Travis said. "I've got to go back and tell you about Stacey and Sam, the way I knew them seventeen—no, it's almost eighteen years ago."

"That long, Bob? I didn't know—"

"I was young," Travis said mildly. "Not a kid, but wet-eared in a good many ways. Stacey was running a big, scattered bunch of cows in West Texas. He had a hardcase outfit. He never asked where a man came from if the man could carry a full share of the load. Anyway, I drifted out that way and tied on with him that winter. Damned lucky for me. I was riding a crowbait and down to my last dollar. I stuck till spring and helped round up Stacey's first trail herd, and when it come time to start north for Kansas, half the crew quit because Stacey wouldn't give the usual wage boost. Hell, he couldn't. He didn't have fifty dollars cash himself. Sam Thompson showed up one morning and hired on, and by nightfall Stacey had his trail crew picked. Me and Sam, five others, and the cook. That's the way we went north. I don't mind telling you it was plain hell. We were shorthanded, we lost half our remuda to Indians, we had more than our share of storms and high water and a grass fire that nearly caught us all. I don't think we slept over three hours a day. But we made it. And Stacey hit it smack on the nose. We came into Abilene, second herd up the trail that summer, and prices were sky high. Stacey sold for big money and that night he called us up to his hotel room and opened a carpetbag and paid us off our wages, and then he handed us three hundred dollars each on top. That was his way of repaying a man for doing a job that meant more than money. He never really gave a damn about money. It was something to use. It was handy to have around, but it didn't mean anything.

"We had a drink and sat around tongue-tied, all of us ready to go out and shoot up the town if Stacey gave the word. Anyway, Stacey was planning ahead. He was going home by way of Kansas City and New Orleans, to start drumming up future business with the commission firms. He told us to have our spree, head south, and see him on the home range in the fall. That was fine with us. We said good-by and I went down and bought my first decent outfit. New saddle, blankets, clothes—and a new gun."

"That one?" Stevens asked.

"The one on the bureau," Travis said. "That's the same gun. I don't use it now, of course. The new Colt is better. But I kept it. You see, that gun made a difference for me.

I guess you know about how things went then, what happened the next summer?''

"I've heard conflicting stories," Stevens said. "You never told us, Bob."

"You never asked."

Stevens smiled. "Well, would you have?"

"Probably not," Travis said. "All right. I'll tell you now we're going all the way. It's better forgotten but too many folks still remember. That next summer we brought a big herd up the trail. Full crew, good equipment, double-sized remuda, plenty of chow. Stacey sunk everything he had made the year before into that second outfit. He got the best, and that meant the toughest crew in Texas. Sam Thompson was foreman. He earned the job over the winter. I don't know to this day where Sam came from, or what he had done, but he knew cows and he knew men, and he wasn't like he is today. Then he could still take a joke, and laugh a little bit. Anyway, we brought that herd up and Stacey hit the jackpot for the second straight year. When we were paid off, we really tore into that town.

"Now you've got to understand that I grew up with guns. I was never slow, and after I bought that new gun I practiced with it all winter and spring. I didn't know how good, or bad, I was myself. So when we got paid off and began ripping into the town, I wasn't expecting to use the gun. You've heard about how Stacey was in that saloon and the trouble started, and he was alone against half a dozen or so, I don't know how many in actual count. I was outside, on the street, and I heard Stacey yell and then Sam came from the hardware store next door, carrying a brand new Winchester he had just bought. He yelled at me and we went through those double doors like a tornado. Sam tripped and fell flat on his face, and just then Stacey had to draw and go for them. It didn't last very long. After things settled down, everybody was in more or less a state of drainage. Stacey had a slug in his left leg and one through his right shoulder, high up. I caught one shallow across the neck, otherwise I was lucky. Six of them were dead."

"Six!" Stevens said quietly. "Did you . . . ?"

"I'm not sure," Travis said. "Truth was then I didn't want to know. They said I got four and Stacey got one. But the bad part was, another one broke for the back door just as things were winding up, and Sam finally grabbed his new Winchester and shot that man in the back and finished it. I didn't think much about it then, being upset myself as you can imagine, but that was the day Sam started to change. But getting back to me and Stacey.

"That fight made us pretty close all at once. The marshal came in and it was just another brawl, self-defense, couldn't call it anything else. Nobody bothered us. We were all set to clear town three days later. Stacey going east again, us riding the trail. I never made the ride.

"Their town marshal was killed in the morning. They came to me at noon and offered me the job. I guess they figured I was about the toughest coot they'd ever seen. I knew better, but the job paid three hundred a month plus all the percentage gravy from fines and rewards and the like, an easy five hundred a month. They offered it to me and I didn't know what to say. I caught Stacey at the depot. He didn't take a minute to make up my mind. He told me to grab it, it was too good to turn down because I couldn't begin to make that kind of money working for him. And I knew what he was thinking.

"With me marshal, he could bring his herds up the trail and get a square deal. So could the others we knew. It was one of those times, Larry, where you didn't have to talk it out and say it. We just understood between us. So I took the job, and that was the last time I went down the trail, that summer. Almost fifteen years ago, and the rest of it as far as I'm concerned is pretty well known. So we'll get on Stacey and Sam, and stick with them.

"You know how the railroad kept pushing west, and how the trail towns popped up one after another. I kept moving with the crowd, taking one job, sticking until the town petered out, going on to another. Stacey kept coming up the trail with bigger herds every year. And every year he was changing, and Sam was changing. In the beginning you've got to understand that Stacey didn't really know what he wanted, or how big he was going to grow. He didn't change much so far as clothes and actions and habits. But his ideas grew with his home range and his herds, and finally with the size of his bankroll. You could see it working in him about the sixth or seventh year. He bought into a big spread in New Mexico along with some eastern money, and Sam ramrodded that outfit during the winter and spring, and they'd build up a big herd at roundup and sometimes bring two and three separate herds up the trail each summer. The money was rolling in and Stacey was getting the feel of power in his hands. And Sam was turning out to be just like you know him now. Sam was just the same to their outfit as Stacey, you see. He could sign checks and give orders, and Stacey never changed them.

"Well, you get to that point where you've got more money than you can ever spend, and more land than you can ever ride across and see, and it starts to work on you inside and out. Stacey got so used to giving orders, and having nobody ever cross him, that for anybody to try it was like signing a death warrant, that is if it was something serious. You heard, I suppose, how Stacey and Sam never called on the law when they had rustler trouble. They just made up their own posse and rode out with some ropes, and there's no doubt they hung some poor innocent bastard for every time they caught and hung a bona fide thief, but that was the way it was down there. Rustlers left them strictly alone inside of three years. The same was true for squatters, and anybody else who bucked them, even towns that tried to get tough with Stacey's crew. He just rode over them all and ground them into the dirt.

"All this time I never had any trouble with them, in all the towns I was in. We could still get together and have a drink when they hit my town, and Stacey's men respected my badge because they knew I didn't care how much hell they raised so long as the killing was stopped. They knew I had been one of them, and that helped. So they tore up towns, Stacey paid the repair bills, and everybody was happy. We'd shake hands when they left, and folks were saying what a fine marshal I was because Goodlove's crew always caused big trouble in other towns. Naturally I said nothing to spoil that talk. I was making big money, spending it, and I got so I looked forward to seeing Stacey every summer because he helped keep my reputation shiny. You know, like shining a little more in the bright light of the biggest sun.

"But as I said, Stacey was changing and Sam was already mean clear through to the marrow. Four years ago, the year before I came up here, Stacey brought his wife up the trail with him to Dodge."

"Wife?" Stevens said. "I didn't know . . ."

"Few did," Travis said. "He got married, let's see, it would be seven years ago, three years before she came along with that big herd, the biggest he ever put on the trail and, as it turned out, the last of its kind. I'd never met her, of course, just knew her folks were ranching in a two-bit way down in New Mexico. Stacey saw her and made up his mind, and that was it. They had a baby, a girl. Anyway, when they rolled into town and one of the crew told me his wife was along, I couldn't wait to see her. I was hoping she might change him back a little to the way he was, and so far he seemed like he was getting worse all the time. He located me before supper and took me to the hotel to meet her. They'd left the little girl at home, on the big ranch, with about sixteen nurses. This was supposed to be his wife's first vacation since their marriage.

"Her name was Ellen and she wasn't much over twenty-three or four then, and Stacey was just about fifty. I don't know now his right age. She wasn't what I expected. She was about the prettiest, stupidest, smartest little bitch all

rolled into one woman that I'd ever met. She had Stacey
wrapped around her little finger when he was with her. Not
away from her, don't get me wrong. Nobody could change
him there. But with her he was a plain blind, damned fool.
She gave me one of those looks while Stacey was shouting
at waiters and ordering supper. Well, I'd had my share of
those looks for almost ten years from all the best and worst
parlor houses in all the towns, and I knew her kind when
I saw her. Understand, I don't mean she had ever been that
way, not in action. She just grew that way down there in
that wild country. But I could see why she'd married Stacey, and I could damn near guess what was going on when
he was gone and she had the chance to sneak out on her
own. She was the kind who'd never pass up a chance if it
was absolutely safe.

"I felt uncomfortable all through that meal. I got away
quick and ran into Sam in the hotel bar. We had a drink
and he asked what I thought of Ellen, and I said all the
usual things, and he just looked at me with that poker face
you've seen, Larry, and we understood. That was the night
Sam told me, not in words, but the way we understood
each other without speaking right out, that as far as he was
concerned Ellen was just a temporary attachment, like a
bull you use for one season and then sell or shoot. He knew
she was no good, and he was just waiting for her to make
a mistake, and then he'd wake Stacey up and they'd get
rid of her—hell, shoot her if necessary, I suppose—and
then go back to living their old way.

"It happened three nights after I met her. Stacey's crew
had pretty well run themselves to death on the town. They
were getting ready to head south, and Stacey was taking
Ellen home by the eastern route, combining business and
pleasure. That night Stacey was invited to a poker game in
the downstairs club room the hotel reserved for the big
boys. I usually played if the street was decently quiet. I sat
in, but about midnight I was called out to settle a squabble
between some drunks. I got them quieted down and had a

cup of coffee in the dining room, figuring on returning to the game. When I came back into the lobby, the night clerk showed me one of the dodgers I got regularly from the U.S. Marshal and always distributed among the business places. He was sure the wanted man on that dodger was upstairs in a room on the second floor.

"Well, there was a five hundred dollar reward and the night clerk was a good boy and I never took rewards but gave them to the man who tipped me. He knew that. So I had to go upstairs and take a look for his sake. I took the dodger and went up and started down the hall to the room—number eight or ten I forget which—it was on the south wing. The hotel was U-shaped and the room was way around in back on that south side. Stacey had two rooms on the top floor on the same side.

"It was quiet by then, past midnight, and I went down the hall on tiptoe, not wanting to wake folks up or cause any unnecessary trouble. The walls were thin and it was damn near impossible not to hear people moving or talking in the rooms if they made any undue amount of noise. I came abreast of room four, never forget that number, and I heard a woman laugh in there and a man say something, and there wasn't any doubt they were having a big time, and weren't done by any means. Of course, that meant nothing. Happened all the time. But I knew her laugh. I'd heard it at supper so often I'd never forget it.

"I stopped and I felt like Stacey would have felt if he was standing there, because he was still close to me in all our old ways. I caught myself just before I began smashing the door down. I backed off and went down the hall to the room this man was supposed to be in. I knocked real soft and he was still up and opened the door right away. It wasn't the wanted man, just a man passing through. I apologized and got away from his door, and I didn't know what to do. Then I knew there was only one thing I could do. Go downstairs, get back in the poker game, make sure Stacey didn't go upstairs until morning. She knew he wouldn't come anyway before three or four, but I had to make sure.

"When I got back down the hall I could hear them, and when I turned the corner on the front hall, I noticed that the corner room door was ajar. Somebody was standing just inside that door. I didn't stop, but I was worried bad then. Well, I just got to the stairs when he whispered to me, stopped me. Sam came from that room and down the hall. He was in his socks, carrying his gun, and his face was like the devil in person. He asked me if I'd heard. I nodded and he touched my arm, there was no begging in his eyes, he was telling me because we understood each other. He told me to go down and keep Stacey in that game until he came down and gave me the all clear.

"I asked what he was going to do, and he just smiled and said the best thing I could do was forget everything I knew, he'd see that things got taken care of. I couldn't think of anything to say except he ought to avoid any trouble, and he promised he would, just let him handle it. So I went down to the game and kept Stacey until six in the morning. Sam came down at five and gave me the sign, but I made sure. I took them both to breakfast and I don't know how Sam and I managed to talk because we were thinking what a bitch she was, staying with that other man until five, apparently sure that Stacey wouldn't come up any earlier. Sure, or else she just didn't give a damn.

"I didn't see them again. I slept until afternoon, Stacey and his wife took the noon train east, Sam went down the trail with the crew right after the train left. About eight that night I was called out to see a dead man in a ravine about half a mile west along the track. I didn't even need to go out, or identify him. It was the man who had that room number four, all right. He was a drummer from Kansas City, young and handsome and well-dressed. He was selling barbed wire and assorted hardware. He'd been shot five times, a full load. A piece of wire from his sample truck had been tied around his neck and used to drag him out along the track.

"About three months later, news came up the trail that Mrs. Stacey Goodlove had been killed in a runaway on the home ranch when her horse went crazy and threw her off. She fell down into a canyon and cracked her head on a rock. Next summer when Sam came up the trail with a small herd—it was beginning to change then, more rail-roads and more markets and the northern ranges opening up—I found out, by asking around it the right way, that she'd been out for a ride and Sam was along. I knew then what had happened. When I saw Sam that night—Stacey didn't come up that summer—there wasn't anything to say. It was all gone between us then.

"We had a drink and he looked at me and said, 'It's all right now.' I couldn't say anything. How could I charge him with the murder of that drummer? How could I come right out and say I knew he murdered her? According to his code, they deserved it. According to Stacey's code, it was the same way, the only thing to do.

"He looked at me funny that night and I knew what he was thinking, and how he had changed over the winter, gotten even worse than he'd been. Two people knew what had happened, me and Sam. And he intended that Stacey would never find out the truth. He wasn't worried about me telling, it wasn't that, but he couldn't bear to think that anybody else should know.

"He left for home in two days. That fall I saw the writ-ing on the wall. The trail towns were done. I headed north and stopped here. You know the rest of it, Larry. I hadn't seen Stacey or Sam from that time I've been telling you about, until they came into town the other night. I hadn't heard anything about them, other than in a business way concerning Stacey's leasing this new northern range and bringing up this big herd to stock it. Stacey has got over losing his wife, I can tell that, but he's a lot worse in all the other ways. And Sam, well, you saw Sam. Both of them are just living for their work and I guess for each other. They can't bear having anybody cross them now. You could tell that.

"Now you're saying, what does all this have to do with John shooting that young puncher? How come Stacey got so damned mad and made that threat to come back and get John? Hell, I've seen a dozen of his men killed in the past and he was mad, sure, but he knew how it went. So why was he like that with John the other night? And why is Sam doing what he is? By the way he came to the inquest and scared Joe, the way Lea Ferguson was shut up, there's something we don't know yet. And why do I say that Sam is somewhere around town right now, looking for Joe? Those are the things you and Ed are asking, Larry, and once you understand about Stacey and Sam and me, and the past, it ought to be pretty clear."

"I can see what you're driving at," Stevens said quietly. "I see them plainly now, I can understand how they might become furious and hold a grudge. But to involve innocent people . . . that's still beyond me, Bob. It seems to me there's something more about this dead puncher—this Dohney—that has a great deal more bearing on the whole thing than we know or you've told us yet—if you really know."

"That's why I got your promise for you and Ed," Travis said. "If it hadn't turned out this way, I had no need to bring up the past. Now I've got no choice. You remember that Dohney was hanging with Sam all the time in town. You could tell Dohney was Sam's boy, that he was growing up under Sam's wing, going to be just like Sam, only worse if given the time. And Stacey was watching the boy, and you could tell that he was the apple of Stacey's eye. Well, I suppose it couldn't turn out any other way. Ellen Goodlove's maiden name was Dohney. This red-haired puncher was her kid brother."

"All right," Stevens said softly. "You needn't say any more, Bob. I'd be a lousy doctor if I couldn't take this case history and tell you what and why. In fact, I can probably explain it a lot clearer than you from this point on."

"About Sam, you mean?" Travis said.

"About Sam's thoughts these past four years," Stevens said slowly. "Here we have a faithless woman murdered to protect her husband from learning the truth at a later date. And a young brother who quite naturally would come to work for his brother-in-law in the course of time. I see Goodlove as being kind and generous to this boy, just as he must idolize his little daughter. And there was Sam Thompson, knowing everything, so that Sam couldn't help hating the brother because he was a living, walking reminder of the woman. And I can see this Thompson adopting the boy—this Dohney—and in his twisted fashion, starting immediately to change Dohney into something like himself, only worse if possible. Isn't that the way you see it, Bob?"

"Only way," Travis said. "Sam wanted to keep that boy around a long time. Must have been the only pleasure Sam had left. I can see Stacey trying to baby the kid, and Sam working from the other end. When John shot that boy it was just the same as killing the one pleasure Sam had left. It's no wonder Sam is hanging around. And I can understand why Stacey gave him permission. Stacey don't know all of it, though. About Sam coming back to get Joe. You know why Sam's doing it, don't you?"

"Because anything and anyone connected with Dohney's death is the same as dead in Sam's mind," Stevens said. "Isn't that right?"

"Has to be," Travis said. "Joe, Lockland, me—even Lea Ferguson."

"I just thought of her," Stevens said sharply. "Bob, we've got to act fast."

"Wait," Travis said. "You go along and tell Ed all this. Can't hurry anything along now. Just let me take care of it for now."

"But . . ."

120

"What can you do?" Travis asked. "Not very much, Larry. Wait till noon, see if Joe comes in. He won't, but I've got to wait. Then I'll see what can be done."

"How long will it take?" Stevens said. "To find Joe, to find Thompson?"

"Who knows," Travis said. "Maybe all summer. We've got nothing but time now."

Fourteen

JIM MURPHY CAME FROM THE LIVERY BARN DURING THE lazy noonday hour, his red face sweating in the rising heat. Travis had kept him on the go for three hours and Murphy dropped into the barrel chair with weary relief.

"I brought a couple of apples for your lunch, like you said. Anything else, Bob?"

"No more," Travis said. "Pablo wasn't back?"

"Not yet. Two horses gone."

"All right," Travis said. "If anybody asks for me, I'll be home by night."

"Sure you don't want me along?"

"I'd like it," Travis said, "but one of us has to stay. Ferguson would raise hell about us going fishing on pay time."

"The hell with Ferguson," Murphy said. "Bob, you be careful."

"Always am," Travis said. "See you tonight."

He took his rifle from the gun rack and paused in the doorway for a last look around the office. He had come down to a full morning's work after his talk with Stevens, papers and letters and vouchers, signatures and answers and routine business. In the old days his job was watching men. Now he seemed to spend more time writing letters and adding figures and lecturing harmless drunks. Times were changing and he occupied the best seat for the show, with the additional knowledge of having lived through the entire cycle of this change from beginning to foreseeable end. He was almost happy that Joe had run away. It gave him a chance to get out of the office.

He crossed Pioneer to the livery barn where his mare welcomed him with her smooth, warm nose and nibbled the sugar cube while he saddled and tied on the lunch bag. The rifle fitted snugly in its scratched, faded boot, and for a moment he felt like past days, heading out for open country and a meeting with the unknown. But only a moment; for the past was gone and this was a miserable business. Leaving the barn, he saw Webb McGowan's wagon beside the blacksmith shop and crossed over to the door. Webb came from the forge and Travis bent down in the saddle.

"Can you do me a favor, Webb?"

"Name it," Webb McGowan said. "Soon as he fixes that share."

"Stop at Fred's," Travis said. "Tell him to look for me tonight. If any of you catch a sign of Joe, I want to know."

"Will do," Webb said. "Just heard the news, Bob."

"Don't spread it around," Travis said. "I'd appreciate that."

He grinned at Webb and rode down Pioneer, waved to Dick Burnett, and crossed the tracks. He skirted the buffalo wallow where the meadowlarks sang and the cottonwood fuzz drifted steadily over the sunscorched grass. A few years ago the wagons had stopped here, the buffalo covered the plain. Now the noon whistle from the roundhouse called men to work and a switch engine pushed empties under the elevator grain spouts. All gone, he thought, like the buffalo. Like himself.

The mare carried him over the first ridge and the town dropped from view into the rolling, endless swells of grass and sky. He rode five miles before turning eastward to begin a circle that would bring him around to the river far east of town. He rode slowly, paying no heed to the land, holding the mare in. He couldn't do much today, just make a circle and cross the river, prowl the north bank a few miles, and stop at Summerhays' to see if Fred had any news. Joe was probably far north of the river, hid out in a crumbled soddy or up a brush-choked draw. He didn't worry about finding Joe. It was the other hideout that mattered. Sam Thompson might have a pair of ears back in town, and once Sam knew he was being trailed the fun would start.

Travis hadn't been down this way in months, and he felt guilty at living in this country three years without covering the south bank more thoroughly. The land south of the river wasn't worth farming and too sandy for running cows beyond river drinking distance. It was wind-blown into dry, sandy washes and spotty grass and patches of alkali that showed up as he swung east. Angling closer to the south bank line of green willows and cottonwoods, Travis crossed the fading trail ruts and stopped the mare, looking down at the twin tracks already half filled and covered with grass and sod.

Forty years ago, he thought, just a wink of the eye since the first ones came this way. Really not first—there were many before the wagons—trappers and government outfits, French and Spanish and the Indians. Now the engines snorted by every day and the buffalo were finished, and the tribes hemmed on the reservations. Still, if a man could forget all that, the land hadn't changed at all. Nor would it, neither here or all the way south to the Rio where part of his life was spent and gone. The land was the same and all the plowing and planting and people moving wouldn't change it a foot. But it didn't do any good to remember how things were, not if a man wanted to live in the present.

He spoke softly to the mare and turned into the willow thickets, batting mosquitoes with his hat and jerking his bandanna over his mouth, plunging down the bank into shallow water, letting the mare pick her way across, half a mile to the north bank, through the sluggish channel and the pools and over the gleaming white sandbars that hurt his eyes. He stopped on the north bank for a drink, and lit a cigar. Now, by the grace of God and the changeable actions of nature in the last few million years, he was for all purposes and within ten minutes ride, in a different kind of country.

North of here and along the river was better land, just high enough to have shelved and held decent topsoil among the glacial sand reefs, clay deposits and gravel beds. It was good graze land, but proper working made it richer for crops and hay and gardens. Travis knew this side of the river better than the south, having ridden it many times with Fred and his neighbors. Not far from here, west about half a mile, was a sheltered draw running back from the river into a little hollow masked by trees. The big catfish and bullheads stayed in the hole under the bank, and Mexican Joe and Pablo came here often during the summer months to fish, have a big fry at night, and carry home a gunny sack for sale. Travis didn't expect too much, but the draw couldn't be bypassed today.

He rode west on the higher rim of the bank, staying in the trees, making no special effort at silence as he closed on the draw and put the mare down and then rode along the narrow bottom path. He saw the tracks in the brown sand and followed them up to the hollow, two horses that had milled around before being tied beneath the trees. Travis dismounted and walked to the fireplace, knelt down and dug up the blackened ends of burned wood, thrust his hands deep into the mixed ash-and-sand between the cooking rocks, and rubbed the sticks together.

Two men had stopped and built a fire and cooked a hasty meal not long ago. No fish because the birds would still be hanging around. Travis led the mare out of the hollow onto the higher slope, following the tracks again. They turned west, toward town, both horses walking for a hundred yards, then breaking into a trot. He relit his cigar and stood beside the mare for a minute, putting himself in their place for the first time since leaving town. It was time to think like Joe and Pablo, plan and talk and act as they would.

They had stopped here, eaten, and left the hollow. Pablo had turned west with both horses, but Joe had struck off north on foot. It was no use trying to dig up Joe's track, nor was it a sure bet that Joe had gone north. He might start and veer back to the river, even cross over to the south bank again; or he could try the third route, go straight north. Pablo was back in town right now, giving Joe a prearranged time to reach a known hideout. Joe and Pablo were starting a game that contained more circles and cutbacks and false trails than a fox could lay. Even if a man understood the game and knew exactly how the circles and cutbacks and false trails could be laid, it didn't help a bit.

Pablo and other friends were watching the town. Joe was hiding out in one of a hundred places. When a man, either Travis or Sam Thompson, came this far, following a clear trail, he would then strike out blind to investigate the hideouts north and east of the river. Pablo or another friend would be riding the same way in a wider circle, at greater distance, converging on a point far ahead of the tracker reaching Joe in ample time to take him farther along. Pablo would then go away with the horses to lay a false trail, while Joe ducked into the next hideout.

It could go on for days, weeks, even months if Joe kept heart and Pablo was able to bring food and stay clear of trailers. For Joe and Pablo the game was simple. They were running from just two men, himself and Thompson. And the two men were divided into definite categories. Joe had no fear for his life from one, and all the fear in the world from another. But the two made up a greater fear because one might lead the other to the right spot at the right time. That made Joe think faster, hide deeper, run farther. Travis knew all the old tricks, the circles and cutbacks, but Sam was handicapped because he didn't know the country.

"North or east," Travis said. "What do you say, Goldie?"

The mare turned her head and nuzzled his boot. Travis said, "Only woman I know who doesn't want her way," and set her to the north. He'd take a swing to the beginning of the sandhills and double back to Summerhays after dark. Sam Thompson could easily be in the hills, and Travis wanted no part of a premature meeting. It was best to stay clear, let Sam sweat for a week, run short of supplies and duck back into town. With luck, he'd catch that move and have his clear trail.

Johnny Cork took a bruising fall late that afternoon and limped out of the breaking corral in low spirits. "Hell with this," he told Herbelsheimer. "I'm going fishing."

"Good idea," Herbelsheimer agreed. "Raus, Johnny."

Johnny Cork took a manure fork behind the barn and dug a can of worms, stopped at Lockland's store for line, bobber and hook, and rode out to the river. He went down the path to the big hole where Travis and Tommy fished for big ones, cut a willow pole and put on a worm. He sat against the big cottonwood tree with his eyes closed.

"Don't bite," he said. "I don't want trouble today."

He was half-asleep when voices drifted from the upper bank, Lea Ferguson and the Elliott girl and the silly giggle of the preacher's daughter. They were picking flowers and Lea said, "All right, go that way. I'm going down here."

Johnny Cork wiggled his pole and watched the bobber jump on the placid water. Lea pushed the willows apart and gave a false little cry of surprise and said, "Why, Johnny. I didn't know you were here."

"Come on in," Johnny Cork said. "The water's fine."

He'd wanted to see her for days and especially the past two days, hearing all the talk and wondering if she had really lied on the stand, or was actually frightened by Sam

Thompson. He didn't know how to start the conversation, and he was always embarrassed around her anyway, so that seemed to put him in a fine position. He felt like a beggar looking at a queen. Lea was smiling at him with that funny look in her blue eyes, the way Big Annie's girls flirted with him and teased him about being a virgin. But that was a silly thought, for Lea was too young and sweet for such ideas. Johnny Cork struggled hopelessly with a hundred speeches while Lea sat on the diving log and arranged her skirt carefully over her ankles.

"Any luck?" she asked.

"Not much," Johnny Cork said. "Where you been hiding lately, Lea?"

"I've been busy," Lea said importantly. "Getting ready for school. Just think of it, I'm going to Chicago."

"What are you going to study?" Johnny asked.

"Oh, I don't know," Lea said. "Whatever they teach. Mostly I'll take music and learn how to be a lady. Just think of it, meeting people, going to balls, wearing all the latest styles."

Johnny Cork wondered what balls and styles had to do with going to school, but held his tongue on some sharp words to that effect. After all, she was a girl and that kind of school evidently taught girls differently than the schools he knew.

"That sounds fine," Johnny Cork said, "But don't stay away too long. I'd like to see you once in a while."

"I don't know," Lea said. "I'll be older, and changed, and Mother says that people just grow apart and have no common meeting ground."

"No common ground?" Johnny Cork said. "What's the matter with me? Not good enough for you?"

"Oh, stop talking riddles," Lea said pettishly. "That's what I don't like about you, Johnny. Sometimes you act like you don't have any manners at all."

"Like those white-collars you'll meet back east," Johnny Cork said sullenly.

"I intend to meet many fine young men," Lea said. "I hope to . . ."

"What's wrong with men out here?" Johnny said. "What do you want in a man, dude clothes or somebody with savvy?"

"I don't consider them dudes," Lea said stiffly. "You're being unfair."

"All right," Johnny Cork said bluntly. "If you're looking for the right man, have I got a chance?"

"Why, Johnny! I don't understand."

"I remember once last winter," Johnny Cork said. "At the school play. You didn't have much trouble understanding."

"That," Lea said. "I was silly that night."

"I wasn't," Johnny said.

He dropped the pole and got to his feet. Lea said, "No, I won't kiss you again."

"If I come over there," Johnny Cork said, "what are you going to do about it?"

"I'll scream. The girls will hear me."

Johnny Cork walked to the log and lifted her by the arms and kissed her harshly, feeling her lips against his sunburned mouth, hoping for a return of his feeling and getting only the placid warmth and finally a giggle as Lea broke loose and turned her head. She was always that way, playing the flirt, but never withholding completely. He had wondered before, that night at the school play, if he ought to go a little farther. But that wasn't like Lea. He might frighten her badly. And yet, he felt even emptier after kissing her than before he tried.

"I didn't scream," Lea whispered, "but I will if you try it again."

"Have I got a chance?" Johnny Cork said doggedly.

Lea touched his shirt with one finger and shook her head sadly. "It's no use, Johnny. Father says my husband must support me in the style I know, give me a good home."

"Ah," Johnny Cork said angrily, "the hell with this

129

talk. You wait . . . just wait and see. All I do is act like a damned fool, and you laugh at me.''

He turned up the path, and heard her soft laughter, and hated himself for being such a hopeful fool. If he just had the money; that was all it took with Ferguson. Money made the mare go, and Lea wouldn't be so far away if he owned a respectable balance in the bank. Heading for town, already planning when he might see her again, Johnny Cork remembered that he hadn't asked her about the inquest. That made him think of Travis, gone from town suddenly during the noon hour. Johnny Cork didn't know what was going on in town, but he'd better find out by nightfall. It was all right to moon over a girl for an hour or so, but he had his friends to think about. Travis would play hell sneaking off to bed tonight without telling him just what was going on.

Travis rode north through the afternoon, winding between the hills and keeping off skyline, working deeper into the open country away from the last homesteads on the west. At six o'clock he was twenty miles beyond the river on the edge of the endless, rolling hills that went north in this monotonous pattern all the way to Fort Robinson and Custer City and Deadwood. There was sufficient water and grass and game, and a man could ride in here and literally vanish from the earth.

Travis turned west as the sunheat dissipated. The meadowlarks sang loudly and the swallows came from their holes in the clay banks and began swooping over the grass, crying their funny song, catching their evening meal. The mare detoured around a prairie dog village, jerking at her reins, wanting to veer southwest toward the waiting hay and water in Summerhays' yard. Travis let her go as darkness came and relaxed in the saddle, chewing a dead cigar and thinking of the good food not far away.

He entered the yard at nine o'clock and Fred called from the kitchen door, "That you, Bob?'' and hurried across the yard with a lantern to take the mare as Travis dismounted stiffly.

"Webb stop?" Travis asked.

"Yes," Fred said. "Go up and wash. I'll take Goldie."

Travis went to the pump and washed his face and hands in the cold water, dried off on the big yellow towel, and followed Fred into the kitchen. Annie had supper waiting on the table, and Mary was just coming from the pantry with a double-sized piece of apple pie. "Sit down," Annie said. "We expected you sooner."

Travis drank the glass of elderberry wine and sat down to a heaping plate of roast beef and mashed potatoes and fresh peas. Fred Summerhays poured himself a cup of coffee and joined Travis at the table. He waited a few minutes while Travis ate the big edge of hunger off, and then said, "Webb passed the word. I took a ride north, Mary went down along the river. The neighbors scouted around quite a bit, but none of us saw a thing. Webb didn't know much about this deal, Bob. Bring us up to date."

"Joe got scared and ran," Travis said. "Pablo's helping him. You understand why we want Joe. That's the size of it."

"Joe'll be hard to find out here," Fred said. "You'll need help."

"That's why I stopped tonight," Travis said. "I need your eyes, but I don't want you riding with me, or riding more than five miles north."

"Why not?"

"There's something else cropped up," Travis said. "This is not to be passed along any further than to Webb and Charley Miller. You know that Sam Thompson scared Joe. Well, Sam didn't ride north and rejoin Goodlove. He's hanging around, too, looking for Joe. And not for my reason. Understand now why I can't have you folks going too far?"

"That Thompson," Fred said soberly. "He's a killer, all right. We can't have him hanging around here."

"Leave him alone," Travis said. "I know he doesn't scare you, but you can't match his kind, Fred. I want your eyes helping me, but no more. And I want your promise on this right now."

Fred looked at his wife, and Mary Summerhays turned to the stove for the coffeepot with a little shiver that Travis noticed. Fred said, "Very well, Bob. But you know where to come if you need help."

"I do," Travis said. "Now, I'm apt to drop in any time. Keep your eyes open, if you see Joe or Thompson, find any tracks or signs, get word to me as fast as possible. If I send any message out here, it'll come with Doctor Stevens or Johnny Cork. Remember one thing there—Stevens knows about Thompson, Johnny doesn't, and he's better off in the dark. He's reckless and I don't want him hurt."

"We'll take good care of him," Mary said quickly.

"I know you will," Travis smiled. "Now, I've got to ride. Thanks for supper, Annie."

He shook hands and crossed the yard with Fred, and slapped the mare lightly on the neck as he mounted. With a good meal and apple pie under his belt, he felt like a new man. "Thanks again," he said. "I might see you tomorrow night, Fred."

"There's more to all this," Fred Summerhays said accusingly, "but I won't pry. Just remember where your friends live, Bob."

"The lucky man can count his friends on his fingers," Travis said. "This house just about takes care of one hand. Good night, Fred."

Fifteen

BACK IN TOWN, TRAVIS LEFT HIS MARE IN THE LIVERY barn, washed hurriedly, and began his customary patrol. He talked with Dick Burnett and had a few words with Johnny Cork who seemed depressed, broke up the usual quota of fights and hauled one drunk to jail. He went home at three o'clock thankful for an uneventful night. He slept dreamlessly and woke at noon of another bright, hot day. Now the search was started in earnest and would not end until he topped a hill, or rode up a draw, and saw his man.

It meant coming home in the night and doing his job, sleeping until noon, rising with saddle-galled legs to dress and ride again. It meant dividing the country into sections, not on paper but in his mind, and searching one piece each day, and never daring to make a systematic search because that cautious, easily followed pattern was a dead giveaway. No, it meant jumping around like a flea, nosing here one day, far over there the next, rooting over old trails and cold fires and scattered rubbish, in the draws and along the river and outside the yawning doors of abandoned soddies.

And with the searching, it meant walking Pioneer at night and seeing—no, sensing really—the subtle change of feeling as the story spread and people understood what he was doing. As the days passed they would whisper that Travis couldn't find his man, and if he couldn't locate one poor damned greaser, maybe all this time he'd been fooling Pioneer Street, maybe he wasn't half the man they believed. This change of opinion could cause trouble on one of those nights he came from the ride and started his patrol. This sort of foolish business, which he could not dodge, would reveal all the qualities he had concealed for three years. For he would get short-tempered and his nerves would fray, and this town had never seen him when he was truly angry.

He considered these possibilities that morning, talking with Murphy, riding out again on a fresh horse to continue the hunt. He rode south of the river that day and found nothing, and saw only one rider, a boy chasing runaway calves on a scrubby little piebald pony. Summerhays had nothing to report, and Murphy was watching Mexican Town and drawing a blank. Travis went through three days of physical agony while his body ached and stiffened, and slowly worked itself into shape. Doctor Stevens caught him at home on the fourth morning, waking him at eleven-thirty, forcing him into a chair and opening the black bag of instruments.

"Now what?" Travis said sleepily.

"Sit still," Stevens said. "Take off that nightshirt."

"What for?"

"I'm impersonating a doctor," Stevens said. "I'm going to tap you and whack you."

"You're wasting your time," Travis said. "I'm all right."

"You're not a young buck," Stevens said. "You've been pushing yourself four days, I don't know how long this may continue, so I intend to inspect your working parts."

Stevens tapped his chest and back, listened to his heart and took his pulse, went from eyes and ears to tongue and on down to stomach and private parts and legs. Finally Stevens grunted, made some notes on his scratch pad, and closed his bag.

"You need more sleep," Stevens said. "Smoking too much, nerves are tight, you're apt to come up with some bad muscles and veins if you ride too much. I prescribe complete rest."

"Fine," Travis said. "I'll follow your orders—next month."

"Listen," Stevens said. "You can get by now, Bob. But not too long, understand?"

"Give me two weeks," Travis said. "No more."

"Ten days."

"I won't split hairs," Travis smiled. "Will I live?"

"Past a hundred," Stevens said. "Bob, you're a tough old coot. You'll be all right. I just wanted to make sure."

"Truthfully," Travis said, "my legs hurt like hell, Larry."

"Soak them at night," Stevens said. "Hot water, towels. I'll bring you some salts for the water. Bob, how long can a man hide out? Ed and I have worried over that for three days."

"How long?" Travis said, beginning to wash and dress. "It depends on a good many things. How much bacon and flour and coffee he can get, how many meals he can cook and eat before he needs more supplies. How much money his friends can spare from wages to keep the supplies coming, how long his friends can last, keeping watch and taking him food, helping him change hideouts. How long can he last by himself, in the brush, watching all around him? Nobody knows. That's the part he can't judge in time. Nobody knows unless he's done it, and even that won't help because conditions are different every time. It starts getting under a man's skin after a while. He sees a gun behind every tree, a man on every hill. He starts running, he can't stop, pretty soon he runs into the man he's dodging, and there's your finish one way or another. How long can he hide out? I don't know. In this case it isn't how long Joe can last, but how soon I can find Thompson before he locates Joe. I've been on this merry-go-round four days. It can't last forever. Next week, ten days, something will bust open. But I'll tell you this. I'll never do it again, no matter how this ends. I'm too old. I haven't got the feel for it any more. Every night I stop at the Summerhays' place and eat with them, see how they live, I know I'm finished with all this. They're living the way I want to live, and when this is over I'm getting my share of that life in a damned quick hurry. Now I've got to get started, Larry. Hold down the fort in town, you and Ed. And for Christ sakes, dig me up a little information. It's bad enough going blind out there and coming back to less."

"We'll try," Stevens said. "We've got a lot of friends helping out. Be patient, Bob. Things will open up."

Stevens was right. Travis rode two more days before the disconnected facts began trickling into his hands. Murphy was cracking down on the small stores, and Johnny volunteered a watch on Mexican Town during the night. Johnny and Murphy, pooling their facts, discovered that Pablo was not only skipping work with the section crew, but staying entirely out of sight. Lupe was buying flour at the store near the depot, and Pablo's wife was buying white beans in a larger quantity than was usual at the railroad commissary. And Nino Gonzales bought two horseshoes at the blacksmith shop, an ordinary purchase except that Nino did not own a horse. The bad part of this was Johnny's growing doubt as to who Travis was actually hunting. The next noon Johnny was at the kitchen door when Travis woke. Johnny cooked breakfast and began asking questions.

"Lot of trouble over Joe," Johnny said. "He'll come back anyway."

"Could be," Travis said. "Pass the bread."

"How do you know he's around here?" Johnny said.

"Lupe," Travis said. "If Joe was gone for good, Lupe would be taking a train. He won't leave her."

"All right," Johnny said, getting red-faced at his blindness to a basic fact. "But it sure looks funny to me, Bob.

You carrying a rifle and changing horses every day, and prowling around out there, just to get Joe back to change that inquest record. Hell, let me and some of the boys help. We'll find him in no time.''

"Eat that egg," Travis said. "It's free, and it keeps a man's tongue busy.''

He managed to shut Johnny up for the time being, but he wondered that afternoon, riding farther north of the river, just how long he could keep Thompson's presence hidden from the town.

He extended his ride that day, going much deeper into the sandhills and coming down to Summerhays on a long angle that took in a big slice of wild country he'd deliberately bypassed during the week. He had found one dead fire in mid-afternoon that might have been laid by Joe, or by Thompson, and it was only a matter of time and luck before he crossed their track. He felt better that night, eating at Summerhays, and over coffee had enough humor to joke with Mary.

"You'll spoil 'em," Travis said. "I'm getting fat."

"I'd like to," Mary said. "We never had anybody who was spoiled. How do they act, Bob?"

"Well," Travis said, "they sleep late and eat big, and don't work, and complain about how you iron their shirts."

"That's enough," Mary said. "Go sleep in the barn."

Travis said, "I can sleep anywhere," and after saying his thanks and good nights, walked across the yard with Fred, who had nothing to report. Joe apparently had vanished, and Sam Thompson was either playing a waiting game far to the north, or holed up somewhere, content to wait them all out.

"We've all been looking sharp," Fred said. "No luck yet, but I've got a hunch Joe is around here."

"What's your hunch?" Travis asked. "Have I missed anything, Fred?"

"I don't know," Fred said, "not being with you. Hit all the old soddies and wells?''

"All I remember," Travis said.

"What about the Dutchman's?" Fred said. "You never knew him, Bob. He homesteaded that piece of ground eight miles east and twenty miles north of my northeast corner-post, section eighty-six I think it is. He was a crazy old devil, said he intended to raise goats. He worked out for all of us, was a good man too, but his well dried up four years ago, and when that happens you're done in those sandhills. He pulled out that fall. He had a soddy and a root cellar, and God knows there's acres of cover around that place. It's just an idea, understand, but you ought to give it a look if you missed it so far."

"I did," Travis said. "I'll go over it."

"Be careful," Fred said. "The soddy's on a little hill, with a big ridge to the north. I'd swing way east and leave my horse and come up on it from the north and east. There's a little ravine runs between the ridge and the hill. If you want, me and Webb'll come along."

"No," Travis said. "But thanks, Fred."

Riding home that night, Travis wondered if Joe might be that far out; and in the same breath thought of Thompson's possible knowledge of such a place. He felt no inner hunch, no feeling that told him Fred had tipped off the right place, but he couldn't ignore the chance. It was a good three days ahead of his planned search, but there was no use stalling. He'd try the Dutchman's tomorrow and work back on succeeding days. Entering town and washing up before the night's work, he rested in the jail office for the length of one cigar and a bottle of cold beer, and spoke to Murphy.

"Reckon Sam's enjoying a smoke and tasting a nice cold beer tonight?"

"Jimson weed and loco juice," Murphy said. "That's what I hope Sam's dining on. Listen, why don't you sleep? I'll make the rounds tonight."

"I can manage," Travis said. "Can't you tell I'm getting into shape again?"

"I can tell you're getting a shape," Murphy said sharply. "Reminds me of a skeleton with ears."

"A few more days," Travis said. "Keep watching, Jim. Joe can't last much longer."

"What about Thompson?"

"Sam's another horse," Travis said. "He might have a chuck wagon hid out there. You never know about Sam. I wish I did."

Lea Ferguson was alone from seven to eleven that night, her parents attending the regular weekly meeting of their Aid to the Heathen Missionary Society at the church. The house was cavernously empty with her mother gone, but Lea sometimes experienced a vague, excessive sensation of freedom during those four hours. Mostly she visited Grace Elliott, or had Grace come over, but tonight she wasn't in the mood for talking about Chicago and new dresses and men. Johnny Cork had bothered her conscience, in truth her senses, but she didn't understand herself at all in that bodily respect.

She changed into her pink nightgown and the light blue quilted robe her mother had made last Christmas, put her hair in curlers, and settled down in the kitchen with a smuggled paper-back romance and a glass of lemonade. Drinking the lemonade gave her a superior feeling; it was very close to champagne if she closed her eyes and smelled the lemon bubbles in her nose. And lemons were a luxury in Olalla that few people could afford. She finished the romance at ten o'clock and went out on the back porch to get cold milk and summer sausage from the icebox, lemonade being fine for the senses but poor for the stomach, and coming back to the kitchen felt a sharp push in the small of her back, the fingernail scratching through the thin robe and nightgown against her bare flesh.

"Get inside," Sam Thompson said. "And keep your mouth shut!"

He spoke without particular violence or threat in a calm,

low voice, but the sound frightened Lea more than the bold finger and the sudden appearance of a man. She wanted to faint and discovered herself turning, looking at him, with terrifying clarity of sight and thought.

Sam Thompson had no resemblance to the man she had seen downtown such a short time ago, wearing a nice suit with those fine Texas boots and hat and white silk bandanna. Thompson was wearing old brown-colored clothes stained and faded by the weather, splotched with dirt and grease and food droppings. His beard was a week long, hiding his mouth and cheeks behind a coppery, dust-encrusted stubble. An old black hat, the sweat band faded and salt-rimed, was pulled low over his eyes, and he had two guns on instead of one. He carried a big gunny sack in one hand, a short saddle carbine in the other.

"Mr. Thompson?" Lea Ferguson said. "I'm not dressed . . . what do you want?"

"Know me, eh?" Thompson said. "You alone?"

"Yes," Lea said. "You have no business . . ."

"When will they be back?" Thompson asked curtly.

"At eleven," Lea said. "Did you want to see Father?"

"You'll do," Thompson said. "Here . . ."

He tossed the empty sack against her chest, and when she backed away, grasping the sack and twisting it in her hands, he spoke in the same even, quiet voice, "Come on, fill it up."

"Up?" Lea said, not understanding at all.

"Grub," Thompson said. "The pantry."

Lea found herself walking into the pantry while Thompson stood in the door, watching the porch and hall doors, giving her quick, continuous glances that took in the shelves crammed with food.

"Sack up some flour," Thompson said. "Cheese, bacon, ham, coffee, everything you can get in there. Hurry up, get a move on."

Lea began dropping food into the gunny sack, reaching at random along the shelves and taking canned goods and a prize ham and everything she could find that fitted the sack. About the time Thompson said, "That's plenty," and motioned her back into the kitchen, Lea began to gather her vanished courage and make sense of this crazy visit.

She knew all about Travis's search for Mexican Joe. Her father was grumbling about that all the time, the waste of time and town money by Travis, doing a foolish and unnecessary thing that amounted, in her father's estimation, to no more than a vacation. Lea remembered the inquest and how this man had stared at her and then at Mexican Joe, and how her father explained that Joe ran away because he had some fool idea that Thompson was after him. For the first time in her life, Lea Ferguson realized that her father was actually wrong about something. He had told her that Sam Thompson was gone, back with Mr. Goodlove and their herd. But he wasn't. He was right here, he'd been near town all the time, and Mexican Joe wasn't such a fool after all. There was more to it, she felt, but she couldn't quite work her way through all the parts of this puzzle.

Thompson took the sack and walked to the porch door. He raised his rifle in a small, harmless gesture and said quietly, "If they notice the grub, tell your father I stopped by. If they don't, keep it to yourself. Understand?"

"Yes," Lea said. "Yes, I'll tell him."

"If they notice the grub, tell your father I stopped by. If they—"

"Oh—oh, yes. If they notice."

"I guess he didn't tell you," Thompson said, and Lea thought for a moment that he was smiling beneath the hat-brim shadow. "Sit down and get hold of yourself. You're not hurt."

He was gone before she could answer, across their back yard into the alley. Lea stood beside the cookstove for ten minutes, staring at the door and then the clock above the china cabinet. She had stood up to a strange man and hadn't been even near fainting, and dressed in practically nothing.

And the funniest part of it was, she wouldn't tell her father unless they noticed the missing food. But she couldn't wait for morning to see Grace. This was something that had never happened to Grace, or any of her friends. Lea began eating her sandwich and rearranging the pantry shelves, hoping her mother wouldn't notice the shortage. If she hurried, she could bring up another ham and more coffee and flour from the basement; and her mother just might be fooled. She didn't really know why she was going to act this way, but she had a strange feeling that she had caught up with something important tonight. In a way, it was the same sensation she had when Johnny Cork looked at her.

Sixteen

TRAVIS MEANT TO GET AN EARLY START BUT DOCTOR Stevens was in the kitchen when he woke, drinking coffee and frying bacon in a state of unconcealed excitement. Stevens made him eat breakfast and took the opposite chair with his coffee and a sugar roll that apparently failed to tempt his famous sweet tooth.

"Important news," Stevens said. "Sam Thompson was in town last night."

"About time," Travis said.

"Well, God damn it!" Stevens said. "Can't you express some wonder?"

"Too tired," Travis said. "Who saw him? That's the thing I want to know."

"Lea Ferguson," Stevens said. "She was home alone. Thompson made her fill a sack of food, evidently warned her not to tell anyone. How she'll fool her mother with food missing, I don't know. "That woman can spot a missing grape at twenty feet." But Thompson made a mistake, he doesn't understand girls like Lea. Early this morning she told Grace Elliot. Grace was in my office an hour ago for her regular six months checkup. While I thumped her flat chest she confided in me. I think those girls expect

143

Thompson to shoot Joe, you, me, the judge, then rape all the women and burn the town. The silly little fools don't see the serious side, they'll spread it around, the entire town will know by night. What do you make of this, Bob?"

Travis finished eating and stooped to draw on clean socks and rub oil into his stiff, dusty boots. "Sam went to Ferguson's when he could sneak into a store for grub? Makes a man wonder."

"I've been wondering," Stevens said. "Do you think Ferguson . . . ?"

"Ferguson's an honest man," Travis said. "Tight, selfish, but an honest businessman. You couldn't bank money in a safer place. But he's all balled up with a lot of bad ideas on running a town and the people in it. I think he means well, but he doesn't understand, and he's got a lot of stiff-necked pride that mixes him up. Sure, Stacey could have sent Sam in that night to see Ferguson, get him to prime Lea not to testify directly. Ferguson would hate to lose a new, big account. He might have thought it all over and decided it wouldn't hurt anybody if Lea followed directions. It could be that way, but I can't see Stacey doing it. He never asked for help in his life."

"What about Thompson?" Stevens asked.

"I'd like to know," Travis said. "Maybe I never will, but it would help."

Stevens said, "Would you stay in town this afternoon? I might be able to find out."

"For that?" Travis said. "Yes, I'd stay, but how can you work it?"

"As a doctor," Stevens said, "I prescribe more sleep for you. You go to bed, I'll bring the results."

"What's your plan?" Travis said. "Will you work on the girl, the mother, or the father?"

"The mother is impossible," Stevens said reproachfully. "The father is impregnable. The girl, well, I'm rather a dog with young ladies when I slick up a bit. Wish me luck."

"Stay away from Johnny," Travis said. "He might get the wrong slant on your intentions."

Stevens smiled and gave his upper lip a finger twirl. "I'd enjoy opening Johnny's eyes. Now get in bed, I'll see you around five."

Travis sat at the table after Stevens had gone, fighting the rising desire to saddle up and leave town, cut Sam Thompson's trail and bring everything to a finish. He couldn't see Goodlove sanctioning such a deal, ordering Sam to hide out and gun for Joe, and stay on week after week, with so much work on the northern range. Stacey had no taste for intrigue or murder, and Sam was attempting outright murder on Joe. Travis had no choice now, knowing Sam as he did. He had to find Sam in a hurry, before Sam got Joe and turned on his next man—and that couldn't be anybody but Lockland. And after Lockland—by that time Sam couldn't stop himself from going on.

Travis oiled his boots, laid out clean pants and shirt, and returned to bed. The meadowlarks bothered him for half an hour, singing in the rose bush outside the bedroom window, but something scared them off—the neighbor's yellow tomcat, he guessed sleepily—and he didn't wake until Stevens shook his arm at five-thirty that afternoon. Travis mumbled, "What luck?" and began dressing before the doctor could answer. But buttoning his shirt, waking up, he saw Stevens's eyes and knew it was all right.

"I just spent two hours with Lea," Stevens said. "She passed my office and I invited her in on the excuse that she looked peaked and that ill health could result from mental strain as well as physical ailment. A dirty trick, knowing damned well she was under some mental strain, but very effective. I finally persuaded her to talk after swearing secrecy on my doctor's oath. Lord forgive me! Ferguson told her what to say at the inquest, but she hadn't seen Goodlove or Thompson in their house or with her father. She met Thompson for the first time last night. To be truthful, she doesn't understand how serious this is. Her parents

145

have got her living in a little dream world above the clouds, a world that will provide a rich, handsome husband and new dresses and big house and even a true soprano voice, if she listens to their advice. I didn't get what I expected, but it was worth the time."

"I can't accuse Ferguson without proof," Travis said. "And I can't see Stacey giving that order."

"Which leaves Thompson . . ."

"If anybody did see Ferguson," Travis said, "it was Sam. And on his own hook. Well, it doesn't matter either way."

"Now what?" Stevens asked. "Going out tonight?"

"I'll start tonight," Travis said. "Stay out tomorrow."

"Be sensible," Stevens said. "This is the time for help."

"You be sensible," Stevens said. "I'll handle things."

"You're the most bullheaded man in the world," Stevens said impatiently. "It could take you another week to find him. Why don't we go out in force and finish the job?"

"It's my job," Travis said. "Between me and Sam. Maybe I can talk sense into his head, maybe I can't. Either way, it's my job."

"Very well," Stevens said, "but what will we do when the news spreads. John will know by night. Ferguson will get it secondhand if Lea hasn't already told him. Then people will begin putting the facts together. They'll know that Thompson's hunting Joe, and you're after both of them. I don't care what happens to Thompson. But Ed raised a point last night that worries me. Assuming Goodlove doesn't know about this, how will he react if he hears that Thompson is—well, you see the point?"

"He'll hear," Travis said. "Somebody will tell it in Cheyenne, the news will go north. If I kill Sam, how will Stacey act? That what you mean?"

"Yes. What about him coming back here with fifty men? With a hundred. Won't that make him harder to handle?"

Travis buckled on his belt and holster, slipped a clean

bandanna around his neck, and stamped his boots down on the rag rug. He had considered all this long before Stevens put the town's greatest worry into words, and his reaction was that of not caring what happened. If Stacey came back, it didn't matter when, summer or fall, it was bound to happen anyway. And when that time came it was not the town who had to stand on Pioneer Street and face the Goodlove crew. It wasn't really John Lockland, for John was just the accidental reason for an inevitable showdown.

"If Stacey comes," Travis said, "it won't matter about Sam. I know you're thinking of the Locklands. So am I. But thinking and worrying can't stop Stacey Goodlove. You've got to take things as they come, don't try to jump ahead of time. It won't work."

Stevens followed him outside and walked in silence along Cottonwood Avenue, kicking at the earth. When they reached Pioneer Street, Stevens said, "If you find Thompson, you have to shoot. What then?"

"That's one problem nobody can answer," Travis said. "What comes after you're dead, I don't know."

"No, man. I mean Thompson."

"Will I bring him in?"

"Yes," Stevens said. "I was thinking . . ."

"You mean well," Travis said kindly, "because you're thinking of Lockland, the town, not yourself. But remember I've known Sam a long time, in good and bad days. If we have a showdown and my luck holds good, I can't do what you're thinking. Dead or alive, I'll bring him in."

"I had to ask," Stevens said. "I knew you'd answer this way."

"Keep an eye on Lockland tonight," Travis said. "Adios."

He turned away quickly and went down Pioneer to the jail office, took his rifle from the rack, and crossed to the livery barn. The mare was waiting, rested and eager, and Johnny Cork was standing beside her in the stall shadows, stroking her neck and bursting into angry speech before Travis lifted his saddle off the peg.

"Played me for a sucker," Johnny Cork said bitterly. "Set me out on the hill, watching a bunch of women while you look for Mexican Joe. I just heard the news. You're going out tonight by yourself with that mad dog in the hills, and your friends are sitting here. Don't you want help?"

Travis reached across the stall and caught Johnny Cork firmly by the shirt front, and jerked him forward until their faces were nearly touching. Johnny was bubbling over with the rare, honest anger which a boy felt for a friend in danger, the anger a man could not condemn. He wanted to slap sense into Johnny, but that was rank injustice, thanks of the worst sort for faithful service. But he could not have Johnny following along, a boy with no chance against Sam Thompson. With Johnny nearby Sam had two chances for the first shot. He held the shirt a moment, then dropped his hand and tried to find a smile.

"Sorry," Travis said gently. "Put yourself in my boots, Johnny. What would you do?"

"Not in your boots," Johnny said stubbornly. "In my own. What are we standing around for? Let's get started."

Travis saw the belt and gun, one of Calderson's old .44's, and the rifle leaning against the stall wall. Johnny had raided Calderson's office for weapons, and even his pockets bulged with extra cartridges, and a skinning knife was sheathed under his belt. Travis swallowed a grin, remembering another boy of twenty years past, riding across Texas into nowhere, loaded down with an old Walker Colt, a rifle and two knives, facing a pretty big world with small equipment. He hadn't differed from Johnny in any way, in the heart, the body, or the mind, in that forgotten time.

"Get your horse," Travis said. "Let's ride."

"You—" Johnny said hollowly.

"Well," Travis said sharply. "Don't just stand there. You want to come. All right, let's hang and rattle."

Johnny lost his angry face and ran across the alley to get

his horse. Travis saddled the mare and led her outside and Johnny followed him with a groaning uncertainty Travis felt as plainly as he smelled the dying heat of the day. He saw Dick Burnett on the Bighorn porch, and others stepping outside in the early gray dusk. Big Annie was down the street, and Calderson, and the dark faces of Mexican section hands were farther along in the shadows of the depot saloon. It didn't take long for news to spread through town. A woman's tongue had the speed of lightning, and one man's business became the personal property of everyone.

He mounted and heard Johnny's boots slap the stirrups at his side. Murphy came from the jail office and gave him a tiny hand signal. Lockland stepped from the store and stared at him. He couldn't see John's face clearly, but he knew what John was thinking. Travis rode over to the jail door, and Jim Murphy moved off the sidewalk and spoke in a soft voice.

"Pablo's been in and out of town, Bob. Three more left with him early this morning. Nino and two others. What you want me to do?"

"Take the town tonight," Travis said, "And tomorrow. If I'm not back tomorrow night, come to Summerhays'. Fred will know what to do."

"Johnny going along?" Murphy asked.

Travis winked with his off eye. "Johnny figures I need a shotgun guard."

"Now," Johnny Cork said furiously, "you cut that out, Bob."

"Well," Murphy said. "Maybe you do."

Murphy stepped back and waved, and Travis went up Pioneer, hating the next stop but having no choice. He pulled up against the store veranda and seeing the fear in Lockland's face, he wished he had time to explain everything.

"Nice night, John," Travis said. "Think it'll rain?"

"I feel like a fool," Lockland said. "You're protecting

me like a baby. Why didn't you tell me about Thompson before?''

"And worry Margaret," Travis said. "That wasn't good sense. Are you hurt yet? Did Sam bother you last night?''

"No."

"Then stop fighting ghosts," Travis said. "I'm assuming you've heard about Sam.''

"The whole town knows," Lockland said.

"Forget him," Travis said. "He won't bother you."

"But you . . ."

"It's a nice night," Travis said, "and Johnny here feels like a ride under the stars. So we're going out for a little ride. You lock up, go home and play with Tommy. You know something, John? I wouldn't be at all surprised if tomorrow isn't a nice day and you'll be selling things as usual.''

"Bob," Lockland said thinly. "I can't have you fighting my battles, risking your life.''

"Jesus Christ," Travis said gently. "Take that look off your face. You're a merchant, not a gunman. I've got my job, you've got yours. And yours is at home, with Margaret and Tommy. I'll handle my end. See that you do as well with your own. Come on, Johnny. Traffic is getting too thick for my nerves.''

Seventeen

TRAVIS CALLED A HALT TEN MILES EAST OF TOWN AND led the way through the willows to a tongue of sandbar that thrust far out into the lazy current. Johnny hadn't talked much during the ride and Travis gave him little encouragement, aware that Johnny was full of excitement, ready to cock his rifle and charge like the cavalry. If the finish were only that easy, Travis thought, watching his mare drink from the river and lift her head to shake the drops back against her face. He might need another week, maybe two, always with luck on his side.

"Time's going," Travis said finally. "We split here."

"Split?" Johnny said quickly. "No trick, Bob."

"For the present," Travis said curtly, "assume I know a little more about this business than you, eh?"

"I didn't mean that," Johnny said. "I just don't want you to ditch me. Tell me what to do, Bob. I'm here to help."

"I'm going along this south bank," Travis said. "You cross to the north. We'll both ride east another ten miles, swinging out and looking. The river turns south ten miles from here. You cross there and meet me. If we draw a blank, we'll try another idea."

"You got a hunch?" Johnny asked.

"I've got a dozen," Travis said. "Take your time, don't bust along like a wild man. There's nothing to fear from Joe. We're after Sam Thompson, and he's worse than poison. If you see him, mark the place and get the hell away and find me. Any more questions?"

"Nope," Johnny said. "Good hunting, Bob."

Johnny urged his horse into the river and seemed to float off toward the north bank, faintly visible as a dark greenish-black line across the glimmering water. Travis rode back to the darkness of the willows and waited there until Johnny disappeared in the night mixture of water and darkness. He had to chuckle, reading the boy's mind clearly.

Johnny had agreed to the split far too readily. Johnny was thinking that Travis was going to ride south for a certain spot, using information he had kept from Johnny Cork. So Johnny was sent across the river to the safe side, and would have no chance to help. That meant just one thing: give Travis time to get started, then cross back to the south side, and follow along. If Johnny wasn't thinking this way, Travis decided he would never understand a boy's mind again.

He stood beside the mare in the cool dampness of the willows, brushing mosquitoes, watching the flickering phosphorous gleam of fireflies, hearing the muted gurgle of water over the sandy bottom. Time passed slowly and the mare poked his arm, impatient to go. Travis said, "Patience, Goldie," and rubbed her neck, kneading his fingers deep into the smooth hair, feeling the corded muscles and the skin, then giving her ear a flick and smiling as she faked a bite on his wrist and nuzzled against his fingers. Minutes later he heard splashing, cupped one hand over the mare's nose, and saw Johnny Cork ride from the mid-river gloom and climb the bank a hundred yards below his position.

Johnny rode carefully through the willows onto the

higher ground, paused for a minute, and then went on to the south. Travis waited half an hour before leading the mare off the bank and crossing over. With six hours of darkness remaining, and one hunch in his mind, he wanted to reach the Dutchman's abandoned claim before dawn. If that hunch was bad, the tough part was coming. But Johnny was out of the way for a little while, and Sam would face just one man.

Travis struck out north and east, starting a wide sweep that should bring him to the Dutchman's from the east. If he found Joe, half the worry was over. He could take Joe to Summerhays' place, put him under guard, and turn back for Sam. If Sam was there, by some quirk of fate, he needn't worry about Joe. Travis held the mare at a steady pace and tried to rest in the saddle. The miles passed, the hills and deep stretches of grass prairie, the ravines and bisecting draws, the rolling, endless land that lay gray-black beneath the sky. Night birds swooped around him, bats and hawks, and occasional larks flushed up by the mare. He judged his time, made the north turn, and entered the rougher country where the sandhills began and the sod was unturned, thick and matted, nearly impervious to the plow, beaded with sun cracks that were clogged with old grass and tumbleweeds and burrs.

He stopped twice to rest the mare, dismounting and walking, stretching his own arms and legs, chewing on the tasteless sandwiches Murphy had dropped in his saddlebag. The beef had turned cold and lardy. It was stringy meat between butterless bread, garnished with salt and pepper and had a faint tongue-drying dustiness. Two sandwiches and an apple, a drink of lukewarm water, and a few snatches of grass for the mare as she bent down and ate without breaking stride. He came up into the overhanging, wind-blown dunes and the alkali patches. There he saw the elderberry brush topping the skyline of a long ridge, just as first dawn touched the east. He was a little too far east, but the ridge appeared to be the right one, for west was the hill that sloped into the ridge, and between was the dark shadow of a ravine that notched on across to the west.

He tied the mare in the ravine, loosened her girths, took his rifle and canteen, and moved up the narrow bottom path. It was a crooked, water-washed place littered with old tumble-weeds, burrs and fist-sized rocks worn smooth by past rains. It took fifteen minutes to reach the summit, crawling the final yards on hands and knees, wondering even then if he was wasting time and skin. He came up through the shallowing ditch and crawled into the high grass looking down the west slope at the deserted farmyard below. There was just enough light for a decent look, but not enough to bring objects into sharp clarity.

He saw the level piece of ground at the foot of the hillside, flanked on the north by the ridge. The Dutchman had built a soddy against that ridge slope, digging into the hill like a gopher, throwing up a roof of willow poles with a few corner and center legs across the big rod squares. The roof had caved in long ago, the log ends sticking upward toward the sky. Rain had washed part of the sod back into the ground, so the house was no longer a dwelling place, but a lump of earth and a few old rotting logs about to disappear entirely. The door was a square black hole, masking whatever remained inside the single room. An old windlass frame stood just outside the door, over the well that had dried up, and on down the draw to the south was the faint outline of the melon patch and garden where the Dutchman had tried to grow his food.

As Travis stood there he saw the horse in a moment of revealing daylight, tied in the high, tangled brush behind the soddy on the upper hillside. Neck and head appeared, rising from the skimpy grass below the plum trees for a sniff of the morning wind. Whoever staked the horse out knew how to pick a spot where the animal could work around a stake and widen the grazing circle with hoofs and teeth, and still remain hidden by the high surrounding brush. While Travis watched, the horse returned to its grazing, head dropping from sight. He couldn't get a clear look at the brand, or even the color, but he knew it was a good horse. It had to be a good one, tough and lasting, to bring a man here and make the rides a man had to take, living off this land for any length of time.

Travis pushed his rifle forward in the grass and estimated the range to the soddy door at less than a hundred yards. He sighted once, brushed a speck of dirt from the notch, and pressed low in the grass, chin on his left fist. If it was Joe, he could walk down and start giving that man hail Columbia. If the horse had a Fishhook brand, there was no more rest until he had his man.

He watched the soddy doorway while the last grayness lifted from the earth, and the pale orange streaks appeared above his head, shooting out across the sky. The birds were up and busy, the wind faded to a slight rustle in the grass, and down the draw from the soddy a man stood up cautiously in the middle of the weed-choked melon patch, folded a piece of canvas tarp under one arm, and plodded stiff-legged up the path toward the soddy, holding a rifle under his right arm and fumbling for tobacco and paper with the other hand. Travis watched him enter the soddy and come out with coffee pot, frying pan, and sack of grub, squat beside the windlass frame and scrape together the unburned ends of last night's fire. When he scratched a match across his dirty brown pants and got his tiny fire going, the transparent flames and the growing sunlight cast a few shimmers of amber reflection on his reddish beard.

Sam Thompson was hungry and dirty and tired. While he cooked his breakfast and rolled his smoke, he stared at the frying bacon as the dying breeze dissipated the smoke.

Travis could see far down the draw toward the open country. He had to admire Sam for coming out here and finding this spot. From the north ridge, Sam could see a big stretch of country. It was luck, pure and simple, that

Joe hadn't ridden up here and walked squarely into Sam's arms. Travis wished he'd crawled farther down the hillside. He was within easy rifle shot, but the soddy doorway was a short jump from the windlass, and Sam was a man who checked all his possibilities. Travis was considering the best way to start when he saw the rider far to the south, just a dot on the prairie, but heading straight for the draw. He couldn't tell who it was, almost a mile distance down the gradual landslope, but it was Joe or Johnny Cork. Travis brought his rifle up and centered his sights on the crouched man beside the windlass frame. He couldn't wait any longer. If Sam wanted to argue, one shot would warn the rider coming on.

"Sam!" Travis called. "Tired of your own cooking yet?"

Sam Thompson seemed to shrink in size. His shoulders inched together and his hands closed tighter on the frying pan handle and the cigarette. Finally he looked up, directly at Travis's position on the hillside, and answered calmly, "That you, Bob?"

"Nobody else."

"Been expecting you," Sam Thompson called. "But not so soon. Saw you twice last week, at a distance. Guess we're hunting the same wolf."

"Could be," Travis said. "But not a wolf, Sam."

Sam gave his frying pan a little shake; the bacon popped and sputtered, and Sam set the pan carefully over the hottest flames. "Well, come on down and eat, Bob."

"No thanks," Travis said. "Not this morning, Sam."

Sam Thompson began talking in a loud, even voice that carried easily up the hill in the morning stillness. "I figure on getting him," Sam said, talking as though they were seated around the same cookfire. "Then that Lockland, and then you."

"Me last?" Travis called.

"No insult intended. Got to be orderly about this business."

"Why me?" Travis asked.

"You know why," Sam Thompson said, almost querulously. "It's got to be that way."

"Catch any sign of Joe?" Travis asked.

"Not a hair," Sam said. "That Mex is smart. I saw his partner once, far off and heading for town, but the Mex is holed up tight. I'll get him. Just takes time."

Sam's left hand moved slightly, dropping along the tight, folded line of upper thigh and bent calf, moving toward the ground for a balance hold. Sam looked straight up the hillside but Travis could read nothing in his face. The beard hid Sam's mouth and cheeks, and his eyes were shaded by the hat. The only thing Travis knew for sure, and this with sad, regretful pain, was that Sam was gone, all the way, not so much crazy as coldly and rationally insane with the desire to kill and even a score that could never be added. Travis on the hillside meant nothing much to Sam. It was just a minor worry that Sam really didn't care about. Sam would take care of him because Travis was blocking his search for Joe, but there was no longer a personal feeling in Sam's hatred. He had gone far beyond that comparatively clean sensation.

"Why don't you ride on north?" Travis called. "You know Stacey's worried about you. He needs you. I'll find the Mex. He'll be here this fall."

The rider coming up from the south was only half a mile from the soddy. Another minute, another few feet up the slope, and Sam would hear or see him.

"How about that, Sam?" Travis called.

"I'd sure like to," Sam said soberly, "but I just can't do it, Bob. You might plug him yourself. I got to do that."

"No use talking then," Travis said. "You won't go, eh?"

"No use, Bob," Sam said. "I know what you're thinking. You think I'm crazy. No such luck. You were last in line, but it don't matter. I'll take you first, then get the

157

Mex. One thing, you can't go back to town. Besides, you never were my match in the brush.''

"Sam!" Travis called. "Don't do it. I've got the cold drop. Stand up and shed that gun.''

"Why, Bob," Sam Thompson said mildly. "You're a six-gun man. You never could handle a rifle.''

He watched Sam crouch low, drop his left hand and use it as a pivot base, and throw himself backward behind the windlass frame. Sam rolled over and hid himself for a second, then dived like a gopher for the soddy doorway. Travis had him centered cleanly in the sights for a full breath before Sam reached the doorway and disappeared inside.

Travis didn't shoot and he knew why. Watching the doorway, he heard the faint scuffle of boots within the soddy as Sam grabbed his rifle and began moving around. Sam was crazy and deserved no mercy, but he couldn't shoot him down like a dog, not while there was the barest chance of taking him alive. The marshal took another look at the oncoming rider and recognized Herbelsheimer's horse and the red, angry face of Johnny Cork. Travis fired three quick shots through the soddy doorway and moved back off the hilltop into the shelter of the ditch. He saw Johnny leave the horse in a sudden dive and scramble behind a rock to look cautiously toward the hill. Then Sam fired, a slug that passed directly over Travis's head. Johnny's face was a blurred picture of puzzled surprise.

"Damn you," Travis whispered. "Come at a time like this.''

He slid backward below the skyline and ran south along the hillside until he rounded the lower end and caught sight of Johnny in the draw below. Travis called, "Get down," and had the wry satisfaction of watching Johnny drop on his face in a patch of burrs and squirm frantically for cover. Travis stood up and waited until Johnny saw him and waved recognition.

"Who is it?" Johnny called.

"Sam," Travis said. "In the soddy. I ought to beat your brains out, but there's no time. Work around to the west, get up on the ridge, watch the back of the soddy and the plum thicket. His horse is in there. Watch the horse. If you see him, shoot him!"

"The horse?"

"For God's sake!" Travis said. "Sam. What do you think this is, a tea party? Now get moving. I'll be around on the hill."

"You tricked me," Johnny Cork said thickly. "I'm not forgetting that."

"Aim low downhill," Travis said. "And change position every time you shoot. Maybe in about an hour you'll wish I did a better job of fooling you."

He turned and ran, hoping Sam hadn't noticed he was gone off the hill, hating Johnny for wasting his precious time. His breath came in ragged gulps as he ran along the sandy hillside, and he felt a sharp pain in his chest. Stevens was right, he thought, a man didn't stay young forever. He worked up to within twenty feet of the hilltop, but a hundred yards south of his first position, and crawled on up to the top, looking for rocks, for any kind of decent protection from rifle fire. When he wormed into a half-decent spot behind a little mound of gravelly shale and looked down at the soddy, the fire was scattered and the frying pan lay upside down beside the windlass. There was no sound from the soddy.

Judge Clark had to work and it was blistering hot at ten that morning. He sat in his office off the courtroom and smelled the pitch oozing from the walls.

In his thoughts he was riding east of town with Travis and Sam Thompson and a little man named Joe. He was fat and fifty, and he had to sit here while Travis did the dirty work for him and everybody else in town. Clark stood in the window and looked down on the town. He watched the people, recognized a back, a head, feet, noses, all the people of the town. Today he didn't give a damn for any of them. They were so many papier-mâché figures and he was looking through them, seeing something else—Shadows on a wall, a whip of spirally dust in the street, a dog sleeping under a porch, an empty bottle in the alley behind Big Annie's, a tall man walking straight who cast a solid shadow while others stooped in their souls—a man nobody looked through. He was looking upon his town, Clark thought, and all he saw was one man who wasn't present.

"By God," he said aloud. "I need a drink."

He turned to the lower desk drawer and had the bottle half out when his clerk looked in and said, "Visitors."

"I'm busy," Clark said. "All morning."

"Mr. Ferguson," the clerk said. "John Lockland and Lea Ferguson."

"In that case," Clark said, "I'm not busy. Show them in."

He shoved the bottle behind the stack of county claim blanks and welcomed the visitors with a wave at the empty chairs. He smiled genially at John Lockland and nodded to Ferguson with the fading corner of the smile as he thought, "You mealy-mouthed old tightwad, what's up your sleeve this morning?" He looked at Lea and had a recurring thought that came and went whenever Doctor Stevens spoke of the girl, "If that girl ever decides to live as she dreams of living, what a time we'd have in this town." Probably he'd preside over the damnedest bastardy case in county history if she ever found out what freedom meant.

"Well?" Clark said. "What brings you good people into this sweatbox?"

Ferguson brought forth a large blue kerchief and mopped his face vigorously. "Judge, about that inquest evidence."

"Yes?"

"Can the record be changed?"

"Evidence can always be added," Clark said. "If witnesses wish to testify of their own free will."

"John and I have been talking," Ferguson said. "Lea has gotten over her fright, haven't you, Lea?"

"Yes, Father," Lea said.

"She apologized to John and Margaret this morning," Ferguson said. "I'm happy to say that John understands. He has forgiven Lea, and now we want to have Lea tell what she saw that night. She didn't mean to confuse things, and she meant no harm to John. You know that's true, Judge."

"I see," Clark said. "John, you're not saying much."

Lockland looked down at the floor and colored slightly, evidently embarrassed by Ferguson's explanation. "I can understand Lea's fear, Judge. I told Henry the record didn't really need changing, but if you think it will help, or do something to stop some of the gossip, I'd appreciate it."

"As the record stands," Clark said, "you are completely exonerated, John. But Lea's testimony would show direct proof of your self-defense. Just as Joe's testimony will help. There's really nothing to the procedure. Go out to the clerk's office and have him take down Lea's story. She can sign it, have it witnessed by two people, and we'll file it with the record and add it to the permanent file when court convenes this fall. Satisfactory?"

"Yes," Lockland said.

"Very good," Ferguson smiled. "We can do that now, Judge?"

"Any time," Clark said, and pawed meaningly at the stack of papers on his desk. They took the hint and hurried out to find the clerk. Lockland held the door for Ferguson and Lea, and as he left Clark caught his eye and winked broadly. Lockland smiled then, and winked in return as he closed the door. Judge Clark sat motionless for a brief spell before grabbing his bottle and taking a shot of straight whiskey from the mouth.

"Now why?" he asked the bottle, "and how, and where, and all the other questions that stem from this?"

He waited until the clerk brought him the newly written testimony of Lea Ferguson, signed and witnessed in legal fashion. Judge Clark read it over hastily, threw it back to the clerk, and said, "File it with the inquest papers. And send somebody for Doctor Stevens. Tell him I'd like to see him as soon as he can spare the time."

Travis had lain on the hilltop for three hours, watching the soddy below, while the sun climbed directly overhead and the day grew steadily into a scorcher. Johnny Cork had taken up a position on the ridge, signaled his spot to Travis, and remained in hiding. The horse up behind the soddy in the plum brush was getting restless, wanting a drink and some freedom, jerking impatiently at its stake rope and nickering for Sam. Travis sucked a small stone and closed his eyes for a moment against the sun glare. The soddy doorway was dark with inner shadow. The frying pan glinted in the sun beside the windlass frame. Sam hadn't moved since his first scramble into the soddy. Travis hated to see the horse suffer, and realized his own mare would need water in a little while. Sam was aware of these facts, squatting down there, a lot cooler and better protected than Travis. Sam was perfectly willing to wait for night and make his break. If Travis wanted to come down now, that was fine too. Sam was crazy, but not foolhardy.

Travis waited another half-hour before slipping off the hilltop and going down the ravine to his mare. He had a half canteen of water and, to his best knowledge, was a good ten miles from the nearest well or pond. He took a final drink and gave the mare the rest in his hat, holding her ear and making her go slow. He hoped Johnny had a full canteen. They might need it by nightfall. Then he stopped trying to fool himself. He couldn't wait for night, and Sam knew it.

"Getting hot," Travis said. "We'd better finish it, Goldie."

He tightened the cinches and rode east until he was safely masked from the hilltop, then turned north over the ridge and came back to the west until he was directly on line with the soddy. Johnny Cork waved and came down from his skyline hole while Travis tied the mare and moved painfully up the slope. Johnny Cork took a drink, extended his canteen, and said disgustedly,

"He's in there, Bob, he won't move."

"How much water you got?" Travis asked, refusing the drink.

"Near full," Johnny said proudly. "Made sure before I left the river this morning."

"Save it," Travis said. "Now I want you to ride around east and climb up in my spot on the hill."

"What you going to do, Bob?"

"We can't let him sit until night," Travis said. "You watch the door. I'll go down from this side and try to kick him out."

"You can't," Johnny said quickly. "There's no door or window but the one. You'd have to walk right into him."

"Don't argue with me," Travis said sharply. "Get around there, make sure your rifle's clean."

"But this ain't no way . . ." Johnny began.

"What's the matter?" Travis said wearily. "Won't it go all nice and regular, like the stories you've heard? We stand back, he comes out, and everybody gets a pot shot? It never goes that way, Johnny. I don't like it any better than you, but I've no choice."

He stepped around Johnny and plodding up the ridge stopped once more to say warningly, "I'll give you twenty minutes to get over there." He went on without a backward look and crawled the last feet on his belly to the ridgetop, where he looked down upon the rear end of the soddy.

He couldn't spot any holes in the roof big enough for a rifle barrel, let alone decent shooting, and he saw no windows or doors on the sides. Dirt had slipped down on the rear and onto the caved-in roof. That meant Sam had very little room inside for maneuvering, maybe an area six feet square, but no more. Travis stretched out in the grass, rolled a smoke, and chewed on it, waiting out the time he had allotted Johnny Cork. Johnny made it in fifteen minutes and showed one hand in signal from Travis's old spot on the east hilltop. Travis waved in reply, tossed his cigarette away, and started down the ridge.

He crawled feet first, watching the soddy closely, his rifle on the full cock. He was about fifty feet from the back end when he noticed the crack between the big corner log and the sods. There was an inch of dark shadow hidden from higher view by the outthrust sods. He aimed at that crack and sat motionless, expecting a shot, but nothing happened. Then he saw, more clearly, that the crack was simply corner shadow laid against the sidewall by the sods forced out of plumb by the sliding earth. Getting spooky, he thought, or suffering from sunstroke.

He went on down, rose on his knees, then stood erect and felt naked as the day he was born. Sweating in the sunlight that burned his neck and raised the little beads of water on the backs of his hands he felt the rifle hot and oily in his grasp. He placed his boots carefully and went on down at an angle calculated to bring him directly onto the roof in the center of the soddy. Ten feet from the rear end he stopped and listened for a minute, heard no sound, and took three more steps.

He shifted the rifle to his left hand, at the trail, drew his Colt, examined it quickly and blew dust from the cylinder head. He was too close for the rifle now, and like Sam had said he was never at home with a Winchester after all the years with his Colt. The rifle was dead weight but he held it just the same, no different from any man in the final summation, clinging to every weapon in the pinch. He came to the edge of the roof, where the soddy pushed underneath his boots into the hillside, and stood, hand on his Colt, thinking out the next move.

He could stay up here and begin talking with Sam, try to flush him out, giving Johnny the first clear shot, or move down on the side where he could cover the doorway and get first shot himself. He decided to stand for the present, because Sam wasn't coming out under the influence of any silver-tongued orator. But after that . . . Travis called down, "Sam, you still kicking?"

" 'bout time," Sam answered, his voice coming up from directly below Travis's feet. "Been waiting for you to come down, Bob."

"It's hot," Travis said. "You hot in there, Sam?"

"Not bad," Sam said. "How's your water?"

"Enough," Travis said. "Your horse needs a drink, Sam."

"Well, give him one," Sam said. "You never let an animal suffer, Bob."

"Come on out," Travis said. "No sense in all this. You're just building it up in your mind, Sam."

"No thanks," Sam said. "I'm fine in here. If you want me, come down and get me."

"Guess I'll have to," Travis said. "Sam, remember what you said about my rifle?"

"Sure," Sam Thompson laughed. "You never were much good with one."

"I won't need it this close," Travis said. "And I'm better than you with the six-gun, Sam. A lot better."

"On the draw," Sam said cheerfully. "Not with me in here. Why don't you wait for night, Bob?"

Travis was through arguing for the present. While Sam spoke he was moving to the right and going down around the corner of the soddy and running out away from the front wall, plunging heavily through the sand and coming directly on line with the front. He was about twenty feet from the corner, another two steps from the doorway, and he could see the narrow rind of shadow cast by the soddy wall.

He stood with his legs wide apart and did not move or

speak for a full ten minutes, just allowing himself the wonderful pleasure of relaxing, going slack-muscled, getting his breath and steadying his nerves. Then he laid the rifle against a bush and drew his Colt, turning his body sideways to the doorway, giving Sam the smallest possible target. He took the time to wipe his face with his bandanna, and slap the dust from his hat. Right then, he thought, a bath was worth five hundred dollars.

"You sound like a jack rabbit," Sam called. "Getting up your guts, Bob?"

"Just taking it easy," Travis said. "Waiting for you, Sam."

"Keep waitin'," Sam said thinly. "I'll come, don't worry, but not just now."

Travis glanced up at the hilltop and lifted his left arm, signaled Johnny to back off and go around behind the ridge and come down on the other side of the doorway. He made his signals slowly, repeated them twice, until Johnny waved understanding and disappeared. Travis could see the boy's face as he started this new run. Johnny was thinking that Travis really trusted him, needed him, to let him come down so close. Johnny didn't realize that Sam Thompson was ignorant of his presence, that Sam knew Travis was on the right side of the doorway, and if, and when, Sam made his break he would come shooting for Travis and nobody else. Up on the hilltop, Johnny might get excited and show himself when the action started, and Sam needed just one careless movement to make a good shot. Johnny was actually much safer down here.

Travis watched the doorway and finally Johnny appeared on the ridge coming fast. Travis moved his arm in a gentle circle, slowing Johnny to a walk, making him approach silently. It took Johnny half an hour to creep down the ridge and squat in the brush fifty feet north of the doorway. Travis nodded approval and held one finger across his lips for silence. Johnny nodded grimly and held his rifle at the ready.

"Well, Sam?" Travis called.

"Getting hot out there?" Sam answered. "Cool in here, Bob. I'm dug in the floor, smoking, feeling like a cow on Sunday."

"One more time," Travis said. "Will you come out?"

"No thanks."

"You're a damned fool," Travis said. "That kid wasn't worth the powder to blow him to hell, Sam. You know it. Trailing you around like a puppy, living high off the hog at Stacey's table. I heard about him. Couldn't ride drag on a herd of goats. Sliding along on her reputation, wasn't he, Sam? Buttering you up, getting that free ride. What do you worry about him for, Sam? She's gone, the kid's gone, why keep it alive? Can't you think of anything else, Sam?"

"Shut up!" Sam Thompson called thickly. "You've got no right . . ."

"Just you and me," Travis said. "Only two who know, Sam. Listen, you're making things tough for me. Maybe I ought to ride back to town and start telling what happened to her and that drummer, and to Stacey, and what happened that fall down on the ranch. Maybe I ought to ride north and see Stacey, tell him everything, Sam. Then I wouldn't need to waste my time chasing a Mex, trying to poke common sense down your throat, trying to keep law and order in my town. Stacey wouldn't believe me, but he'd damn well chase you to the border and past, and hang you by the ears. How would you like that, Sam?"

He straightened up, gun ready, watching the doorway. He hated to speak of the past and people better forgotten, to the man who couldn't forget. But he knew no other way of angering Sam to the point of uncontrollable rage. And even this might not work. He waited, feeling the sweat turn cold on his neck, and Sam moved suddenly within the soddy, one boot thumping against a loose board.

"You can't," Sam said. "You can't tell it, Bob."

"Why not?" Travis said coldly. "I owe you nothing. Guess I'd better go back and start for town."

"Wait," Sam called. "What if I come out?"

"We'll head north," Travis said. "Until I know you won't come back. Then you keep going, I'll turn south. Fair enough?"

"Without my guns?" Sam asked.

"Without your guns," Travis said. "Think I'm a fool?"

"What about this fall," Sam said, "when Stacey comes back?"

"Come along," Travis said. "Do you think Stacey will pull a fool play like that? Give him more credit, Sam. Those days are finished. Stacey will cool off. If you want to come along, I'll be in town. But give yourself three months to cool off, you'll see I'm right. Well, Sam?"

"Stacey's coming back," Sam said. "He told me he was."

"When?" Travis asked.

"That night."

"What night, Sam?"

Sam kicked restlessly at the same loose board. "That night I rode in and tried to find the Mex."

"And saw Ferguson?" Travis asked quickly.

"That bastard!" Sam said contemptuously. "What do I want talking with him? I never saw him but twice, on the street. Him and that fancy-pants daughter. I don't know their kind."

Travis looked at his gun and thought of Ferguson warning his own daughter not to testify, not from threats, but through his own selfish fear of losing Goodlove's business. He said gently, "No, Sam. You don't know their kind. You don't want to. Come on now, let's not waste time."

"Stacey's coming back," Sam said again. "He told me he was. He's got to. That Lockland shot the kid, and the kid was mine. Don't you savvy, Bob? The kid was all mine. I was bringing him along the way I wanted, watching him close so he couldn't hurt Stacey like she did. When the right time come, I was going to take care of the kid. Lockland had no right. Stacey's got to come back and even the score.''

"All right," Travis said. "Let him come back. You're crawfishing on me, Sam. Are you coming out, or do I ride for town?"

He waited an eternity, his last chip played, while the sweat gathered in the dirty hair on the back of his neck, and dripped, oddly cold, down his spine. He saw Johnny Cork in the brush, young face tight with puzzled wonder, holding a steady aim on the doorway. Finally boots moved inside the soddy, the sound of a man getting to his feet and shaking himself loose.

"All right," Sam Thompson said.

"Throw your guns out," Travis called.

He waited again, and then the rifle glittered in the sunlight, coming through the doorway and landing in the dust beside the frying pan. The Colt followed, a shorter arc and quicker shine of sun on metal, and thumped beside the rifle.

"Anything else?" Sam called petulantly. "You want my pants?"

"All right," Travis said. "All right, Sam."

They sat in the courthouse office with the bottle on the desk between them. "After all," Judge Clark said, "Ferguson knew about Sam, and if he promised Sam to prime Lea, now he's in mortal fear that Travis will find it out. No wonder he decided to get back on the right side of the fence in a hurry."

"Yes," Stevens said, "but say that Sam didn't threaten him, say that Henry didn't promise anything. Then it's just his conscience bothering him, Ed. Bob says that Henry is an honest man. I'm inclined to agree. So it must be his conscience."

"Now we're getting philosophical."

"Practical," Stevens said. "Like Ferguson. Say he

fought it out in his mind, conscience against business, and conscience won this morning. I'd like to think so."

They were talking to kill time. They both knew it, waiting for the sound of a horse, a voice in the hall. The town dozed through the noon hour, and the office got hotter by the minute.

"John wasn't excited about it," Clark said.

"Why should he be?" Stevens said. "Lea's conversion meant nothing to John. He knows her too well."

"Then why did he come with them?" Clark asked.

"He's sick of trouble."

"From Ferguson?"

"From anybody," Stevens said. "Hell, he's not thinking today. He's waiting, just like us."

"But lacking the genial conversation," Clark said.

"Genial," Stevens said. "Try harder, Ed. We're as genial as two undertakers discussing longevity."

"I wonder," Clark said, "What all this will do to us, Larry. I don't mean the present. I mean in the future. Funny how one incident will affect people in many ways for many years to come. Look at us, we're in this with Bob, but what will it do to our future actions? Make us better men, greater scoundrels, what? Twenty years from now I'll be a bad picture on the courtroom wall. Old Judge Clark, remember him, they'll say. And a hundred years from now people will look up, in a new courthouse, and remark about that funny old bastard in the Dundreary whiskers and wonder what he did to earn his salt in those days. Hang horse thieves, take graft, was he good, bad, or indifferent? Yes, what did he do, and what made him do it?"

"And what about the good doctor?" Stevens asked.

"All doctors are good until proved otherwise."

"And proof comes along. Why, twenty years from now—"

"You'll be the same," Clark said. "Lecherous as ever."

"Forty then, to remove all probability."

"But not attempt."

"Never mind," Stevens smiled. "What will they remember of the doctor, Ed? Not much. Time moves too fast. But I hope the memory has some smell of good done in it. I've tried. One thing, in backing Bob I know I'm right. But is that enough good? Ah, hell. We're just talking to hear our voices. I wish Bob would get back."

"I can tell you how to work some good," Clark said.

"How?"

"Woo and marry Lea Ferguson."

"Jesus Mary!" Stevens said, reaching for the bottle. "The heat's got you."

"No. Take her from her mother's arms, awaken her, make her a woman, change her, change her mother, change Henry. If that doesn't come under the heading of a holy miracle, nothing short of sainthood, then I'm a liar."

"You're getting drunk," Stevens said. "Come on, we need a breath of fresh air."

Leaving the office, going down the steps under cottonwoods, they listened unconsciously for a sound from the east. Clark said heavily, rubbing his red face, "Even if this comes off right, I wonder if it's finished."

Johnny Cork saw the rifle and six-gun land in the dust, and stood up in frozen surprise, forgetting his duty, watching the doorway and looking beyond Travis who stood in a strange, stiff way, right hand holding the Colt at his side.

Johnny Cork heard boots and saw a hand grasp the side of the doorway, and remembered himself. He dropped on one knee lifting his rifle, and watched Sam Thompson appear suddenly in the doorway, hands at his sides, head bent forward a little in a strained attitude of listening for some sound nobody could hear.

"All right, Bob," Sam Thompson said.

He walked slowly from the doorway shadow into the bright sun glare and turned south, his dirt-caked shirt back to Johnny Cork, facing down the little slope toward Travis, arms still loose at his sides. Johnny Cork started forward and saw Travis take a step, swinging his body from its sideways position until he directly faced Sam, and in the same step raise his Colt and start shooting.

Johnny Cork cried, "No . . . no!" hearing the shots, three of them fired in a drum-roll from the heavy gun, watching Travis's arm jerk and settle with each shot, watching his big thumb work the hammer, sending the shots into Sam Thompson's body. While Johnny Cork watched, frozen in place, Sam was pushed backward by that invisible hand, pushed by each shot in rapid succession, and finally slammed on his back in the dust, dead before he struck the ground. Johnny Cork dropped his rifle and began running, anywhere, anyplace, blindly, unable to believe what he had seen. Shoot a man down without a chance into the dust, after he'd given up. Johnny came against the soddy wall with painful force, wanting only to hide and forget what he'd seen.

"Johnny!" Travis said. "Snap out of it!"

Johnny Cork rolled his bruised face away from the soddy wall and looked up. Travis was standing in the same place, looking at Sam's body, lowering his Colt and levering out the three spent cartridges, extracting three more from his belt and shoving them into the empty chambers. Travis's face was shadowed by his hat brim, but Johnny saw his mouth and jaw, and knew real fear for the first time in his life, and indecision with it, the first doubt about a man he had never doubted before.

"Why?" Johnny said. "Why did you shoot . . . ?"

"Come here," Travis said brutally. "Over here."

Travis walked forward until he stood over the body. Johnny stayed against the soddy wall, and Travis said once more, "Johnny, come over here."

"No," Johnny said. "You shot him down."

"Come here!"

Johnny came forward slowly and stopped a pace from the body and looked across at Travis.

"Look at his face, Johnny," Travis said.

"I can't . . ."

"Listen," Travis said. "You're too old to be sick. You haven't got the time, and you'd better swallow it and grow up. Look at his face."

Johnny Cork looked down, moving his neck in short jerks, feeling the bitter bile in his throat, against the back of his tongue that was pressed flat in his dry mouth. He swallowed hard and finally looked down upon Sam's face, upturned in the sunlight, the old hat lying a foot away, half-covering the six-gun. The face was a different thing to Johnny Cork, not just eyes and nose and mouth and jaw, but something else that had no relation to a man. He saw the deep wrinkle lines beneath the eyes and cutting down along the front ridges of the cheeks into the cross wrinkles that surrounded the mouth and dipped under the jaw into the leather-brown neck, all filled with the dust and the sweat and the substance of a man, and all cruel, all laid bare to the sunlight in which there was no shadow to lurk and hide what lay beneath the skin in the mind and heart and soul. Johnny Cork saw the cruelty, the wildness and the absence of all pity. He began vaguely to understand what Travis wanted him to see.

"He was done, Johnny," Travis said gently. "No matter what might have happened, he was done. He knew it, too. I know what you're thinking, Johnny. It's in your eyes, son, but you're wrong. Open his shirt, Johnny."

"I can't," Johnny said. "I don't want to."

"You've got to," Travis said. "You wanted to see it to the finish. You came along. Open his shirt."

Johnny Cork knelt down on one knee and reached out gingerly and noticed that the shirt was already unbuttoned at bottom and top, held together above the belly by one button. He took it carefully and rolled the eyelet loose and threw the shirt open.

"Well, Johnny?" Travis said.

Johnny Cork saw the six-gun, cocked and ready, thrust

against the bare skin under the belt, hidden by the shirt buttoned by one button. The cocked gun, ready for the loose hand that had dangled at Sam's side when he walked from the doorway and faced Travis. Johnny Cork swallowed again, his eyes smarting with the tears that were welling up, the shame at himself for having the doubts about a man he would never entirely understand.

"Bob," Johnny Cork said. "I . . ."

"Know why now?" Travis asked.

"Yes," Johnny said. "I know why."

"Then we'd better get the horses and take Sam to town."

----------------- Eighteen -----------------

THEY CROSSED THE RIVER AT EIGHT O'CLOCK AND
walked the horses slowly into town, coming down the alley
behind Lockland's store on the east side of Pioneer. Sam's
horse was between them, and Sam's body, swaying gently
across the saddle as they moved along, no longer bothering
Johnny Cork so much with the finality of its motion. Travis
saw a cigar glowing ahead, in the alley behind the jail, and
heard Judge Clark's voice say, with deep relief, "Here he
is . . . yes, it's Bob."

"And Johnny," Doctor Stevens said. "Bob, that you?"

"Yes," Travis said. "Don't strike a light."

He dismounted stiffly and moved over against the jail
wall as John Lockland came from the wall darkness and
took his arm in a sharp quick grasp. "Are you all right,
Bob?"

"Do I look it?" Travis said. "Certainly I'm all right."

"And . . . ?"

"On his horse," Travis said. "Anybody got a drink?"

Doctor Stevens thrust a bottle into his hand, and tilting
it up, he smelled the faint trace of whiskey on the doctor's
breath. The waiting for these men hadn't been an easy
business either. He swallowed deeply and felt the whiskey

175

warm his stomach, as he handed the bottle up to Johnny Cork.

"No thanks," Johnny said.

"Drink," Travis said. "Tonight you drink."

"Well," Clark said quietly. "You finished it, Bob."

"All done," Travis said. "We'll fix it up tomorrow, Ed, if you don't mind waiting."

"Any time," Clark said. "We just wanted to see you."

"Better take Sam to the hardware store," Travis said. "Nels can take charge. Johnny, will you look to the horses?"

"Sure," Johnny Cork said proudly, aware of their glances, knowing he was possessor of a story they wanted desperately to hear, so that tonight for the first time in his life, he was the envied man and not the envier. "Sure will, Bob. Anything else?"

"Yes," Travis said. "You can tell these gentlemen about it if you're not too tired . . ."

"I'm not tired," Johnny said quickly.

"You are," Travis said flatly, "but I guess you can tell it straight. Understand, Johnny? No fancy additions."

"Yes, sir," Johnny Cork said. "I couldn't do that now, Bob."

"Sam wouldn't give up, would he?" Stevens asked softly.

"He couldn't," Travis said. "I'll see you all in the morning. John, go home and sleep easy. And tell Margaret to do the same."

He touched Lockland's arm, smiled in the darkness and went through the back hall to the front office. He racked his rifle and gave the books a disinterested inspection. Murphy was on duty along the street, two drunks were sleeping it off, nothing had changed. He wanted to go home and stay there, but he couldn't do that tonight. It was one man's pleasure to run, and another's to face reality. He stepped outside and walked down Pioneer toward the Bighorn, not thinking yet, refusing himself that right for the present. A few more hours, he thought, hold off the thinking, blow off the steam. Walk the street, do the job. Then go home. Because it'll come fast when it starts, and it won't be good.

He paused outside the Bighorn doors and heard voices inside, loud and half-drunken. The horses below him on the rail were marked with the trail brand of another outfit from the south. Not a herd, he guessed, but a few punchers already going home from the Dakotas or Wyoming. He was moving on when Murphy's voice sounded angry and sharp above the crowd, telling a man to stop talking like a fool. In the following silence, the man answered Murphy boldly, "Well, where's this marshal? We been hearing about him, not such a big stick, after all. Letting a Mex buffalo him, not to mention other things."

"I'm warning you!" Jim Murphy said.

Travis pushed through the swinging doors and entered the Bighorn. He saw Murphy beside the bar, facing a big-shouldered man with yellow hair and a red, smiling face. He was facing Murphy and grinning meanly as he waved a bottle in his left hand. The crowd had already moved away against the far wall, and Dick Burnett was edging down to get the loaded pool cue from its hiding place beside the beer taps.

Travis said, "I'll handle this, Jim," and passed Murphy as the latter seeing Travis, opened his mouth in glad surprise. Travis went on, not stopping now, and said, "Enough from you," and hit the big man on the jaw with a vicious, brutal blow that dropped him flat and carried Travis directly over him as he fell, facing the other punchers who were grouped behind. He saw anger and surprise, then recognition in their faces. The man stirred as Travis reached down, yanked his victim up and threw him back at Murphy without turning.

"Lock him up, Jim," Travis said. "Drunk and disorderly. Now, did somebody say a few words about me . . . ?"

Whatever they saw, they looked away, and moved.

177

"You know me?" Travis asked roughly.

"Why, sure."

"Then don't forget me," Travis said. "I'm the big stick here. Now get out of town. Your friend will be released in the morning. Better be in if he can't pay his fine."

"How much?" one asked.

"For him?" Travis said, all the bitterness, anger and sadness entered his voice, with the bitterness overriding the feeling of futility of all this. "One dollar, friend. I fine them exactly what I think they're worth."

They met his look for a moment, broke and passed around him, heading for the street. He looked at Dick Burnett and said, "Sorry, Dick," and waited until the horses galloped up Pioneer in a bunch before going outside. He hadn't meant to do it, but all day long the anger built up in a man until it had to come out or blow him skyhigh.

He walked the length of Pioneer, crossed the tracks, and followed the sandy path until he stood in the cottonwoods above Mexican Town. Then he heard the familiar sound of a guitar playing in the still night. He would know that guitar anywhere, the player's individual finger touch against the strings, the hand butt slapping gently against the wood as the beat was held, with the voices joining the chorus that followed. He wasn't alone here on the path, he knew that, and down below in the little houses they were singing again and passing the bottle.

Travis stood on the path a long time, listening to the music, taking off his hat and letting the wind cool his face. He felt the dried runnels of sweat, salty and harsh, on the inside of his legs and down his back and under his arms, where part of his insides had dribbled away during the morning and afternoon—a part of him that was going to be remembered for too long a time because each drop of sweat had been a pound of worry and fear. Mexican Joe, who hadn't sweated that much, was home tonight, playing his guitar and drinking with his friends, coming out of nowhere and slipping back into his daily routine as if nothing had happened.

Travis wanted to go down, take Joe by the neck, and make him scream for forgiveness in terror; but that was no good. By his own lights, Joe had done the only thing he could: run and hide and wait for his friends to help. Being a friend, Travis's share was not so much an obligation as a part expected and, now finished, part of himself that would always be in their hearts. No, he couldn't go down there tonight. Tomorrow or next day, maybe in a week, he'd talk with Joe, and Clark would get the true testimony for the record. Not that it was needed now, but Joe would want to tell the truth.

He turned back for town smelling the cinders and coal smoke from the roundhouse, and heard the distant pounding of a freight approaching from the east, coming off the midland run for water and coal, and the long climb west toward Cheyenne. A section hand came from the depot, hunched over with the weight of tools and lunch bucket and sack of coal picked up along the tracks. Travis said, *"Buenos noches,"* and saw the head come up and the eyes flash white, and heard the soft answer, *"Buenos noches, Señor Bob,"* and the tiny, giveaway hiss of breath as the section hand quickened his steps, heading for home with the news that, to his chagrin, would be twice told before he dropped the coal sack importantly on his back step.

Travis looked into the depot and saw the night operator tilted back in a chair under the Seth Thomas clock, reading a book and tapping one finger absently on the sleeve-worn telegraph desk. Everything was quiet in the depot as it was in town. Tomorrow the news would raise a little storm of gossip and the curious ones were sure to visit the hardware store for a look at Sam, laid out neatly in his pine coffin. The rumors would start then, how it happened, how it really was, then the inside version of what took place in the hills. The legal geniuses would argue that Travis shot Sam without proper authority or good cause, even in cold blood.

Others would try to put together the separated pieces of a puzzle they would never understand, and finally give up in disgust. Because Clark and Stevens and Lockland would never tell, and Johnny Cork was safe. Ferguson didn't know; all he could do was guess. Shot while resisting arrest, the record would say, and that was best for all concerned. Mexican Joe was safe, Lea was safe, and Lockland could forget his fear for a long time. Most of all, Stacey would never know the truth now, thank God. Sam had died with all the hatred of an old, festered revenge, which he hadn't passed on to Stacey. All Goodlove would hear was the story of Sam's death, enough to anger him more than before, but much better than breaking down all his memories of the past. He didn't expect Stacey to lose his best friend and his brother-in-law in the same month and think kindly toward the people involved but there was still a chance that Stacey might change by summer's end.

Travis walked around the depot and kicked an upturned nail keg left by some loafer beneath the wide station eave. The sound was no different from Sam's boot kicking a loose board inside the soddy. All sounds tonight were alike in their beginnings, repeating themselves over and over in his mind. He was jumpy to think that way, remembering the morning and the look on Sam's face when he stepped from the soddy. Sam had stared at him and he knew that Sam hadn't given up. It was the hardest thing he'd ever done, lifting his gun and making the shots good.

"Stop it," he said. "Got to stop it tonight."

He went up Pioneer and came to the cul-de-sac leading into Big Annie's, and heard the piano tinkling in the parlor. He stood in the darkness outside the front windows and watched the girls and the customers. He wanted to go inside but couldn't. He walked around the house and stood on the storm cellar door and glanced into the kitchen through the big window above the sink. Annie was pouring a drink for Doctor Stevens who sat at the table in his shirt-sleeves, holding a glass and looking vacantly at the bottle as it tipped and poured. Stevens had gone through a great deal today and was taking it off like a sensible man, getting drunk and sitting in Big Annie's until the sour early morning hours when the last customer started home and the girls thought longingly of rest, and Annie turned morose herself, because at that time of morning she always saw, too clearly, the dirty linen of the past. With a wealth of grimly acquired insight, she didn't like the look and sound and smell one bit. Yes, it was a good way to loosen up, but not for him tonight. Stevens deserved a good drunk, a good talk with Annie. But for himself, he'd better go home, take a bath, and lie down. Not that sleep was going to come easy when he thought of Stacey and what could happen in the fall. It might be finished for the town, but not for him.

Long after Travis had gone away, Doctor Stevens looked across the table and waggled one finger solemnly. "Time to say good night, Annie."

"Almost," Big Annie said. "This time of morning I see all the dirty linen, Larry."

"All of it?"

"Well," Annie said judiciously, "I can't see that far down the clothesline. But you've got to admit, in all fairness, I'm the washerwoman's best customer. If I can't see all the way, it's not my fault. A few others have been hanging their own on the sly."

"And theirs is the same as your own," Stevens said. "Don't feel badly, Annie. We're all the same in the end. Heat up some coffee and I'll go home."

Nineteen

As the summer days passed, Travis watched the town settle into humdrum living. July was dry, with barely enough rain to sustain crops and keep the river wet in mid-channel. With the heat people gradually forgot the big excitement and the dead men. Life moved on evenly, a comforting condition for Travis, who wanted no lingering reminders of the past.

But with a special, grim laughter he remembered the morning they held Sam's inquest. Judge Clark presided and Johnny Cork, in the opening moments, was sole and willing witness. Clark was carrying it through delicately, showing that Sam was shot while resisting arrest and that Travis was literally racing time in his search for Sam, to save the life of Mexican Joe. Clark piled up the circumstantial, extenuating evidence and just when they were ready to close the books and put the legal tag on a tricky piece of business, the door opened beneath the balcony and Mexican Joe came sheepishly into the nearly empty courtroom. Travis met him halfway up the aisle and took his arm in a firm grip, and Joe looked at him with that innocent, trusting smile and flash of those white teeth, and Travis couldn't stay mad.

"Where were you?" Travis asked, leading him down the aisle to the witness stand.

"All over," Joe said. "Couple of times, Señor Bob, you near spit on me."

"A shame I missed," Travis said. "Weren't near the Dutchman's at any time?"

"Once," Joe said, and Travis stopped him abruptly in the aisle, just outside the swinging gate, and looked down at him wonderingly.

"Just when?" Travis asked softly. "Like yesterday morning, for instance?"

"I knew he was there," Joe said. "Pablo sneaked up on him one night. I was just a little way from Johnny, buried deep like a gopher. I had Pablo's rifle, Señor Bob. I, too, had my sights on the *cabron.*"

"Well," Travis said. "There's a lot more you and I are going to settle, Joe. But right now I think you'd better step up here and tell the judge everything you know. And Joe . . ."

"Yes, Señor Bob?"

"Those new guitar strings sound pretty good," Travis said.

So Mexican Joe took the stand and added his testimony to both inquests. That bolstered the records and did away with any circumstantial doubt in either case. Travis sat back in his chair and listened to Joe, and wondered at the change in a man when fear and death disappeared from his heart. Yesterday Joe was running for his life. Today he would be hard put to remember how that feeling had started and grown in his own mind. Travis listened intently, but Ferguson was the most interested onlooker that morning. Ferguson tried to understand everything about Joe, and at the same time was examining himself and his daughter in the light of all these strange events. When Clark adjourned the inquest, Ferguson stopped Travis outside the courtroom and tried to discuss the thoughts that had never troubled his mind in past years.

"Sam wasn't acting on orders, after all," Ferguson said. "Was he?"

"No," Travis said. "He just went loco, off on his own hook."

"But why?" Ferguson said. "It doesn't make sense."

"It did to him," Travis said dryly.

"But he was a smart man," Ferguson said wonderingly. "With a fine job, and a great future. Goodlove praised him to the high heavens. I can't see how the death of that puncher would turn him berserk. You'd think, with all his experience of violence in the past, that he'd have learned from the mistakes of other men he saw killed."

"You don't learn anything from others," Travis said. "If you do, it won't be anything that counts up to much. You learn all the things that count by yourself, Henry, or you never get them kicked deep enough into you to make a profit from the pain."

Ferguson looked up shrewdly, considering Travis's words. Travis had spoken so casually that Ferguson almost missed the truth. But only for a moment. Then Ferguson blushed and nodded with a kind of dour resignation. "I'm a stubborn man," he said, "but don't misunderstand me, Travis. I can always learn and I know when I've guessed wrong, and when I should make a change in my business or my thinking. We're never too old to learn."

"If I ever got that way," Travis said, "I might as well die young and get it over with."

"I see your point," Ferguson said. "What I want to ask now is, when will you resign—in light of what's happened?"

"I named the first of July," Travis said.

"I know, but you must admit things have changed."

"Let's slide along awhile," Travis said. "If the town board doesn't mind paying my salary, I'd like to stick around a little longer."

"I'd prefer that," Ferguson said, surprising Travis greatly. "So we'll just forget that July first date."

Travis had never understood Ferguson's change of thought and feeling on that morning. As the days passed he discovered that Ferguson was actually becoming more genial with people. As Clark described it one night, "I think he's trying to discover that being human isn't so bad. He'll never make the grade completely, but at least all this has shaken him loose a little bit."

"Natural reaction," Stevens grumbled. "Afraid of his hide if Goodlove does come snorting down again. Bob, we've deliberately avoided that subject for two weeks. Think he is coming back?"

By that time Travis knew that Stacey Goodlove had the news about Sam. The funeral had been quiet, with just the three of them present to lay Sam away, but it was done with all decency and kindness, and Travis himself paid for the headstone. Stacey knew, all right, but nothing came down the trail from the Dakotas. Whatever Stacey was doing up there, those plans were strictly secret.

"I could be wrong," Travis said.

"But you think he'll come?"

"Yes," he said.

"Don't tell John," Stevens said. "He's just starting to act normal."

"And we'll keep him that way," Travis said. "No use worrying, trying to guess if and when, trying to fix the day. When you put all your thoughts and hopes in the future, you waste the present. We just live today, we can't live tomorrow. I'm too damned old to play the fool and waste today. So stop worrying—yes, both of you are. Cut it out. If Stacey comes, he comes, and I'll worry about it on that day only."

"You're right," Stevens said. "It's summertime and we ought to take it easy, be thankful we're alive and kicking. By the way, did I tell you my conversation with Lea the other day?"

"No," Clark said. "but I notice she's stopping by your office pretty regular."

"My charm," Stevens said modestly. "Well, this is interesting from the standpoint of her father acting different these days. I was asking her about her school plans, and telling her about Chicago as I remembered the city, and quite suddenly she said she didn't think she wanted to go back there to school. So I immediately said, nonsense, of course she did. But she said no, she thought she ought to stay here. But why stay in this cow town, I insisted, what of the balls and her music and the handsome young gentlemen she'd meet? So she said because she thought Olalla was her home, she didn't know why, but she thought so."

"The heat," Clark said. "It got her."

"Believe me," Stevens said, "that was my thought. Then I began probing and I discovered that she wouldn't object to a good Omaha school for genteel young ladies, but for some reason Olalla was suddenly a better town than she had realized. I inquired as to her mother's reaction to this change of plan, and she told me her mother had a case of the galloping vapors when she heard the news. That was expected. So it must be that Henry is reweighing his daughter and trying to decide about the future of this town in terms of making a good match for her here instead of hooking some Chicago pork king."

"And I know exactly why you're worrying about the problem," Clark said.

"You do?"

"You're wondering just who Henry has turned his eye on," Clark said. "That's an interesting question, Bob. Who could it be?"

"Line up the young men," Travis smiled. "Then check their bank balances. That'll give you the answer."

"Maybe," Clark said slyly. "Would you consider Doctor Stevens eligible, or slightly long in the tooth?"

"Now . . ." Stevens said.

"No," Travis said thoughtfully. "He's getting up there, but I'd still judge him sound."

"By God," Stevens said, "the way you two talk, I ought

to carry the girl off and force Henry to load a shotgun. Be serious."

"We are," Clark said. "You're just evading the issue."

So they talked through the hot days and nights, gradually forgetting the past in the pleasure of the present. Travis rode to Summerhays' for Sunday dinners and spent the evenings talking with them, seriously discussing a farm against the value of a business in town. There was no use placing a mark on one calendar day in the fall and telling himself, "After that, if Stacey comes, what's the use of planning?" It was better to talk cows and pigs and crops, and a house, and what they could all do to make the country better. Johnny went along a few times, but he was still watching Lea, and he talked with Mary only because it was polite. One Sunday night riding back from dinner, Johnny broke a long silence and said, "Know what I heard yesterday?"

"No idea."

"Lea's not going to Chicago," Johnny said. "Going to school in Omaha."

"Good idea," Travis said. "It'll save Henry money."

"Well, hell," Johnny said. "Don't that prove something else to you?"

"What?" Travis said.

"Plain as the nose on your face," Johnny said. "Ferguson is betting this country will get richer. He's keeping her near home instead of putting out the hook for one of those eastern dudes."

"I'll back Ferguson's faith in this country," Travis said, "but I doubt that marrying his daughter locally will grow more wheat per acre."

"Aw," Johnny Cork said disgustedly. "Never mind."

Rain fell in August and kept the crops alive, dropping here and there with the typical carelessness of the country, wetting the earth, putting new life into corn and grain and cows, then coming down in a big gully-washer that nearly ruined everything overnight. But things hung on and August spent itself in a listless, hot succession of lazy days, and September 1st came before Travis realized the even, deceptive flow of time. The grain was cut and threshed, and Fred reported fifteen bushels to the acre on his barley, and others had equally promising returns from land that had grown nothing worthwhile short years ago. Ferguson did a brisk trade in new accounts, as heavy advertising by the land companies brought a stream of families out from the east, farmers and tradesmen and fiddle-feet, some stopping, some looking, some going on west, but always providing new, strange faces on the street. The blacksmith couldn't handle all the repair work, and the implement dealer sold plows and wagons and a new type of disc cultivator faster than he could pull them off the freight cars and set them up. Lockland did a fine business in winter supplies, overshoes and underwear, woolen shirts, mackinaws, canned goods, cream separators, shotgun shells, shovels, buckets, everything farmers with ready cash wanted badly. And for the first time the town ladies began thinking about extra help in their houses. Farmers with several daughters were approached with the idea of hiring out the girls in town. That was the first step of real change, Travis knew, the coming of the hired girls. And, by God, if the town ever needed something new and strong and good, it was a big infusion of hired girls, girls like Mary, honest and willing, lacking foolish vanity, eager to get ahead, unafraid of work, thinking always of their families and how the money earned would be used to buy more machinery and stock and feed and supplies, to make the farms better. Fred stopped by one day and mentioned that Ferguson had asked about Mary going to work in his house when Lea went to school in Omaha. Travis had to make a quick decision. While he was for the good of all, he thought wryly, he was still selfish about somebody he cared for deeply.

"No," he said that afternoon. "Not there, for Mary. I'll

name you half a dozen other families Mary would like, but not Ferguson's."

"You object to Ferguson?" Fred asked.

"Not him. His wife."

"So do I," Fred said mildly. "Just wanted to hear you say it. Mary laughed when I told her. Besides, she don't like it in town and I still need her until the boys get bigger."

But a few girls hired out and injected a fresh breath of life in town. Through the long, hot weeks the street seemed to grow quieter and less inclined to violence. Dick Burnett stopped by occasionally to smoke a cigar and discuss the change, how his business had dropped off in one way, but in return he was getting a steadier, more sensible bunch of customers, farmers and townspeople and visiting drummers, with fewer itinerant punchers who caused the big trouble and kept the jail filled at night. The other saloons were feeling the pinch and by September three folded up, being jerry-built in the beginning, and within a week's time different merchants were dickering with Ferguson for the lots. Big Annie had to ship three of her girls up the line to Cheyenne. She told Travis one night that if business got any worse she was going to change her curtains, buy Singer sewing machines, and make an honest living. When Big Annie started talking that way, Travis knew it was just a matter of time before she sold out to some smaller madam and moved on to greener pastures. He'd hate to see Annie go in a way. She wasn't as bad as the breast-beaters liked to paint her. There were no arguments for her kind that would stand up under the moral guns, but on the other hand there were many kinds of morals in the world, all shapes and sizes and levels, and Annie's code was stricter than most in her own way—and above all she always stuck to her own code.

Yes, summer was almost gone and the street was changing before Travis's eyes, and he hadn't made up his mind about that business or a farm. The word had gone up the line that he was resigning, and about the time summer heat faded, the letters began arriving from the places with the names that still sent a little thrill into his bones. They wondered if he wanted the job as marshal here, and there, and way out there, name his own price. They needed a man like him badly, not many were left—God, he thought, how true that was—and they'd meet any price he set. So it wasn't all gone yet, it was still the same farther west and north and down in the southwest, but it was going fast, and if he wanted any more he'd have to hurry. He didn't hesitate over a single letter, just read them and balled them up and tossed them in the wastebasket. He hadn't believed he would ever be able to do that, but it had finally happened. The last letter came from a Nevada town, so new he could smell the canvas-and-wood streets from a thousand miles, offering him five hundred and all fines, and he threw it away without a second reading. He knew he had broken away from his past that afternoon. Johnny Cork stopped in, coming from the breaking corral, and Travis felt so good he poked Johnny in the ribs and said genially,

"Let's buy a farm, Johnny, and raise pigs."

"The heat finally got you," Johnny Cork said. "You take the pigs. I'm after bigger game."

"Listen," Travis said. "I've found out something, Johnny. There's no bigger game in the world. I've been making up my mind for three months. I just did. I'm buying a farm."

"You serious?" Johnny asked.

"I am," Travis said.

"You better have a drink," Johnny Cork said. "I ain't so sure you're sane today."

-------------------- Twenty --------------------

JOHNNY CORK CHANGED TO CLEAN CLOTHES THAT NIGHT and returned to Pioneer for supper, and then stood on the boardwalk, glancing up the street toward Ferguson's bank. That was just as close to Lea as he could get these days. He turned south to the Bighorn, looking for a pickup job, and Burnett called immediately from the cash register, "Mulligan's doctoring a sore tooth. Will you fill in for two hours?"

"Two dollars," Johnny Cork said.

"All right," Burnett grinned. "You robber."

Ten minutes later Johnny was drawing beer and washing glasses, exchanging insults with the other bartender, watching the customers enter and fan across the long room. Travis stopped in with Judge Clark and Doctor Stevens, and smiled in approval. "Another dollar, eh?"

"Two," Johnny said. "I'm skilled labor."

The Bighorn filled slowly and the games broke into steady play as nine o'clock rolled around; in the rear, at the battered pool table, the younger men began their nightly game of call shot, flicking the wooden counters on the overhead piano wire. Burnett sat in the dollar limit poker game, and Travis argued good-naturedly over the drinks with his friends, and finally Clark said, "All right, let's draw for it."

Johnny watched him break three matches in different lengths, shuffle them, and hold the three, ends on line and uncovered. Travis said, "Short stub pays," and drew. Stevens drew and they both laughed as Judge Clark opened his fist and grinned ruefully at the shortest stub.

"Always let the other man call the shot," Travis said. "Thank you, gentlemen."

They left the Bighorn, and Johnny Clark stared at the discarded matches thoughtfully. He drew beer and washed glasses until ten o'clock, collected his pay from Burnett when Mulligan returned to duty, and walked up Pioneer to the jail office. Travis found him at the desk two hours later, making figures on a tablet and staring sharp-faced into space.

"You belong in bed," Travis said mildly.

"I've got an idea," Johnny Cork said. "Let me tell it, Bob. I got to thinking about those matches after you left the Bighorn. I thought how everybody likes to take a chance, gamble on something. How many people live in town and around?"

"Fifteen hundred in town," Travis said. "Another thousand or more around. Why?"

"I've saved two hundred and ten dollars," Johnny said flatly. "I need two thousand to start anything worthwhile. I'll be gray-haired before I get that much breaking horses or tending bar. I thought about those matches and about gambling, and I got an idea. I'm gonna hold a raffle."

"A raffle?" Travis said.

"Sure. Sell tickets, give a prize."

"No," Travis said. "For a turkey, a horse, a gun—fine and dandy. You could net a hundred or two, but never two thousand. And a raffle is only worked once by a man in the same place. The novelty wears off."

"I'll sell tickets at a dollar each," Johnny said stubbornly. "I say I can sell twenty-five hundred tickets."

"And what's the grand prize?" Travis said. "The bank, controlling interest in the railroad? Blow those dreams away, Johnny. What could you offer?"

Johnny Cork said, "Me."

"You!"

"I'm the prize," Johnny said quickly. "I'll offer one year of my time, working for the winner free. I'll sell those tickets. I know I can. Burnett will help, you will, everybody will pitch in. I can live a year on three hundred dollars, even less. I'll finish with a decent stake. I've figured it every way. Tell me it's a good idea, Bob."

Travis said, "I'll be damned!" and paced the office, slapping one hand against his thigh. Finally he turned and smiled broadly. "By God, I think it'll work. I've never heard anything like it, Johnny. Just crazy enough to catch everybody the right way, and at the right time, too. Summer over, crops in, folks are looking for a little fun. And we can use a little around here. I'll get those tickets sold. Dudgeon will print for you. I'll buy ten to start the ball—" Travis grinned, "and if I win, you'll be feeding those pigs. Now, there's just one thing . . ."

"What, Bob?" Johnny Cork said eagerly.

"What if you can't do the work?" Travis said. "Or don't like the man who wins you?"

Johnny Cork said, "I'll worry about that, Bob. See you tomorrow."

When Johnny Cork ran from the office, Travis stared reflectively at the gun rack. "Raffle himself?" he said. "Now why didn't I think of that twenty years ago."

Johnny Cork worked the next morning in his usual manner, finding tough going on a hammerheaded little horse that hated mankind and all restrictions; and wondered through the hot afternoon if it was going to come off. Travis had been good as his word, getting up early and making the printer rush the tickets through, then going down the street and setting up the ticket sales and spreading the word around. Travis set the drawing in two weeks, and told Johnny Cork at noon that a longer time would only ruin interest. The tickets had to sell in two weeks or the raffle was no good. Johnny Cork agreed, and sweated through the afternoon, dreaming of the day he could say good-by to the danger of the breaking corral.

The town loafers came in mid-afternoon, grinning and talking about the raffle, lining the corral fence. Johnny went about his business and Herbelsheimer cast angry glances at these idlers who threatened to upset his carefully planned Teutonic routine. They shouted at Johnny and he returned the questions, and finally Herbelsheimer understood. At quitting time the fat man walked to the barn with Johnny Cork, rubbing his stomach, looking worried and angry.

"This is true, John?" Herbelsheimer asked.

"Sure," Johnny said. "But I'm not letting you down cold, Gus. I'll have another breaker for you, don't worry."

"Yah," Herbelsheimer said. "That I know. Men come along. But you, I like you, John. You work hard, do your best. I hate for you to try something like this raffle and maybe go pfttt!"

"I won't," Johnny said. "When those loafers came down this afternoon, I knew it was started the right way. You buying a ticket, Gus?"

Herbelsheimer shook his head violently. "Nah, John. I don't throw money away."

"Worth a chance," Johnny said. "Well, see you in the morning, Gus."

Washing and crossing town to his room, changing clothes for the night, Johnny wondered how many men would think like Herbelsheimer. He couldn't back down now. The tickets were printed, Travis was spreading the news and the town would be filled with it tonight. Johnny Cork worried through supper, refused apple pie, and wandered north in the light dusk, passing Ferguson's and hoping for a glimpse of Lea. He walked to the edge of town where it was quiet and was haunched over on the ditch bank, chin in hand, when Mary Summerhays pulled up her team and light wagon, and got down to shake hands. She had come to town for a load of barbed wire and some staples, and she stood before Johnny, brushing at her thick brown hair, standing straight and strong in her man's trousers and work shirt.

"For a raffle prize," Mary said. "you don't look healthy."

Johnny said, "When'd you hear, Mary?"

"From John," Mary said. "You've stirred up more excitement than a hanging."

"What do you think?" Johnny asked. "Am I crazy or smart?"

"Smart," Mary said firmly. "Sure I heard those loafers talking, making fun of you. I know they talk that way. They're jealous of you. You're going somewhere and they sit on the nail kegs and whittle, and never do anything."

Johnny Cork looked up with gratified relief. "You make me feel a lot better, Mary."

"The tickets will sell," Mary said. "Every last one. You'll get the stake, Johnny. What then?"

"Haven't figured that far ahead," Johnny said.

"Remember what Dad's been telling you," Mary said. "We've talked about it enough this summer, you and Bob and us. The real future here is farming, feeding stock on the side. You even doubted we could grow a decent garden. Well, we did. You ate out of it all summer. The same thing happened with the grain, and the corn. Johnny, those two sections east of our place are still open. Why don't you grab one, come out after you work that year, and start farming?"

One thing about Mary, there was no subtlety in her; only the honest truth about her feeling for him, and the plain, clear question in her eyes.

Johnny Cork said, "I don't know . . ."

"I just saw Bob," Mary said. "He's going to buy a farm. You know that?"

"Yes," Johnny Cork said. "He told me."

"Not looking for the easy way, are you?"

"Did I say that?" Johnny asked sharply.

"No," Mary said bluntly, "but you're thinking that way. There's no easy way to make good. You're not scared of work, Johnny. The land is good. We'll all help you. There's the best future in this country, better than anything in town."

"Maybe," Johnny Cork said.

Mary Summerhays flushed and turned to her wagon, climbed the seat and gathered the reins. She said, "What's in town that you call better, Johnny?"

He looked up and felt her strength and affection hold his body for a brief moment. Then he thought of Lea's soft white skin and her way of life.

He said, "Maybe a thing or two. I could be wrong, but I want to know for sure before I make my move."

Mary spoke to her team and headed north for the river, making a lot of clatter as the wagon rattled over the small rocks and through the washboard blowouts. Johnny Cork walked back to Pioneer, passing the big white houses, looking at the curtains and the lamplight. He knew what was gnawing at him tonight. He could enter the Bighorn and be among friends, but he could not walk six blocks up Pioneer and enter those homes; not tonight. Maybe two weeks from now, he thought, when he had the money and the big chance. He hesitated outside the Bighorn doors and heard the loud talk within.

Travis was answering a railroad man who said, "Sure and what would I do with the young scamp if I won him, Bob?"

"Take a year off, Brady," Travis said. "He'll work your job while you sit in the shade and collect the wages and grow fat. Is that worth one dollar?"

"You won't be argued down," Brady laughed. "I'll buy a ticket, Bob."

"And spread the word," Travis said. "We'll hold the

draw in two weeks. First come, first served. Tickets won't last long.''

Johnny Cork wiped his suddenly wet face and moved quickly across the street, up the alley to his room. Travis was going far past ordinary friendship, doing all this for Johnny Cork. He slept soundly that night, went about his work the next day, and looked vainly for Lea after supper. He was standing on the hotel veranda when Herbelsheimer came ponderously from the dining room and patted his shoulder.

"I yust changed my mind, John. I'm buying a ticket, maybe two."

Herbelsheimer smiled and waddled down the street, and Travis passed a few minutes later and said, "Tickets selling fast, Johnny," and went on about his rounds, leaving Johnny Cork alone with the wonder of a dream actually coming true. Then he couldn't wait any longer. He went down to the Bighorn and got no more than three steps inside when somebody roared a welcome, "I feel lucky, Johnny. If I win, son, all I want is for you to rub my back every night."

"That I'll do, Red," Johnny Cork laughed. "With a currycomb."

Bill Calderson turned from a poker game and called, "Big Annie just bought twenty tickets, Johnny. What do you think of that?"

"All I can do is pray," Johnny Cork answered, and the laughter rose loud and friendly.

Dick Burnett waited until the noise settled back to normal and leaned over the bar. "Guess how many we sold tonight?"

"I wouldn't know," Johnny said. "I hope plenty, Dick."

"Over three hundred up to now," Burnett said. "We'll spread the other two hundred stocked here within three days. Travis just made a tour of every place in town. Over five hundred sold elsewhere.'' Burnett chuckled softly. ''Everybody's buying tickets, even Ferguson.''

''Him?'' Johnny Cork said.

''Why not?'' Burnett said. ''Free work for a year if he wins. Hell, we might make a regular guy of Ferguson if we could get him away from that wife—and that daughter.''

''She's all right,'' Johnny Cork said curtly. ''Not her fault.''

Burnett stared impassively at Johnny Cork. ''You're no town man, Johnny. You belong in open country. Listen, you got a taste of this town last winter and spring when things were still popping. You got your craw full of excitement this summer. But the town is changing, has changed the last three months. And once that happens, the town'll be like all the others. Ferguson and his kind think they run these towns, and maybe they do in a way for a while, but wait until the farmers take over and Ferguson is dependent on them for his business. Remember that, Johnny. Where do the fine girls come from to work on upper Pioneer? Off the farms. And they go back and raise their families. You watch. Ten years from now Ferguson will stand on his doorstep and bow them inside, happy to get their trade. Ask Bob. He knows. So do I. Give me five years more and I'm going north across the river on my own place. And then I'll look for a big strong girl and hope she'll marry me, and the hell with town and all these white-faced women who can't carry water from the well.''

Johnny Cork said, ''You'll eat those words, Dick,'' and left the Bighorn in a rage of uncertainty that carried all through the next day. He slept late, it being Sunday, and then walked along the river to be alone with his thoughts. Travis had caught him at breakfast and given him the total sales for the first night—a thousand and twenty tickets gone, with indications pointing toward a sellout by next Saturday night. Johnny Cork sat on the high bank above the deep pool and stared across the river. About an hour later, thinking of Lea, he saw her coming down the path, carrying an armful of late flowers. She pushed the willows aside and sat on the diving log fanning her face with one hand.

"I'm ashamed of you, Johnny," Lea said sharply. "I've never heard of such a thing. Raffle yourself to someone, like a—like a slave. What on earth possessed you to do such a crazy thing?"

"To get my stake," Johnny said.

"Stake!" Lea sniffed. "How much can you possibly make from such a hair-brained scheme? Johnny, I had high hopes for you. Now I don't know what to think."

"Give me time," Johnny said. "I'll show you."

"Sell yourself!" Lea said. "For a year. Thank goodness I won't be here to watch you working for some dirty farmer or worse."

"Omaha school?" Johnny asked.

"Yes," Lea said. "I couldn't stand another winter here."

"Thought you liked it," Johnny said.

"I do, but I've got to get away for a while."

"How many years you going to Omaha?" Johnny asked.

"I don't really know," Lea said lightly. "Two or three. After that . . ." she laughed and looked at Johnny with that stare of promise that seemed to invite so much without realizing how much it offered.

"After that you'll get married," Johnny said boldly. "Won't you?"

"Well, I suppose so."

"Why waste three years?" Johnny asked.

"For heaven's sake," Lea said. "I'm not throwing myself at the first man who comes along. And certainly not here."

"Not even if the man could support you?" Johnny said.

"He'll have to be a smart man," Lea Ferguson said, and now it was her mother talking, "and make a lot of money. And be a gentleman, too. Goodness, it's late. I've got to run, Johnny!"

"You're always running," Johnny Cork said. "Mostly from me."

"That's not true."

"Oh hell," Johnny Cork said. "Beat it. I want to think."

She gave him a quick, surprised look and started up the path, and stopped a moment, watching his back, but he didn't turn. When her steps died away, Johnny Cork got up and started for town. He remembered Travis's words the night he drew the matches with Clark and Stevens: "Always let the other man call the shot."

He hadn't thought seriously about those words before, and now he began to understand that all of Travis's life had been built upon something like that, letting other men call the shots and either show their worth or their weaknesses before Travis declared himself. Like the past summer, Johnny Cork thought soberly, letting Sam Thompson call the last shot. And with memory of that day coming back for the first time in days, Johnny Cork thought of Goodlove and looked up at the turning leaves. Fall was here, and he suddenly realized that nobody in town seemed to remember Goodlove's promise to return.

---------------- Twenty-one ----------------

THE WEEK PASSED SWIFTLY FOR TRAVIS, FILLED WITH rumors that raced through the lower town and sneaked discreetly up Pioneer into every house. Johnny's raffle was a shot in the arm, he thought, a breath of fresh air badly needed; not only for the town, but himself. He hadn't laughed freely for a long time until this week, and cooler weather helped lift the general spirit, as the leaves turned yellow and orange, and folks began fall housecleaning. Eighteen hundred tickets were sold by Friday night; twenty-three hundred and fifty after Saturday night. Fred stopped after church on Sunday morning and bought twenty-two for all his friends east of town, and twenty-eight were sold during Sunday afternoon in the Bighorn. When Big Annie heard the news that night, she called Dick Burnett down from the saloon and offered to split the final hundred and close the game. Travis walked along and laughed at Big Annie's jokes, and bought another ten himself, letting them split the final ninety.

"What's he going to do with the money?" Annie asked.

"I know what he should do," Dick Burnett said. "Question is, does he?"

"Give him time," Travis said. "He'll find the right thing."

"Like you?" Annie asked.

"Didn't know I had," Travis smiled.

"The word gets around," Annie said. "You're buying land out east."

"If you say so," Travis said. "Truthfully, I guess I will, Annie."

Big Annie looked around, at her garish parlor and bright curtains and overelaborate furniture. She sighed deeply and said, "I know how you feel, Bob. Sometimes I get so tired of looking at faces and hearing voices, and thinking back over too damned many years and thousands of faces and voices, that I feel like buying a farm myself. Get away from all of it, be alone if I want it that way, go to town if I want a little noise. You get that place out there, Bob. It'll do you good."

"When will you resign?" Dick Burnett asked, after they left Annie's and started up the street toward the Bighorn.

"Soon," Travis said. "Pretty damned soon, Dick."

"No reason to hang on," Burnett said. "The summer's gone, and there's more that went with summer. We sure saw the old days die this year, Bob, you and me and Annie, and I can't say I'm sorry. You know, I was just thinking of all the big nights I've seen in the past down the trail. And thinking of this coming Saturday night that's apt to be the biggest of all, and for a different reason. Instead of brawling and shooting, we'll raffle Johnny off and folks will go home with a smile. That's a pretty good way to end one kind of living and start another, isn't it?"

"Yes," Travis said. "Come to think of it, Dick, it is a pretty good way to end."

But through that week, knowing he wanted to buy the farm, putting off formal notice of his resignation, he waited for Saturday night with a strange feeling of increasing tension. Dick Burnett had said, "No reason to hang on," but Dick was forgetting, too, like all the town that fall was not yet spent and only now, to the north on the new, sprawling ranges the Texas men were finishing a year's work and thinking about taking the long ride for home. He sat in the jail office and watched the street, talking at night with Clark and Stevens, and the days crept past with shortening twilights and cooler winds.

Johnny Cork was working faithfully each day at the breaking corral, with twenty-five hundred in cash deposited in his name at the bank. Every merchant in town was preparing for the biggest Saturday night in history. Big Annie had ordered a general housecleaning, and John Lockland received a huge shipment of merchandise on the Thursday freight from Omaha. Johnny Cork was the butt of a thousand jokes that week, bearing them all with a grin and quick comeback. Saturday noon Travis walked over to the corral and led Johnny aside for a last minute talk.

"What are you wearing tonight?" Travis asked.

"Same clothes," Johnny said. "Why?"

"Good," Travis said. "Wear your oldest pants and shirt. When I call you, get up on the bar beside me. I'll handle everything. After we make the draw and get the winner, you better go home and stay out of sight."

"Good idea," Johnny said.

"And then what?" Travis asked soberly. "You've got the stake. How about that farm? You coming out and be my neighbor?"

"Don't know yet," Johnny said.

"Seen Mary lately?"

"Yes."

"Let's call the spades," Travis said bluntly. "Let the queens go for a change. She's in love with you. Know that?"

"In love with me?" Johnny said.

"The finest girl in this country," Travis said. "And you can't see her for—never mind. We'll just start arguing."

"We will," Johnny said shortly. "And while you're so

damned eager to get me out there, how come you haven't bought your place yet, Bob? What're you waiting for?"

"For the first snow," Travis said oddly. "All right, be at the saloon on time: nine o'clock."

He turned away and went through the alley to the jail office, taking his chair behind the old desk. All right, he thought, Johnny called my bluff. What was the use of waiting any longer? Helping Johnny out tonight had been a fine excuse for keeping the star until today. But what then? John Lockland was his old self again, apparently unworried about the once frightening future. Everybody but himself had forgotten. Why sit here any longer, thinking of the past, juggling the human values of men dead and gone, and their effect upon one living man who had gone north in June and sent no word since of his intentions? Get Johnny set tonight, turn in the star, and start thinking of the future.

He pulled a deck of cards from the right-hand drawer and dealt a hand of solitaire. He played a black eight on a red nine and saw two jacks come up on the right-hand piles. Also he saw, through the window, the approach of Clark and Stevens, walking swiftly down the boardwalk on the west side of the street, then crossing over toward his door. He pushed the cards aside and stood up, and his fingers touched his gun butt as they entered the office, an instinctive movement that curved them as he gave the holster a firm slap.

"In a hurry?" Travis said. "Who raped who?"

"Shorty Carpenter just rode in from Scottsbluff," Clark said. "He crossed a big outfit twenty miles west and north of town, about fifty men riding south, pack horses and remuda."

"Going home for the winter," Travis said calmly. "Too bad we don't have more tickets for sale. If they come in to wet their whistles, we could sell another hundred for Johnny."

He spoke without excitement but he knew, before Clark

went on, exactly what the next words would be. Clark said, "Half of them are Fishhook. Goodlove's crew. The others are all Texas brands."

"He see Stacey?" Travis asked.

"Yes," Clark said. "They were making night camp south of the river. Stacey was giving the orders. They were holding the remuda tight, not opening many packs."

They watched him and waited for his words, while Travis tried to think of something that would ease this feeling between them. They were blaming themselves for having ignored the danger, having allowed time to fool them into false security. Most of all, they were thinking of Travis and all his plans, and thinking of John Lockland who would have to know.

"Well," Travis said quietly, "it was a nice summer."

"Good God!" Stevens said. "If Carpenter hadn't spotted them, think of . . ."

"No," Travis said. "Stacey wouldn't pull that, Larry. He'll be in town this afternoon. You watch. He wouldn't come in that way. And don't blame yourselves. I can see it working in you. I'm equally to blame. I didn't forget, hell, how could I, but I kept thinking that Stacey wasn't going to do it. I was wrong."

"We've got time," Clark said sharply. "We can have two hundred men armed and ready inside of two hours."

"No," Travis said. "I told you once, Ed, it's no good that way."

"But why . . ."

"Listen to me," Travis said. "Go up the street and tell John. Tell him to take Tommy fishing, stay out of town this afternoon. Let him think it all out. If he wants to catch the six o'clock train east, we'll see that he does. If he wants to stay, I'll expect him in his store after supper."

"But . . ." Clark said again.

"This is a big night," Travis said. "For Johnny Cork, for the town. In a lot of ways. Johnny's raffle is going through on schedule, I don't give a God damn what happens. You understand me? That raffle goes through. It means a lot and nothing is going to stop it. You understand?''

"Yes," Stevens said slowly. "I understand you, Bob."

"Then tend to those things for me," Travis said.

They looked at him helplessly and turned away. He watched them go up the street and looked down at the jumbled cards. When he noticed the jacks and the eight spot he smiled without humor. He faced a long afternoon of waiting and he was all alone in the jail office that, quite suddenly, had become all the office he had known in the past years. Really he wasn't alone, he thought, not with all the ghosts hanging around to keep him company and wonder if they might not be greeting a new member in a little while. Matter of fact, it was getting crowded in the office, not enough chairs to go around for Sam and a red-haired puncher named Dohney, and a moustached drummer and a woman who loved no man and loved them all. He had a lot of company, at that, and time ought to pass in a hurry.

Twenty-two

He HEARD THE HORSE AT FIVE-THIRTY THAT AFTER-noon, coming down Pioneer from Cottonwood, slowing outside and then stopping as a big man dismounted, boots hitting the ground with a solid thump. Stacey Goodlove pushed the door back and looked inside, saw Travis at the desk, and came on in and closed the door. Stacey was dusty and unshaven, wearing his old trail clothes, and packing his gun. The summer had been hard on him, cut-ting his face lines deeper, making his skin redder and tougher, adding more flinty steel to his already hard eyes, slicing off some of the excess poundage around his big hips and thighs.

"Well," Travis said. "You made it, Stacey."

"I was goin' to come in cold," Stacey Goodlove said flatly. "Couldn't do it. You knew I was coming?"

"I heard," Travis said.

"How come no troops?" Stacey said. "I expected wire on the streets, rifles on every roof."

"Why?" Travis asked. "You're heading for home, your crew'll want a drink and some fun. What's wrong with that?"

"Nothing," Stacey said. "Nothing at all, except it won't do any good to talk easy."

Travis placed both hands flat on the desk. "All right, Stacey. The town is yours, as always—below this office. Check all guns with the saloonkeepers and have your fun."

"Funny," Stacey said. "I never did see that line."

"I'll show it to you," Travis said. "If you wish."

"All right," Stacey said suddenly. "All right, Bob. We're back and Lockland's still here. My crew'll be in town in half an hour. Take my advice and go for a little ride along the river. You can't stop me. I respect you, Bob, I'm not even thinking about Sam now because I know you had no choice there. But there's things that can't be let go. I've got fifty men and we'll have Lockland or tear this town apart."

"Do you have the time?" Travis asked.

Goodlove said, "It's about six."

Travis lifted his watch from his shirt pocket and studied it slowly, replaced it more slowly, and stood, arms loose at his sides. Travis said, "Five minutes after your crew gets here, I'll be on the porch of Lockland's store. Any man crossing the line with a gun will spend the night in jail. Any man with a gun below the line on my rounds will spend the night in jail. Is that clear, Stacey?"

"Clear enough," Goodlove said. "You're a fool, Bob. Why didn't you resign and clear out? I couldn't stop my men if I wanted to—and I don't. I'll be with them."

"Then you've got time for supper," Travis said easily. "Try the apple pie tonight, Stacey. They usually make it pretty good on Saturdays."

Goodlove looked at him, and then turned to the door. Travis did not speak as Goodlove went outside, jerked roughly at his horse and led it down the street toward the Bighorn. They hadn't said very much, Travis thought, with so many words between them, so much that might have been spoken, all the years of it that stretched back into the shadows. It was a strange thing that he had misjudged

Goodlove for the last time, and Goodlove in a sense had misjudged him. John Lockland had started everything and actually John meant nothing much to Stacey. John was just the figurehead that had broken down Stacey's long-stored up anger and hate, which he let roll out in a flood, all summer and early fall, so that Stacey no longer had any common sense at all.

He stood at the window, listening, finally hearing the sound that had to come. Stacey's crew came slowly, almost sedately, walking their horses around the corner of Cottonwood and down Pioneer, a flood of riders, fifty strong, filling the street from wall to wall, moving quietly past the jail without a glance, fifty dusty, bewhiskered men who tied their horses in a long line before the hotel and the Bighorn and half a dozen other places. Then they just stood around in little groups, rolling smokes and causing no trouble. He had never seen them like this, and he wondered how the town felt in this moment. Buggies and wagons filled with riders were pouring into town. Other people were already trading briskly in the stores—until Goodloves's crew turned down Pioneer. Then the boardwalks were lined with their frightened faces, and all the happy laughter died away.

Travis smoked a cigar, sitting quietly behind the desk, watching the street and glancing at his watch, now laid on the desk. Jim Murphy came from somewhere to the south and slammed recklessly into the office.

"I been up and down the street," Murphy said. "The boys will be at their windows, Bob."

"That's good of them," Travis said. "I gave orders to the contrary. There will be no shooting from them. You understand me, Jim?"

Murphy shook his head. "No, Bob. You can't buck that crew alone."

"Go up the street," Travis said quietly. "Give them my thanks and tell them to clear everybody out of the way, and kindly tend to their own business."

"And me?" Murphy asked.

"You sit here," Travis said. "If I need help, you give it to me. That's our job, Jim, not theirs. When men, no matter their good intentions, take the law into their own hands, it defeats the purpose of the law. That sounds stiff as hell, I know, but I mean it. I'll handle this myself."

"Bob," Murphy said tonelessly. "For Christ sakes . . ."

"Go on," Travis said. "Will you do your job?"

Murphy could not argue with this man he had known three years, and did not know tonight. He said helplessly, "I'll tell them," and ran from the office.

Travis looked at his watch, lifted the double-barreled shotgun from the rack and checked it carefully, loading both barrels with buckshot. He placed the cigar between his lips and walked up the street toward Lockland's store, carrying the shotgun under his left arm. He mounted the wide steps to the south corner post and leaned the shotgun against the post on the inside, and stood loose and angular in the thickening dust, smoking his long black cigar and watching the street that, within minutes, was totally empty. The screen door scraped behind him and John Lockland spoke calmly, "I'll be just inside or beside you, Bob. Which shall I do?"

"Inside," Travis said, without turning. "In back, in your office."

"No," Lockland said. "I'm no coward."

"You didn't take the train," Travis said.

"Margaret and I talked," Lockland said, and now his voice showed strain. "We decided we couldn't run now, Bob. I've got to stay."

"I knew you would," Travis said. "Now go to your office."

Lockland shook his head. "Not alone, Bob. You can't do it."

"It's my job," Travis said. "I know a little about it, John. Get into your office. They're coming now."

Lockland turned inside reluctantly and disappeared in the

store depths. Travis stood very close to the post, shoulder brushing the smooth wood, and heard the first sounds from far down Pioneer. He heard the slow, rising mutter and then, overshadowing the mutter, boots walking deliberately and heavily on the dusty street from curb to curb. Travis puffed on the cigar and blew smoke straight out from his lips—and waited.

Stacey Goodlove led them up Pioneer Street to a point even with the invisible line opposite the jail, and on up the street toward the store. Stacey was out front, as Travis had known Goodlove would be. Whatever qualities these men contained that appeared foolish and wild to the onlooker, cowardice was not included, and this was good to know when one man faced fifty. It was good to understand these men and not be forced to look for a bullet in the back from a coward who would not walk up the wide street and play his hand in the open. Travis moved slightly, until one shoulder touched the post and his left hand dangled just above the shotgun. When Goodlove reached a point ten steps from the porch, Travis said, "Hold up, boys!"

Goodlove raised one arm and the men stopped behind him, fifty of them filling the street completely. These were fifty dark-tanned wild men from Texas, enough of them to engulf and destroy Travis in one short moment. Goodlove dropped his arm and smiled faintly.

"Right on time," Goodlove said.

"Turn around," Travis said. "Check in those guns with Murphy and get back across the line. I'll give you one minute to start, Stacey."

Goodlove said, "You wouldn't listen to me, Bob. All right, we've got no quarrel with you. In one minute we're going inside and get Lockland. We'd like to go without trouble. If you make trouble," Goodlove opened the fingers of his right hand, "we'll take you."

Travis said, "Forty seconds now," and lifted the shotgun in one smooth motion, cocking both hammers and bringing it flat across his left arm, the barrels resting on his forearm and two fingers on the triggers. Travis dropped his right hand to his Colt and stood before them, waiting, watching every man of the fifty with the quick sweep of his gaze.

Stacey Goodlove stared at the shotgun and stood his ground, but some of them shifted nervously behind Goodlove, and Travis swung the shotgun in a short arc and said, louder now, "Thirty seconds. Still time to cross over and check your guns."

Goodlove did not move, and Travis waited, with time slipping away. The marshal thought of the past and his own inner knowledge of how he had been bound to end some day, like this perhaps, on a store porch in gunfire. There was no way a man could turn back. He had to do his job, and if he failed in it, he did not fail those who hired him or depended on him, nor did he fail the job. He failed himself then. Travis waited. They all knew what was coming, knew exactly where both barrels would swing and send their charges. They all knew that Goodlove as he stood there, held by his foolish stubbornness and his blind anger, was a dead man, also the man on the porch. And it had to break one way or another. The seconds were going. Goodlove stood firm and Travis waited on the porch beside the post.

He saw the boy coming down Pioneer then, running from the north alley into the street. He dropped the shotgun, muzzle down, and said, "Hold up, Stacey," and half turned to face the boy.

Tommy Lockland came down the street, bare feet kicking the cooling dust, carrying a big catfish on a pegged string, walking proudly with his blond hair over his eyes and the dark sweat stains showing under his arms. He looked curiously at the crowd and came up on the porch from the north end and held the fish high for Travis's inspection.

"I caught him," Tommy Lockland said proudly. "I caught the old grandad, Bob."

"A big one, all right," Travis said gently. "Where'd you get him, Tommy?"

"In the big hole," Tommy Lockland said. "Father went home early for supper, but he said it was all right for me to try a little longer because I'd been getting a few nibbles. I had him on the hook once, last summer. I knew he was down deep. He always comes up at suppertime for the bugs, so I took off my worm and stuck a big bug on the hook, and I sure got him. I bet he weighs ten pounds, Bob. I'm gonna show him to Father."

"Pretty close to ten pounds," Travis said. "That's the best fish caught all year, Tommy."

"Where's Father?" Tommy Lockland asked. "In the store?"

Travis looked at Goodlove and said evenly, "In the store, Tommy. Show him the fish and then run along home. Your father is busy tonight."

The boy grinned and brushed his hair back with his free hand and hefted the catfish with his other arm. He said, "All right, Bob. Mother said not to forget the coffee cake tonight after the raffle."

Travis said, "I won't, Tommy. Now run along."

The boy passed behind Travis, carrying the fish higher now and went through the door and into the store depths, his bare feet slapping quickly on the board floor. Travis lifted the shotgun and gave them the full rising anger and vicious rising rage that welled deep in him at all times, slow to surface, but unstoppable when begun.

He said, "All right, Stacey. Give the boy a minute to clear and then start your ball."

Stacey Goodlove stepped back a pace from the steps, stared at the ground, and then shook his head. Goodlove said, "You win, Bob," and turned, facing his crew, and called, "Check in your guns, get across the line!"

They hesitated one moment, a darkening sea of faces,

and then the men in the rear wheeled slowly and formed a loose, irregular line that flowed down Pioneer into the jail office and trickled out and on down toward the Bighorn. Goodlove watched them go, and turned to the porch. Travis dropped the shotgun behind the post and stood wide-legged, feeling for the first time the wetness of his palms.

Goodlove said, "I forgot about that boy, Bob. Why didn't you remind me?"

"Why," Travis said wonderingly, "I never figured him, Stacey. He wasn't part of my job."

Goodlove considered these words soberly, a quiet and thoroughly sensible man now. He smiled with great relief and slipped off his dusty hat and began mopping his sweaty forehead. He said huskily, "You never saw my little girl, did you, Bob?"

"No," Travis said. "I didn't."

"God," Goodlove said. "Sometimes I wonder . . . no, that don't do no good. I guess I'm just a wild-tailed cat. You sure won't need no guns tonight, Bob. I'll stand the drinks."

Travis murmured, half to himself, "You never know when."

"How's that?" Goodlove asked.

"Talking to myself," Travis said. "Stacey, I'll see you at the Bighorn in a little while."

Goodlove said gruffly, "Bob, tell him to stop worrying. I'll be in tomorrow to buy supplies—without a gun."

Goodlove turned and walked rapidly down the street. Travis reached down and rubbed his fingers across the shotgun barrels and knew he had to keep moving, that something had gone from him in a few brief seconds that could never return. It had been all over there, all of it for him, for Stacey, for everything he had planned and dreamed. And now he had it all, for keeps, and he couldn't really thank anyone for the gift. Jim Murphy came up the street and looked at him and tried to speak, and nothing came from Murphy's open mouth. Judge Clark and Stevens stepped from the doorway across the street, and Ferguson appeared in the bank door. Still the street was silent, watching him.

"Well," Travis said quietly. "We're wasting good time, with a raffle coming up. Let's all get down to the Bighorn and start the fun."

"Yes," Murphy said. "Start the fun!"

────────── Twenty-three ──────────

H E WALKED BETWEEN CLARK AND STEVENS, ACUTELY conscious of their hands holding his arms as if he might fly off at any minute; and then they were pushing through the crowd before the Bighorn and entering the saloon. Travis saw Johnny Cork in the back room doorway, waiting white-faced and worried. Off on the side, in a chair against the wall, Stacey Goodlove held a full bottle of whiskey between his knees which were drawn up on the tilted-back chair. Travis said, "Time for the draw," and started for the bar.

Johnny Cork came from the back room, slipped behind the bar, and stood near Burnett, who banged a bung starter on the closest barrel and shouted, "Bar's closed for the big draw! Everybody get his ticket stub handy! . . . All right, Bob."

Travis mounted the bar and raised one hand while Burnett boosted Johnny Cork up beside him. Johnny stood in his faded shirt and worn pants, grinning at the upturned faces. Travis called, "Can you hear me?"

From the far side of the room, near Stacey Goodlove, one of his riders answered. "Too damn well!" and grinned sheepishly at Travis.

"Ladies and gentlemen," Travis said, with a courtly bow to Big Annie and her girls who were watching from the back room, "you know the rules of this raffle. We're going to have Bill Calderson's little girl, Rachel, come up and draw the lucky number. But first, I want any two of you to inspect this box and the numbers. Where's an honest face?"

"Here!" Herbelsheimer shouted.

Amid catcalls, Travis laughed, "Come up, Gus, and you there, Billy McGee! Roll up your sleeves before you lay a finger on this box."

They came forward and inspected the box, then the second open box containing the ticket stubs; after which Travis poured the stubs into the box, closed the top flaps and held the box high, showing the circular hole that had been cut in the top.

"All right, Bill!" Travis called. "Where's Rachel?"

Bill Calderson lifted his nine-year-old daughter to the bar and said warningly, "I've got ten chances, Rachel. You better draw lucky for your pa."

"If she does," Travis said, "she'll draw again. Rachel, I'll shake the box good, then you reach in and get one ticket."

Rachel thrust a chubby arm through the hole, fished around and twisted her pink face with concentration, and finally drew a wrinkled stub. Travis placed the box on the bar, rolled up his sleeves and showed his open hands to the crowd, fingers separated. Then he accepted the ticket from Rachel and read the number silently, passed it to Dick Burnett, who read it and passed it to Calderson, who read it and held it aloft.

"Rachel drew number six hundred and seven," Travis called. "Who's the lucky man or lady? Step up and claim your prize!"

In the following stillness, the breathtaking silence, heads turned every way, looking and waiting. Johnny Cork looked around and saw an arm go up near the door, and heard the voice, "For God sakes! That's my number!"

"Doctor Stevens!" Travis shouted. "The doctor wins!"

Dick Burnett called, "All right, folks. Bar's open and ready. Let's drink to Doc Stevens and good luck! . . . Johnny, get down!"

Johnny Cork leaped behind the bar, followed by Travis and felt the strong fingers nudge his back. "Get out of here," Travis said softly, "before they start tearing the town apart."

He stood behind the bar and watched Johnny duck through the back door and disappear. Everybody was pushing up to the bar, laughing and talking loudly, and a big group surrounded Stevens kidding him about what to do with Johnny Cork's year. Travis turned to leave the back bar and saw Goodlove at the end, standing in much the same position he and Sam had stood that night in June when they drank together, and started everything. Goodlove was holding the bottle and waiting for him. Travis walked to the end and ducked under the getaway slab and stood beside Stacey, looking down the long bar at the faces and glasses and windows beyond.

"Let's have that drink," Goodlove said quietly.

"I need it," Travis said. "Three fingers, Stacey."

"Mine—or yours?"

He remembered that past night and smiled. "Yours tonight, Stacey."

They drank and Goodlove refilled his glass staring somberly at his hands. "What kind of a damned fool was I?" Goodlove said. "All summer long I been acting like a fool, Bob. Christ, I came down here and started thinking a few minutes ago. I got to think about my daughter. I can't keep blowing up like this."

"You will," Travis said. "You won't change, Stacey. But just blow up with your fists. That'll do the trick."

"Yes," Goodlove said thoughtfully. "It's time for that, Bob. Well, there's a lot you and me can talk about, but this is too soon. We'll be leaving in a few minutes, got a long ride ahead. What I wanted to tell you—I'll be passing through spring and fall from now on. Maybe we can work out something for this place of yours."

"You heard about it?" Travis asked.

"Just," Goodlove said. "What's wrong with you taking a bunch of nice steers every spring, fatten 'em up, ship from here, we'll work out a split deal."

"I'd like that," Travis said. "It's worth thinking over, Stacey."

Goodlove poured another drink, downed it in one gulp, and turned against the bar, his big face red and ashamed. "Bob, I been thinking about Sam. I guess it was the only way for him to check out, the way he was getting to be. But there's one thing that throws me. When we left that night, he come back in for that inquest at my orders, but he stayed around on his own hook. That's God's truth. And that's what I can't figure. What the hell difference did that Mex make, or the way Sam went loco and tried for you and Lockland? What was going on in him, Bob? What was it he was trying to dig up, or stamp out? All these years I thought I knew him like I know myself, and I never did. What was it, Bob? You know?"

"I don't know," Travis said. "He just went loco, Stacey. That's the only thing it could be. It's all done now. Forget it. Now good-by, Stacey. And I'll see you in the spring."

Travis shook the big hand and went through the back room, outside into the alley night. He was starting to tremble now, beginning to feel everything that had to come, and he had to get home and lock the door and maybe pray a little bit. He was the luckiest man in the world, and from tonight on he wouldn't ever forget that luck.

---------------- Twenty-four ----------------

JOHNNY CORK GOT UP AT EIGHT O'CLOCK AND WALKED up Pioneer Street to Doctor Stevens's office, went around back, knocked smartly. Stevens answered, still wearing his nightshirt, and led Johnny into the kitchen. Johnny Cork didn't say a word, but stacked five hundred dollars in gold pieces on the table between his hands. Stevens rubbed his red eyes and looked questioningly at them, and said, "What's all this, Johnny?"

"I'll tell you, Doc," Johnny Cork said. "I can do the job, whatever you need, but you don't need me. Here's five hundred cash, in gold, on the table. A fine return for a dollar investment . . ."

"Ten," Stevens said.

"All right, ten," Johnny said. "What do you say, Doc? Will you take the money and release me from my promise?"

Stevens thumbed his jaw, regarding the gold, and coughed gently. "You had this figured from the start, Johnny?"

"Yes," Johnny Cork said. "It's legal, Doc. There was nothing in the rules said I couldn't buy off, was there?"

"Well," Stevens said softly, "I'll tell you what, Johnny. I'll release you if you make me one promise."

"Name it," Johnny Cork said.

220

"That you will not decide to study medicine and open up another practice while I'm in business here," Stevens said, his eyes laughing behind his sober face. "I can buck most anything, but not the man who figured this raffle. I want no part of that ambition or competition."

"I promise," Johnny Cork grinned. "Shake, Doc. You're a real gentleman."

"Why, no," Stevens said gently. "You're the gentleman, Johnny. It's about time you understood that. And Johnny . . ."

"Yes, Doc?"

"A gentleman should have only the best," Stevens said. "There are many ways of interpreting that, but I think you know what I mean?"

"Maybe," Johnny Cork said. "Maybe I do, Doc."

"Going to church?"

"Yes," Johnny said. "I'll wait for you, Doc."

"You go on," Stevens said. "Bob is there, with the Summerhayses. They came in this morning."

Johnny Cork flushed and left the office. He walked slowly up Pioneer toward the church, wearing his new suit and white shirt self-consciously, knowing that everything was different for him today, but in what way he wasn't sure. He sat far in back during service, unnoticed, and followed the young people through the side door after the final prayer, onto the street. Lea Ferguson came with her father and mother, saw him, and hurried across the grass to take his hand. Johnny Cork saw Travis and the Summerhayses come down the steps and walk toward their buggy under the cottonwood trees.

"Johnny," Lea said brightly. "You're a famous man this morning. Pa told me last night he believes you'll be one of the big men in the country in five years."

"Don't set a time limit," Johnny Cork said.

Lea realized she was still holding his hand, but Johnny was looking past her, watching Fred untie their team.

Lea said nervously, "I'd better go now. Won't you come to dinner, Johnny? Mother says she'd like to have you."

"I'm a smart man," Johnny Cork said absently. "I'll make a lot of money, won't I?"

"Of course you will," Lea said.

"And I'm a gentleman, too," Johnny Cork said softly. "Overnight, just like that. I don't think so, Lea. Thanks just the same, but I'm busy."

Johnny Cork walked swiftly through the trees and stood beside the Summerhayses' wagon, shook hands with Travis and Fred, and looked at Mary. Travis was wearing a fine dark gray suit and looked different this morning. Then Johnny Cork realized that it was the way the coat hung over Travis's right hip, smooth and unwrinkled, covering nothing but the trousers where the belt and holster had always been in the past.

"Well," Travis said. "We're all heading for a big dinner, Johnny. Clark and Stevens are coming out, we'll have fried chicken and about everything you can imagine. How does that sound?"

"Got room for another plate?" Johnny asked.

"I'll tell you," Travis said, and Johnny saw their heads turn slowly as Travis went on, "there's room for another plate—and another farm right beside the one I'm buying tomorrow."

"I guess we can talk business," Johnny Cork said. "If it's all right with you folks?"

"There's always room for you," Fred said simply. "You know that, Johnny. You haven't been out much."

"I know," Johnny Cork said. "You go ahead. I'll be out this afternoon—Mary, why don't you ride in about three miles and meet me?"

Mary Summerhays smiled and looked at Johnny squarely, an honest and completely warm stare of new happiness and understanding. "I'll meet you at Webb's gate," she said, "and tell you the truth about that section of land before Pa and Bob can fill you full of lies about it."